KINGS OF HELL

LEIGH HADDINGTON

TOMBTOME PUBLISHING

For Claire, Jamie and Charlotte for having to deal with all my crap and this just being another "thing" to add to the list of constant other "things" that dominate my time.

For Mum, its been months since you closed your eyes and still painful but its what you wanted, I hope you and Dad are enjoying your peace together. Both of you were loved and will be forever missed.

FOREWORD

This journey started over three years ago now, commuting from Leeds to Castle Donnington, the home of Monsters of Rock or now known as the Download festival. I started to listen to audiobooks on the train. I was never a reader growing up the focus was always on music, metal mainly but I would dabble with all various genres.

So at first it would be just the autobiographies, I went through about one every two weeks, I enjoyed them and it helped pass the time. Apart from the Harry Potter books that I got to read to my children, who didn't take to them but I was mesmerised by them, I wasn't really interested in reading fiction.

Then I remembered the Sandman comics I read when I was a teen, Neil Gaiman, so I started listening to his work. It started with American Gods, then Neverwhere, I was loving the worlds and characters, I was lost in another place, making being away from home easier to deal with.

Then someone suggested John Scalzi and I was lost in future worlds, stretching my imagination even more. One book after another, there were times where I would get through a book in less than a week and on to the next. Then I found Scott Meyer and his wizards, what an idea for a story. Then horror and James Herbert, Stephen King and so on, all new scary worlds and I loved everyone.

Then it happened, it came from nowhere, the smallest of ideas, then it grew, it morphed, multiplied, and it wouldn't stop. I thought about it twenty-four-seven. I fell to sleep thinking about it, woke up thinking about it, work, travelling and home thinking about it. So I began writing about it.

Twenty-one months later and its arrived, a lot of work, anxiety, stress and self-doubt, a lot of self-doubts. If you're sat here reading this book, thank you.

It's not for children, it covers a lot of dark areas that felt very strange to me, one part I wrote on a crowded train, standing with my iPad, I just hope no-one saw what I was writing.

And finally, remember this is fiction, it's not real, it came from my disturbed mind and it is designed to give you some escape from your normal life like Neil, John and Scott did for me.

1

OFFERING

"I am very sorry, Mrs. Fitzroy, but there is nothing more we can do for your son; it seems that the subacute meningitis has already started to damage his spinal cord and brain. He is not responding to any of our treatments, and I truly do think you need to prepare yourself for the worst. We will make him comfortable, and if there is anything we can do, please let me know. Again, I am very sorry, Mrs. Fitzroy."

After the doctor left the consultation room, Mrs. Fitzroy sat staring at a young nurse, numb with the news from the doctor and her words bounced round her head, slashing every memory of Nick.

"Mrs. Fitzroy, why don't you go down to the restaurant and get a coffee, we have to reposition Nick, and it will take at least ten minutes."

Mrs. Fitzroy thanked the nurse and nodded, accepting her advice. As the nurse went to leave, Jude grabbed her hand.

"Thank you, for everything you're doing." Smiling despite the tears in her eyes, Jude broke-down, "What will I do without him? I don't know what to do."

The nurse handed her a small box of tissues.

"Don't think about that at the moment; you still have a bit of time. Go get a coffee. Please, get something to eat too. He will still be here when you come back."

Jude let the nurse's hand go and smiled wiping the tears away from her wet cheeks with a tissue. As she stood up, the nurse gave her a hug.

She grabbed her bag and left the room, heading towards the hospital's restaurant. She rummaged through her pocketbook and retrieved a new pack of tissues, pulled one out and wiped her face, cleaning her tears from her reddened cheeks.

Jude bought herself a coffee and a small biscuit and sat down away from the other customers, towards the back of the restaurant.

It had been only five days since Nick had been rushed to the hospital. He had been fine that morning; the illness seemed to take hold almost immediately and Nick crashed quickly.

Jude emptied the sugar into her coffee and stirred her cup.

"Excuse me miss, do you mind if I join you?"

Jude looked up into the face of a tall, thin, pale man. His friendly smile relaxed her nervousness; he looked young but with an old soul charm.

"I'm sorry, I don't think I would be good company," Jude mumbled.

"That is fine, I'm not looking for good company. To be honest, I saw you leave the ward, you looked crushed. I thought you could do with a friend. I gather it wasn't good news?" he sat down opposite, ripped open three packets of sugar and poured them into his tea, stirring as he listened.

His voice washed over her like a warm blanket, cosy, familiar.

"It's my son, he has meningitis; the doctor has just told me…" she started to cry again.

The man touched her hand for support, and a warm glow radiated up her arm.

"…he won't last the night…"

Jude wiped her tears off her face with another tissue and added it to the others gathering on the table.

The man looked at Jude, still holding her hand, and smiled; this relaxed her and eased her thoughts.

"It's cruel, I'm very sorry. How old is he?"

"Two, just two."

"If there is anything I can do…" he squeezed her hand and added his second hand on top for reassurance.

"I wish you could."

The man's face lit up, he leaned forward on his seat.

"Wish? Funny you should say that. Maybe I could help you." His smile changed into a knowing smirk.

Jude looked up from her coffee, saw his smile and felt her stomach drop.

"What? Do you think this is a joke? My son is dying and you think it's funny?" She snatched her hand back from the man.

"No, no, you misunderstand; if you are willing, I believe I can help you."

"I don't think I misunderstood. My son is lying upstairs, dying, and you approach me with wishes and smiles. What is wrong with you? I think you had better leave before I make a scene."

The man stood up to leave; he looked around at the other people sitting at their tables drinking, crying, laughing, and he examined his plastic cup, now empty of the weak tea, and tapped it twice on the table in thought and sat back down.

"Jude, I can save Nick, but you have to be willing to give

something in return. How much do you want your son to live?"

"How do you know my son's name? Who are you?" Jude stood up to leave.

"Jude, please sit, I can explain everything," he gestured for Jude to sit back down. "Please, sit down and listen to me, I am not a mad man; I am your only option now. But before I tell you anything I need you to sit and have a very, very open mind."

Jude decided not to sit.

"Sit!" The man demanded.

Jude, without voluntary movement sat.

"Who are you?" she asked shocked that she was sitting.

"My name is not important, what is important is that you believe me and we save your son's life. I am here to help you, I can remove your son's illness and save him, but you will need to give me something in return. I do not normally do this, I normally would sit back and watch your son die. Tonight you are very lucky." He sat back in his chair and placed his fingers together under his chin waiting for her response.

Jude asked again, "Who are you?"

The man snapped, "Really? Why can't you just let me save your son? Honestly, this is not worth it. Anton was right, he knew you wouldn't believe me."

She let out a little laugh, covered her mouth, "I'm sorry, I didn't mean to laugh."

The man looked at her with anger in his eyes. "Are you stupid? No one laughs at Lucifer! With one snap from my fingers, your son could live or die, but if that isn't what you want, then I will leave." Lucifer stood up his plastic cup melting in his hand.

She made a grab for his arm, "I'm sorry, did you say Lucifer? Is that who you think you are?"

"Think? Think?" The melted cup dripping from his hand onto the floor, Lucifer started to walk off.

Again Jude grabbed his arm. "No, please wait. It's not that I don't believe you, but, you have to admit this is a little farfetched. If you are who you say you are, why me? What do you need from me?"

Lucifer stopped and turned around, "This is not about you Jude, this is about your dying son. I don't think you want my help, I don't think you want your son to live."

Jude started to cry again. "I do, please, I do. What do you want from me?"

Lucifer held her arm and escorted her back to the table.

"For a long time now, I have been looking for an heir to my throne, someone to take over so I can leave and live a normal life. This wouldn't come into play until he was eighteen. I feel that Nick could be perfect for the role."

"What? I would never put my son through that, no, even if you could, no."

Lucifer shrugged his shoulders, "Shame, you would never have known either. Maybe you should return to your son, he only has about an hour left, anyway." He stood and started to walk away again.

Jude paused as she watched him leave. Could she let this chance go? Was this real or just some freak preying on someone at their weakest? He said she had only an hour left before her son died; she didn't want to lose her son.

She left her cup, grabbed her coat and bag and ran after the stranger. As he left through the restaurant door, she followed, grabbing him by his shoulder and pulling him back, "I will do it. I can't lose him. You say I get to keep him until he's eighteen?"

Lucifer turned around and smiled a half-smile, confirming his arrogance, "Yes, when he becomes eighteen, I will swap places with him, and I will live as Nick, whilst he rules Hell. You will never know it's happened, only at the time of the swap. Up till then you will remember that the time will be coming, this will give you time to make him understand what will happen on his eighteenth birthday. The main thing here is, it will give you a life with him and a very solid, powerful future waiting for him to embrace. OK?"

Jude looked at her watch and flustered with her hands while she thought of her son dead or alive, knowing the clock was ticking, and after all this could just be a very sick joke. She looked at Lucifer, his half-smile, his confidence.

"Ok Jude, forget it! I can't stand here all night waiting for your answer. You better get back to your son to say your final goodbyes." Lucifer again started to walk away.

"OK, OK, what do I do?" Jude let a tear trickle down her cheek, she wiped it away in denial.

"Let's do this somewhere less crowded." Lucifer snapped his fingers and they reappeared at the side of Nick's bed in his hospital room. The room was filled with the sound of machines beeping, keeping him breathing. Lucifer reached inside his coat and pulled out a pen and roll of parchment. "Would you like to read it first?" Handing the parchment over to Jude.

Jude opened the roll and skimmed through it, she flicked through the words quickly, but none of it really registered. She pointed at the section at the bottom, "Do I sign here?"

Lucifer nodded. Jude signed it and handed the scroll back. Lucifer placed the scroll and pen inside his coat and reached over to Nick, placed his hand on his forehead, closed his eyes, smiled and removed his hand.

"Done. Enjoy him and I'll see you both in sixteen years. I

will be there to collect at midnight of the last day of his seventeenth year, not a minute earlier nor a minute later. Don't forget Jude, I will return, and I will complete our transaction. Make sure he knows about this and is fully prepared to embrace it; it will make things easier on him."

Lucifer stood up and shook Jude's hand, snapped his fingers and with a loud crack he disappeared.

Jude sat there staring at Nick, waiting for something to happen. Ten minutes had passed, and Jude realised nothing was going to change. She broke down in tears again, placing her head on the bed at the side of dying son, keeping hold of his hand.

"Mummy?"

2

THE BIRTHDAY GIFT

Sixteen years later...

ᴡᴥ

He squinted into the bright sunshine as he slowly opened his eyes. Looking around until his surroundings became clearer. His ears where overburdened with a deafening noise like interference. He could see a man standing over him; he asked a question, but he struggled to hear it as the noise still deafened him. A warm glow filled his chest, and he stood up and stroked the man's face with his hand as he walked past. Crossing the veranda of a beautiful white house overlooking a perfect, white sand beach; he stood at the railing of the balcony, closed his eyes and lifted his face to the sun. Feeling the heat drench his face, he smiled broadly. The noise stopped, and he could hear the lapping of the waves below and the song of the seagulls above him. He turned towards the other man again.

"Ok, one more for the road, Anton."

Nick Fitzroy caught his breath and awoke, feeling the wet on his pillow from his sweating head and drooling mouth. He lay for a moment trying to relive the strange feeling of confidence and power that gripped him after his very vivid dream. He still felt the power tingle through his body, the strength of his mind felt greater, clearer. He rubbed the necklace that he always wore, a charm on a leather strap that he had bought from a man on a beach when he was young. Ten years later and he still wore it; it made him feel safe.

Nick had been the quiet child, always the last one picked. He had spent most of his teenage life avoiding people, hiding away in his bedroom and engulfing himself in reading comics, books and consuming horror films. He watched people, understanding their patterns when they were around other people and when they were alone. As a loner on the outside of his social existence, he had experienced a lot of bullying, vowing that one day he would exact his vengeance on those that had tormented him.

As he got older, he let go of his vengeful appetite and focused instead on digging deeper into what made people click, what turned someone from a nice, approachable person into a prick. He knew the signs and the triggers; Nick read everything on understanding the human psyche, studied his fellow pupils and from time to time tried a few experiments. The experiments didn't always go according to plan, and occasionally ended up with his face being smashed against a wall or floor, but this just reinforced what he had known for a long time: Humans are evil.

This was the seventh night straight that he had had a vivid dream, some were graphic and horrific while others seemed powerful and magical, but always leaving him feeling that the dream meant something more. He felt sick the following day and his mood seemed determined by the direction of the dream. But this last one felt different; it felt final, as though this were the conclusion for some reason.

Nick dragged himself out of bed, got dressed and went downstairs.

In the kitchen, his mother, Jude, stood at the stove cooking bacon, the way Nick liked it, crisp, a shade off being burnt.

"Morning sweetheart, one more day to go until you're eighteen; bet you're excited for tomorrow?"

Nick shrugged in his usual despondent way, "Mum, I had another dream last night."

"Really?" Jude continued to cremate his bacon.

"But this time it felt different like it won't happen again."

Jude placed Nick's breakfast on the table in front of him.

Nick poked at his breakfast, "He said 'One more for the road, Anton', I think that was his friend's name."

Jude froze, her smile left her face, and she turned drip white.

"Anton?" Jude chocked.

"Yeah, I think that is what he said, Anton. Why?"

Jude sat down in front of Nick and grabbed his hand, "Did you see the other man? The other one who said it?"

Nick snatched his hand back, "No, I think I was him, why?"

"No, nothing, sorry, just asking; it seems to have upset you, that's all. You better get off to college"

Nick had noticed a nervousness to his mother that he hadn't seen before; she always seemed relaxed all the time, but not this morning.

He left his breakfast half-eaten and walked out of the kitchen.

"See you later mum." Nick grabbed his coat and bag and left.

Jude stood watching her son leave as her panic and tears took control.

♔

Later that afternoon Nick arrived back home, grateful it was a Friday and tomorrow he would be eighteen. He had felt that if he could get through to being eighteen, his life would change. He would be different and more confident. Nick knew it was just another birthday, but something inside kept telling him that things would change for him, and he believed this with every fibre of his being.

He walked into the kitchen to see a couple of bags packed, and his mother wiping her face with a tissue.

"What's going on? What's happened? Are you ok?"

"I'm fine, just realising how old you are and that tomorrow you will be eighteen. So, I just thought we could go away for the weekend, celebrate like you always want to do. Spend your birthday somewhere different."

Nick was a little taken aback by this. His mother never wanted to go anywhere, and it had always been a fight to get her to go on holiday.

"I guess so, but are you sure?"

"I just want to treat you, you deserve it." She went to hug Nick but he turned quickly to put his coat and bag away.

"Anyway hurry up, go get a few things, and I will start packing the car."

"Where are we going?" Nick asked.

"It's a surprise."

Jude got up and started switching things off, grabbing the bags and coats and then she rushed them into the car. Nick ran upstairs and threw a few things into a bag, looking around for anything else he needed; he stood, rubbing his necklace in thought. Happy with the sudden change of his mother's heart about going away, he shot back downstairs to the waiting car.

Hours later they pulled up outside a cottage in a very small village. Nick stepped out of the car and stretched. Looking around at his new surroundings, he noticed the neighbourhood was only a few old cottages, a pub, a bridge and a small church with a graveyard, the latter being directly opposite the cottage.

"Great mum, this place looks... err... lively."

"Nick, it's nice, and there are a few other villages nearby. Reeth is over that hill, and it has a few more shops. It's nice to get away from everything once in a while."

"I know, I say that all the time to you. But mum, there is a graveyard, just there!" Nick pointed at the church.

"And a pub, you will be eighteen tomorrow, we can go for a drink."

Nick stood staring at the graveyard, rubbing his necklace.

Nick sighed, "It's fine mum, really, it is. Well, at least the cottage looks nice."

Jude smiled again.

They unpacked the car, Nick closed the boot and stood staring at the church, rubbing his necklace between his thumb and forefinger.

"A fucking graveyard of all things. Jesus, what was she thinking?"

As the night enveloped the small village of Grinton, Nick and Jude were sitting down to a cup of tea in front of the television. Jude had just lit the fire in the old stone fireplace, and the room was warming up nicely.

She had been quiet all evening, barely speaking to Nick. She seemed jumpy and looked out of the curtains at every noise, never sitting down for long.

"Mum, are you ok?"

"I'm fine Nick, just fine," Jude replied as she looked out of the curtains into the village. Soft rain coated the pane, and the soft glow of the overhead street lights flooded the road and graveyard opposite.

"So why are you so jumpy? Are you expecting someone?" Nick stood up and joined his mother at the window.

"What? What do you mean?"

"It's like you're expecting someone; every noise, you're at the window."

"What time is it?" Jude asked, now starting to get twitchy.

"Eleven forty-seven."

Jude let the curtains close and she started to pace as she began to cry.

"Mum, what's going on?"

Nick was now getting worried, he had never seen her act like this before. The calm exterior was cracking, and he could see panic starting to seep through. Jude grabbed Nick by both his arms, holding him in place so he listened.

"Nick, I need to tell you something before its midnight and I... I don't want you to be scared or hate me. You have to understand, I have always loved you more than anything." Jude sobbed, struggling to get each word out clearly.

"What? What is it?" Nick grabbed his mum's elbows acknowledging her panic.

"When you was two, you were very ill, as you know, and I was told you only had a couple of hours left. I was approached by a man who promised me you would live if I made a deal with him, I'm so sorry." Jude broke down and dropped to her knees. "He's coming Nick; he's coming to take you."

Nick dropped to his knees and held his mother as she shook in his arms.

"Whoever it was who you spoke to, it was a long time ago, and we are in the middle of nowhere."

"Nick, you don't understand." Jude shook with fear; she held onto him as tight as she could, "He said he was Lucifer."

Nick laughed nervously. "It's ok Mum, I don't think we have anything to worry about. I really don't," Nick said calmly, trying to relax his mother from shaking. "Lucifer isn't real; he is part of a story told thousands of years ago. He is no different from Voldemort."

The grandfather clock in the corner chimed midnight, as the notes rang through the air, Jude jumped in shock.

"Run" she screamed, "you need to go now!" Her hands shoved into his chest, pushing him away from her.

"Mum, stop this; everything is fine. It's just you and me, no-one else is..."

A deafening sound hit the room, like a clap of thunder; it knocked Nick into the wall. He tried to grab his mum and run, but fear paralysed her and she stayed frozen to the spot.

The room filled with a hazy mist as the smell of sulphur slithered in, slowly the fog began to form a dark figure and as the shape became solid, as the haze cleared the room. Standing in front of both Nick and Jude was a tall, thin, immaculately dressed middle-aged man. Nick pulled his mother's arm again only for her to remain frozen to the same spot, looking at the visitor in horror.

"So sorry I'm late Jude, what must you think of me?" The intruder apologised, brushing his hands against the cloth of his pants to remove any loose dirt. He stood up straight and approached Nick with his hand out to shake it, a charming grin stretched across his face.

"Hello, Nick. I hope your Mother has told you all about me. Are you ready? Hell is waiting?" The stranger winked.

Jude grabbed hold of Nick, screaming at the man in fear. "GET OUT! HE ISN'T YOURS!"

"For God sake Jude, please be quiet. Nick, please shut her up; she's making my ears hurt."

Nick let go of his mother arm and stood to shake Lucifer's hand. Realising he seemed to be in a trance, Jude grabbed him back.

"Nick don't speak to him, don't trust him, don't even touch him!" pleaded Jude, as Nick shook himself free from her grasp.

"Nick, again let me apologise; how rude of me. I'm just so excited to meet you. It's not every day you finally get to retire and pass everything you have over to someone else, you must have lots of questions?" Lucifer grabbed Nick's hand with both of his and continued to shake.

"First things first, my name is Lucifer, but I am sure you already know that. I'm a Scorpio; I like long country walks and playing with people's soft inner bits," Lucifer drifted off, caught up in a world of bloody dripping entrails for a few seconds, "only joking I HATE the countryside, too many weirdos!"

Jude was sobbing on the floor, holding on to her son's leg as though her life depended on it. Her words were quieter, almost inaudible as if all of her energy were slowly being depleted.

"I... I don't understand what is happening here," Nick's

voice cracked as he broke his trance and started to regain his focus.

"I'm a little confused myself. Your mother, Jude, should have told you about me, should have been preparing you for a while now; it was part of our deal. Jude, have you been keeping this a secret?" Lucifer confronted Jude as though she were a naughty child, wagging his finger at her in disappointment but knowing full well that Nick hadn't been told before tonight.

Nick's mind started to place all the times he had seen this man's face, the different events in his life when he had been there but only in the background, hiding in plain sight.

"You haven't just told him now have you?" Lucifer said in fake shock.

"NO!" Jude screamed at Lucifer, launching herself at him. With a lazy flick of his wrist, Jude froze mid-flight, as if someone had pressed a pause button. Her face was contorted in a scream of anger, her body shaped like a pouncing animal launched at her prey.

Lucifer sighed. "Honestly, Nick your mother has such a bad temper, I do hope it hasn't filtered down to you."

"What the fuck did you just do to my mum?" Nick asked in shock as he prodded his mother trying to understand how she was hanging in the air, mid-flight.

"Relax Nick, she's perfectly safe. I've just given her a time out; it gives us time to talk," explained Lucifer.

"I'm not talking to you, just let my mum go," Nick demanded, trying without success to move his mother, who was still locked in the same spot.

At that comment, Lucifer stopped grinning and looked at Nick with a tired look on his face.

"OK Nick, let me explain something to you. We can either sit down like mature adults and you can sign this little contract, or I can snap her like a twig, slowing it down so that the images will stain your brain and continue to haunt you every single fucking day for the rest of your life!" Lucifer's patience was running low now, and he was eager to rush things along.

"So Nick, what will it be? Sign the contract, or your mother's death?" Lucifer asked.

Lucifer clicked his fingers and two chairs appeared at either side of a small table, big enough to sign the contract. Lucifer sat, Nick, didn't. Lucifer made a hand motion and Nick sat immediately, against his will.

Lucifer relaxed back in his chair, crossed his legs and tapped his fingertips together, "So Nick, tell me what exactly has your mother told you about me and this deal?"

Nick stared at his mother still floating in the air, "Nothing, until about five minutes ago."

He remembered the strange feeling that he always had about his future and how he knew he was different from all the other people he had met.

Nick looked at Lucifer, "But, I always knew there was something else coming. A different life when I turned eighteen."

Lucifer sat forward, "I knew I got through, I knew my influence would seep in. Great, so let's get this signed." He pulled the parchment out of the air.

Nick panicked, waving his hands at Lucifer. "Whoa!! What happens if I say no?"

"Nothing, you say no and I leave."

"Really?" Nick shocked with Lucifer's reply.

"No, not really! I haven't been waiting around for sixteen years for you to come of age only for you to say no."

"I literally have no say in any of this?"

"Look, I get what I want, your mother gets to keep you. You are merely a pawn."

"I just don't understand what you get out of this. She never explained that." Nick asked.

Lucifer explained the deal to Nick, how he would swap with Nick, and Jude wouldn't remember a thing, Lucifer detailed his need to start fresh like a human and how Nick would take his place in Hell.

Nick paused over the signature line, and asked, "What's in this for me?"

"Power, magic, control. Nick, you will be able to live out your fantasies. But there is work to be done too; nothing comes for free. You will need to adapt and deal with some difficult lessons, but I am sure you will be perfect for the role. However, it can't be shown to you until you sign."

Nick looked again at Lucifer, and then at his mother. "She won't be hurt?"

"No," Lucifer replied.

"Ever?" Nick said.

"Never! I can't do anything to her whilst you stay away, and if you do come back, the deal is off and I can do whatever I want." Lucifer stood up and walked over to Nick's mother and stroked her hair like she was a frozen, floating, dog. "Listen I want this to work just as much as you want your mum to live"

Lucifer patted Jude's head and spun to face Nick, "Now sign the fucking contract!"

As soon as Nick finished signing the contract he looked up, where Lucifer had been standing, now stood a mirror image of Nick.

"Holy fuck!" Nick was shocked to see himself. This new Nick had the big grin on his face, an evil sadistic smile.

"Nick, it's been nice doing business with you. I will look

after Jude, you have my word, as long as you stay away."
Lucifer slapped the frozen, hovering woman's arse.

"I might be you now, but I don't share the same love for
your mother as you do, so you'd better be good." Lucifer
looked back at Nick, "Also, you never really read the contract
in detail, I think you had better spend some time going
through that puppy!" He looked at the watch on his wrist then
looked up at Nick, "Now then off you go, you fucking evil
bastard; enjoy the good life!"

And with a clap of Lucifer's hands, there was another
sound of thunder and the room went black. Nick felt the floor
and walls of the room disappear beneath his feet and he
dropped into the void.

3

COASTAL RETREAT

Nick slowly opened his eyes and quickly closed them again, the brightness of the room blinding him. It took him a few seconds to adjust to his new surroundings. No longer was he in the cottage in Grinton, but in a very large room, on an extremely comfortable bed, bigger than any other bed he had seen before. The room had high ceilings and a window that spread across the entire wall in front of him offering an unforgettable view of a very calm, blue ocean.

He slowly raised his body up from the bed to take in the scene. Nick stepped out of bed and soaked in the sunlight and the panoramic feast. The ocean lapped the spotless white beach below; there were a few birds in the sky and a calmness that can only be found on a deserted island. He stopped breathing for a few seconds in awe, but it didn't last for long as the reality started to hit him.

Nick remembered, what had only seemed to be the night before, his mother crying, begging him to run, an image of the stranger and his smile in the room flashed in his mind. His memory was patchy at best, and he couldn't remember exactly what had happened, but all he wanted to do now was to get back to his mother. Could he believe that she would be safe with him? Could he believe that if he did get close that Lucifer would actually kill her? Was he even who he said he was?

His heart was pounding loud in his chest as he tried to get his bearings. He had no idea where he was or where his mother was. He tried to calm himself, taking deep breaths and looking around the room. Nick saw two doors, one to his left which was ajar, this seemed to be the bathroom, and the second, he presumed, was his way out. A neatly folded pile of clothes, that he didn't recognise, sat on the dresser in the corner of the room. Standing naked in the open room, feeling vulnerable, he rushed to the clothes.

Sitting on the top of the pile of clothes was a note:

"Morning Nick,

I wasn't sure what you would like to wear today, so going on the attire you were wearing when you arrived, I have put these together.

We can discuss your wardrobe once you are ready.

Anton"

Nick quickly got dressed.

As he reached the other door to the bathroom, he caught a glance of his reflection in the mirror, fearing that he wouldn't see his usual face, as he had vague memories of the stranger taking his likeness after he had signed the contract with Lucifer, but he looked no different. He still looked and felt like himself, and he hoped to stay that way.

Nick went to grab the door handle but at the same time the door swung open, and in walked a short, portly gentleman, dressed like a butler, sporting black trousers, black jacket, white shirt and tie, he looked like he had just stepped out of an early Victorian-era drama.

"Ah, good morning, sir, you're awake. Let me introduce myself; my name is Anton, I am your assistant, guide, hand-holder, right-hand man, so to speak. I will also be helping you adapt to your new life, surroundings and most of all powers. If you have any questions, which I am sure you will have, I will try to answer everything you need to know."

Anton stepped back out of the doorway to allow Nick to pass through.

"If you would like to follow me, and as it is such a beautiful morning, I thought you would like to eat outside on the veranda."

Nick followed Anton through the living area, open kitchen and through the doors on to the veranda. A table sat outside overlooking the white, glistening, sands of what seemed to be an enclosed bay. Anton pulled out a chair and proceeded to steer Nick into it.

Nick sat down, not sure how to behave in this unusual situation. He thought about making a run for it, but had no idea where to go; he didn't even know where he was.

"Anton, where am I?" Asked Nick.

"Your coastal retreat, sir," Replied Anton.

"Ok, but where exactly is that?"

"Ah, well, it's not something I can explain, exactly; it's not a real place, more like a parallel universe of sorts, but not." Anton tried to explain, but it seemed to go over Nick's head.

"Is this... Hell?" Nick asked confused by his surroundings.

"Oh God no, this isn't Hell. *This* is your haven, well the previous king's haven; you might want to change at a later time. Once you start to understand how all this works, you can have it more your own style?" Anton replied with a smile.

Nick's mind started to stray thinking about his home and his mother.

"Right, I'm sorry, this feels so wrong, I'm trying to listen but I'm really worried about my mother being left with him, Lucifer. How do I get home?"

"I'm sorry, sir, you can't go home; did Lucifer not explain everything? If you were to return, he would hurt your mother. You signed the contract. It can't be broken. You must stay here and fulfil your obligations," Anton warned Nick.

"I know the concept, Anton, but it's not that simple; I can't just switch off from worrying about my mother."

"I understand, sir, but you will need to learn to embrace your new life. You must be the King of Hell sir."

Nick paused as he took in the last Anton's last phrase.

"Hell, right, so how does this work? Is Hell real?" he asked, expecting the answer to be filled with fire, blood and brimstone.

"What were you expecting?"

"You know, fire, torture, the usual inferno"

"Not really, sir, Hell isn't a physical place, it's more a state of mind. Hell is the place where you think things can't get any worse, but they can, and that is where you step in; you make it worse." A smile crossed over Anton's face, "The best part about your job is to remove the soul, however possible."

"What happens to the soul?"

"It is passed to Hades; he then decides who has been naughty and who has been nice, so to speak."

"I thought that was Santa's job," Nick smirked.

Anton gave Nick a smile as he poured some orange juice into Nick's glass.

"I'm not really sure this is for me. Look, this can't be

right; I really need to get back to my mother." Nick stood up in urgency trying to get back on track.

"I see," Anton said as he continued to lay Nick's breakfast, "What do you intend to do? Rescue your mother from Lucifer, who, in her eyes is you now. And your mother, now has no idea who you are as she won't see you as you but someone else. Also, not to forget, returning would lift the magic that hangs over her protecting her from any danger."

"Look, I know what he said, but surely that's not real, I mean magic, that's not real, is it?" Nick mocked.

Anton laughed at this, "No, of course not!" He said almost sarcastically.

"Have your breakfast, and we will then move onto what wonders you signed up for." Anton lay a napkin over Nick's lap. "Bon appetite, sir."

Nick ate very little and spent most of the next thirty minutes looking around nervously; he prodded at his food not trusting it or Anton or his new home.

Anton returned shortly and after collecting the various untouched plates of food, he carried them into the kitchen. Once all had been cleared away he came back and sat opposite Nick.

"So, sir, would you now like to know what exactly you signed up for? What you have to gain?"

Nick looked at Anton; he had questions constantly building in his head, each one more important than the last, but one took precedence: He needed to know his mother was ok

"I need to see if my mum is ok? How can I do that without hurting her?"

"Pick up the computer tablet on the table. Yes Nick, we have technology too. Now ask what you want to see."

Nick looked disappointed with Anton's response.

"Really? I thought you would use something more magical."

"You have this because it's easier for you to accept science over magic, as you develop your skills you won't need this," Anton explained.

Nick picked up the tablet, "Is my mother ok?" The screen blinked to life; it showed the living room of his house, his mother sat on the sofa laughing whilst watching the TV. She shouted to someone in the kitchen, "Don't forget the biscuits." As he watched, another person walked into the room carrying two drinks and a packet of biscuits; he sat at the side of his mother. She leaned on him whilst they sat, laughed and enjoyed their drinks and the program they were watching. She looked relaxed and happy; they both did.

"She doesn't even know it's not me; why can't she see it's not me?" Nick held back the tears as every inch of him ached to see her, not knowing that she was in danger.

Anton looked at Nick, "What did you expect? Lucifer has planned this for a very long time. He's tired of being what he is; he's done it for thousands of years; he wants to be human; he wants the human emotions; he wants to feel. He wants to be mortal. When he became you, he got everything he has ever wanted; your mum has everything she wants too. If you try to interfere with that the repercussions would be fatal."

Nick laid the tablet face down on the table; he placed his head in his hands, "What do I do now? I thought that this might be what I wanted, but it doesn't feel right, I always felt different, but not like this." Tears started to well up in his eyes but the anger forced him to wipe them away quickly and hold them back. "I will find a way to get my life back; this isn't the end of it."

"Nick, I know you won't be finding any of this easy but I

can help you. I can ease the pain, even make you see just how good the deal you have is."

Nick stood up and walked to the end of the veranda and looked over the view, gripping the railing between him and the cliffs below. His body ached of loss but his pride kept him strong. So many times in the past when he had taken a beating, he had held everything in knowing one day he would get his revenge.

Nick was still holding his head trying to make sense of everything. He slowly lifted his head up and looked at Anton. "Can I beat him?"

"Now? No. In time? Maybe."

"Teach me, train me so I can beat him, make him beg, I want to destroy him, Anton."

Nick saw Anton squirm slightly, "What's wrong? I presume that isn't what you want me to do?"

"Sir, I don't think it's wise for you to build your anger up just yet; your powers need to be developed, you need to be stronger; right now you are weak, you need to learn first."

"I know this won't be easy for you, but remember it's me and you now. He has abandoned you too leaving you with me."

Anton nodded in agreement, Nick could see disappointment in his eyes.

"It's not going to be easy; you will need to embrace this new life, develop your new skills, let your feelings, morals, doubts, loves be changed. To beat him, sir, you will need to become him, I am sure over the years he will be changing too, becoming more human, soft, weak, like you."

"So it's possible? It won't be easy but it is possible?"

"Yes, but you have a lot of work to do; you are soft and weak now, mentally and physically," explained Anton, "I will leave you to think, sir. Enjoy your new surrounding and let me know when you want to start."

Nick nodded in acceptance and watched Anton leave through the kitchen doors.

Nick looked out over the clear, calm ocean, taking in the odd bird in the sky, the white glistening sands below. He scanned the view around him, the hillside behind the white-walled home was just as beautiful with picturesque palm trees like you would see on postcards. Nick felt the sun beat down warming his body. He thought it wasn't a bad place, and he realised that this thing did have some benefits and decided it was time to take a further look around and understand the full picture here.

Anton was in the next room; the room was again large with an immaculately clean kitchen area, he was just clearing away the washing up from the breakfast.

"Ok, Lucifer mentioned power and magic, but didn't give me any details, honestly. I don't remember reading the contract, so I will need to understand that later. If this is my life, I want control of it, I want to know what I can do."

"Sir, you have the power to have or do anything you want; no one will challenge you; no one will ever have anything even close to the power and wealth that you have."

"What power do you mean? Is this like supernatural power? Or like Mafia power?" Nick questioned.

"The supernatural type, if you want the type of Mafia power then you just need to take it."

Nick's eyes lit up in anticipation.

"You have been given amazing gifts; for example, if you want something you just need to ask for it. In time you will learn how to ask for it in silence, and your power will develop too," Anton explained. "Also, it helps that you are revered worldwide; people worship you, people need you, people crave you. You can make someone's dreams come true, or you can destroy them; you can control people or kill people; nobody can do anything to you. You are in complete control."

Nick could see the delight creep into Anton's face as he explained.

"How do I do it? Just ask?" Nick asked Anton.

"Yes, start small, an apple for example"

Nick held out a hand.

"I want an apple," Nothing happened. He tried again, "I want an apple." Still nothing.

"Don't just say 'I want an apple.' Demand it! Don't forget you are the King of Hell. Demand," Anton instructed.

"I want an apple!" Nick demanded still holding out his hand, still nothing.

"Ok, try it with a click of the fingers too, that might be your style."

Nick was becoming impatient, "I WANT an APPLE!" At the same time, he clicked his thumb and middle finger together. As he did he felt the power surge through him and in through his palm. A slight crack was heard and a perfect apple sat in his opened hand.

"Oh shit! Anton!" Nick stood shocked, and it was at that point his mind started to turn, he imagined developing his newfound power and watching a cowering Lucifer in front of him begging for mercy.

He took a bite of the apple and spat it out immediately.

"That needs some work!" Nick laughed.

"I don't know how I will be able to do the things he did. It's not in my nature to do things that will hurt people," Nick said looking down at the bitten apple which was rotten inside.

"I know, but you will find a way. Look we have time at the moment. I will teach you skills that will help you control all your abilities. It's not just about making things appear at will; it's mind control, its persuasion, seduction, manipulation, altering reality and more. You have all this embedded inside of you, and I will help you release it all. It won't be easy and you will need to work very hard, but we will get you there."

Nick and Anton continued to discuss the options of where to start the training and began to formulate a very loose schedule. Nick kept thinking about his mother and what kind of man he would be when he could return to his normal life. What would be left of the son she loved deeply and how much of his mind would still be normal and not twisted into some unrecognisable, cold, heartless mess?

Over the next few months, Anton taught Nick how to hone his skills; he trained every day. His magic abilities grew and developed faster than Anton had expected. He knew he would have to face tasks outside of the retreat soon, but he didn't realise just how soon.

4

SCARRING OF THE SOUL

The beeps began hidden by the darkness; her eyes blinked open surrounded by the usual machines and lime green concrete walls. The smell of hospitals and flowers crammed up her nostrils as she coughed on the concoction of fragrances. The cough hurt her throat and chest and woke up her stomach.

She felt the sickness rise and she made a grab for the pan on her bed, what was left of yesterday's soup presented itself in the silver bowl. She closed her eyes and slumped back in her bed. Breathing heavily as her stomach swirled around, she made quick little swallows trying to keep the sickness at bay.

She opened her eyes again and squinted at the clock. Looking around she noticed a woman asleep at her side in a comfy chair. Who was she? She was someone she was sure she knew, but it wasn't clear – maybe her mother? The cannula in her arm started to feel large, the pain started again in her head. She closed her eyes and welcomed the darkness.

The rain lashed down from the late November night sky on the small town of Hollywell in Eastbourne, England. Thunder rumbled in the distance over the ocean, and Jennifer Clarke was standing facing the sea, soaked to the skin, hands clenched, tears rolling down her face.

She had spent the last two years in remission from lung cancer; she now lived her life to the fullest, and couldn't think of ever going back to the sick, painful, hair-loss days of her cancer again. She had fallen in love after her ex left her when things got bad. Her 10-year-old son had really been her rock, kept her up when things got her down, and her mother never left her side. Chris, her new man, had been like a father to her son and had been the everything that Jennifer needed – caring, loving and understanding.

But today the news from the doctors had been bad; cancer had returned and this time it wouldn't be treatable. There wasn't a clear length yet on how long there was left, but, to put everyone through the hell they had endured the last time and not to have a happy ending just wasn't fair.

So here stood Jennifer, 34-years-old, close to the edge of the world, close to beating cancer once and for all, in control of stopping the pain of telling everyone the diagnosis; she would end it before cancer did. It would be better for everyone else.

She had been here for the last fifteen minutes, building up the courage to jump. The heavy rain lashing her clothes, she felt the wetness on her cold skin, her fists were now so tight she could feel her nails starting to cut her palms. Tears mingled with the rain that streamed down her face.

"Excuse me?"

A voice shouted to her through the wind.

"Whatever has put you here today isn't worth it."

The man ran to her but stopped a distance from where Jen stood.

The man shouted again, battling with the weather.

"What's your name? Mine is Clive."

"Please, don't stop me, please. I have to do this; I can't go through this again," Jennifer yelled back as her words came in between deep gasps of tears and wind.

"Ok, just tell me why this is your path? What has put you here tonight?"

Clive had talked many final-moment victims from the edge of Beachy Head; unfortunately, he had also failed on several occasions, and he wore these heavy losses on his heart. Twenty years of volunteering to help people who came here, just to help them rethink their issues. This place had been a popular suicide spot, and a small team made sure there was always someone there to help. A group of volunteers helping lost souls from the edge of a very steep drop.

Tonight Clive had a good feeling about this one; she just needed a hand, some guidance.

As Clive got close, he slowed down trying not to intimidate her.

He asked again, "What's your name?"

"It doesn't matter. I don't matter..."

She took a step closer, slowly looking over the side to the sheer steepness into the black.

She could hear the darkness calling her. Almost pleading with her.

"Why don't you come with me and have a small drink? Just two minutes, talk to me and see if you still need to do this. Please, if you're going to do this, two minutes won't matter. You see if you jump, we have no details, and the paperwork is a nightmare; trust me, please." He said, trying to bring a small joke into a very dark moment.

"Please, just two minutes?"

Clive had stepped a bit closer almost enough to be able to grab her if things changed for the worse.

Nearby, watching, stood a dark figure; he was calm, just absorbing the atmosphere. The rain was pounding down hard now, but, no drops seemed to fall on him. He moved to sit on a nearby bench, just close enough to hear the voices in the distance.

This was his first soul; he wasn't going to rush things. He was nervous, feeling a little sick, but the task was there to be completed one way or another. The vision had come earlier, strong and clear. He was here for her; it didn't feel right, but, he knew he didn't have an option and this had to be done.

Clive made a small step closer, making sure he didn't get too close to Jennifer or the edge of the cliff.

"Come on just two minutes. What's it going to change, huh? Please lady, at least if you do decide to go, I will be able to tell your loved ones that you didn't go without talking it through. Give them a reason otherwise they may never know."

Jennifer's son's face came into her mind again; what were two minutes? She shuffled a little further back from the edge, but with the rain and the mud under her feet she slipped suddenly. Clive made a grab for her arm, but her weight pulled him down and his feet slipped away too.

Nick nearby sat up straight, engrossed in the scene; his instinct was to run and help. However, he needed to stay put; he needed to make sure the story played out as expected.

Jennifer panicked and tried to grab Clive, but his feet couldn't get a grip and his body weight was now dragging him to the edge. Jennifer's foot caught a rock in the ground; she had found stability. Now holding Clive's arm, she tried to keep him from slipping off the edge.

"Stop moving!" Jennifer begged, "Keep still, please."

Clive stopped trying to get a hold of something, as Jennifer pulled now with all her strength, and his slipping stopped. He had one foot hanging off the edge. One little slip would take him over, and it would all be her fault.

"Ok, two minutes. I will come, we have just got to get out of this mess. I don't want you to die, even if I do."

Nick strolled close to them, dry and not slipping on the wet mud.

"Hey, how are you folks doing?"

"Help us!" screamed Jennifer. Still keeping tight hold of Clive and Clive remaining deadly still.

"Please?" begged Clive.

Nick stood there, holding his clenched fist to his mouth, trying not to be sick, debating for what seemed to be a couple of minutes. The task was to take Jennifer, but Clive was now part of the package.

He stopped thinking about the two in front of him and remembered his mother's face, her laugh and Lucifer's smile.

Who was Clive?

Did he deserve to die?

Did Jennifer?

He closed his eyes, holding in the bile now rising in his stomach.

"Sorry, I really can't help you. Not directly anyway."

He crouched at the side of Clive.

"Jennifer is her name, Clive. She came here tonight to give me her soul. She was meant to be my first; it should have been easy. But you have made things difficult. The question I have now is: Do I take you too? Jennifer's grip is loosening and you can feel it, can't you? Clive, I think your time's up, mate." Nick's voice was calm and clear.

"No, please, I have children, a wife, they need me," Clive pleaded.

Nick laughed to himself.

"Clive, whilst you have been saving lives here, your wife, Karen is it? Well, she has been fucking your brother. She ain't going to miss you! Your son might, but he will grow up to hear the story of how you died saving another woman when you should have been at home with them, trying to save your marriage."

Nick stood up, without slipping in the mud and stepped back from the two to think. He put his fist to his mouth; he could feel the bile rise again. He closed his eyes and clicked his fingers; this paused the moment. The rain stopped and there was silence.

Nick gathered his thoughts and calmed his stomach. He took a few deep breaths and decided to only take one soul; baby steps he thought.

Nick clicked his fingers and the rain raged down again.

"Ok, Clive, tonight is your lucky night, you have a choice. I take your soul or hers?" Nick pointed at Jennifer, "Bear in mind that she had come here to end her life, not yours, hers."

Nick looked at Jennifer, "Well, this hasn't gone to plan has it?"

"Who the fuck are you?" Jennifer asked in shock, "I mean, you appear from nowhere and act as though this is a fucking game! Like it's your fucking game."

"You don't need to know who I am, and this is no game. This is reality, Jen. You wanted to end it all tonight, well that will still happen just not how you planned it."

Nick looked back at Clive, "Ok, Clive, have you decided?"

Clive started to cry.

"I have, please save me. I'm so sorry Jennifer, I tried to help, I just don't want to die. I'm so sorry."

Nick put his hand down to help Clive up, Clive grabbed it eagerly. The mud around his feet dried, allowing him to stand. Nick then helped Jennifer up, both covered in mud and soaked from the constant rain, Clive looked ashamed of his decision.

"I thought you were just going to save me and let her die?"

"Clive, I am disgusted in your cowardice. She saved your life, and now you repay her by letting her die. I mean, you could have just walked away in the first place, but no, you had to stick your fucking nose in."

"Jen, I bet you would like to change your mind now? To hold your child for the last few months you have left? And let's just say what if I told you I could cure your lung cancer? But, you had to kill him for me to do it?"

"Just who the fuck *are* you?"

"My name is Nick. I am really not sure what I am yet. I just know that one of you will go over that edge tonight!"

Nick walked over the edge of the cliff and stared into the blackness.

"What?" Jen spat.

"It really is that simple. Clive has decided to watch you fall, knowing he could have saved you to live out what is left of your life with your boy. But his life is in danger, so he decided to let you die to save his skin, so he can live, even though his brother is boning his wife."

"Stop saying that!" whimpered Clive.

"Stop fucking crying, man. He is and has been for years. So, Jen, what's it going to be?"

Nick stepped up to her; he grabbed her hands gently, "I can make it all go away; you could live your life and never get caught?"

"Are you fucking kidding me? You could cure me, and I would never get it again? I would be free?"

She looked deep in his eyes, tears flowing down her face, using her wet sleeve she wiped her face.

"Forever!" Nick said softly lifting her chin up to his eyes again.

For that moment Nick's feeling of sickness had gone; things were clear in how he could do this job, this life. He would help the right people, and he would punish the bad and help the needy, the underdog.

"What's the catch?" Jennifer asked quickly.

"No catch, its either you or him," Nick explained whilst stroking her cheek, at this point Nick could see that Jennifer was already planning her life.

"I'll do it!"

Jen let go of Nick's hands and charged at Clive, both arms out to push him off the cliff's ledge. Clive tried to stop her from grabbing him by pushing her away; he tried to turn to run, but the sloppy mud was back under his feet and he slipped. Clive tried to grab Nick to help him but Nick just watched.

Like a wolverine, Jen attacked Clive, pushing and scratching at his arms and face, cuts were forming, and blood was starting to drip from his cheeks and lips where she had clawed at him. His arms flailed trying to stop Jen from inflicting more damage to his face.

Clive was really close to the cliff's edge but somehow he managed to grab Jennifer and scream at her.

"I'm taking you with me, you fucking whore!"

They both grabbed, clawed and screamed at each other, the mud under them still dragging them to the fringe. Clive threw a punch at Jen, it caught her on the jaw stopping her movements forward for a second, but it only served to heighten her anger. She threw one last kick at him; he lost his grip and panicked. He flapped his arms around trying to grab something but nothing was there; he lost his footing and fell backwards, screaming, off the edge of the white cliff's sheer drop and into the darkness of the void below.

Jennifer, crying into her hands in hysterics, was covered in mud and blood. Nick picked her up and carried her to the bench where he had sat earlier.

"What have I done, I... I... just killed him! What happened to me? That wasn't me!"

Jennifer broke down in tears; she was in shock at what she had done. She had turned into an animal, devoid of remorse or fear at that moment. She was scared that she could do that. She looked at Nick.

"Did you make me do that?" She asked with a whimper.

"No Jen, that was all you. We all have that in us; I just help raise it to the surface, but it was already in you. All humans are born with evil inside, some nurture it, some suppress it, but it is always there."

Nick was at the side while Jennifer leaning forward with her elbows on her knees.

"You still want cancer?" Nick asked.

"No, please take it away," she begged Nick.

Nick turned to her and held her face softly and kissed her gently on her lips. At that moment she could feel her body slowly get lighter almost floating; she was feeling her head become very light as though she were about to pass out.

After a few seconds Nick pulled away slowly, and he could still feel her soft, full lips on his mouth for a few seconds after.

"You're cured. I recommend you go back and get checked again. I can't prove it any other way."

Although Jennifer could feel a difference, she was still slightly dazed from the kiss; she had never felt anything like that before.

"I don't know what to say?" She gushed, stumbling for the words to express what she was feeling.

"Don't say anything. Just get in your car and go. I will clear up here. Enjoy your life, enjoy your son. Have a good life."

Nick stood up and walked away to the cliff edge and jumped off.

Jennifer quickly ran over to the cliff edge where Nick had just disappeared. Watching her footing, she looked over. Nick reappeared floating in the air in front of her from the darkness below.

"Jenny, I told you to go. Now fuck off!"

She ran in the opposite direction towards her car.

Sitting in her car in silence for a few moments, trying to get her breath back, trying to take in everything that had just happened, she remembered Clive. He just wanted to help, she could have given him two minutes. She reflected on the demon she become for those few minutes. She kept thinking back to how her heart was racing, the blood lust pumping through her veins, how it felt attacking him, and then the shock at what she had done.

The kiss, God, the kiss, the gentleness. The kiss was so deep; she felt as though her soul had been touched; she couldn't shake it.

Her mind jumped back to the reality that she was a murderer and needed to go, now!

Scrambling for her keys in her pocket, ramming them in the ignition, she started the car on the first attempt and with her wheels spinning to get a grip, she sped away.

5

BENEATH THE SKIN

Anton waited in the portal room for Nick to return. Within seconds Nick crashed back into the room and slammed into the hard floor. His head banged against the cold stone, and he instantly threw up. Vomit ran in-between the carvings on the floor, slowly making its way to the edge of the circle. Nick watched it run, spreading in the contours of the portal's carving. He looked up at Anton and struggled to his feet, paused, but the room didn't and the walls spun forcing him back to his knees.

"FUCK! FUCK!"

Nick screamed at the floor in rage as another mouth full of vomit forced its way out.

"Anton, I fucked that up so bad!"

Anton handed Nick a handkerchief, Nick patted his lips hoping not to trigger another flow.

"FUUUCCKKK!" Nick continued to scream.

"It's not that bad, Sir. You took a soul, forced another one to do it. That was pretty good for your first outing."

Anton smiled at Nick sympathetically. "Go get a rest and some food; we will analyse this later."

Nick gathered himself and left the room.

"Sir, what are you going to do about the girl?"

Anton asked over his shoulder as he mopped the puke up off the floor.

"I don't know what you mean?"

"Don't make it a habit of saving the damsel in distress; they don't always stay the same."

Anton finished chasing fluids with the mop in the portal room and dragged the bucket behind him, closing the door.

Nick walked into the kitchen and grabbed some cold chicken from the fridge and some fruit from the fruit bowl and sat outside. He had been here now for four months but the view still took his breath away. The warmth from the sun started to soak through his skin and within a few minutes, he had started to feel less like emptying his stomach.

He kept thinking back to how Jennifer had changed when her survival instinct had been on display. It shocked him to see she was like a wild animal. Her arms and legs were just attacking Clive with so much anger he couldn't gain control. All he could do was try to block or push her but her attack was too intense.

And the kiss to cure her cancer, how she felt, he could still feel the deepness of the kiss. He had kissed before but not like that; there was something more to it. As he sat there reliving the moment he realised that he could sense her faintly, as he could still feel her touching him.

He stopped analysing the moment in his mind and started to eat. Nick picked up the butler's bell on the table and rang it. Within a moment Anton appeared beside him.

"You rang, sir?" Anton asked.

"When I removed her cancer, I decided to do it by a kiss," Nick stated.

"I saw, sir. Nice touch," Anton said.

"But for some reason, I still feel her on my skin, why?" Nick said touching his lips lightly.

"Ah, sir, I see. With the desire and yearning to be cured so much and with the murder of Clive, the soul would be more to the surface. Then with the kiss and the cleansing of cancer, there will have been contact with your soul. Normally, the yearning alone would have raised the soul, and the contact would have created what humans call, love." A slight repulsion fell on Anton's face.

"However, as the soul was raised due to the selfishness of her actions, it may have just been one way, and she won't be able to stop thinking about the moment for a long time. I have seen this before. Humans crave the feeling of it so much it pushed them over the edge. The want to relive the moment so much, they would go to any end to replay the moment." Anton explained.

"My advice, sir, would be to stay clear of her; let her path play itself out."

Nick couldn't stop thinking about how warm Jennifer's kiss was on his lips, the wetness of her skin on his hands. He tried to refocus his mind on the view, his food, anything else but her.

"Would you like to discuss how your first undertaking went, sir? Or would you prefer to do this after sleep? You must be exhausted?" Anton enquired.

Nick thought for a moment. He was tired but awake, and his mind was still racing. The initial plan had been a simple one; he would guide Jennifer over the edge of the cliff and her soul would be his; it was that simple.

The chance of that self-righteous arsehole jumping in and messing the whole thing up was not expected. Nick wanted to wring his interfering neck himself, but he wasn't ready for the guilt. Even though he had the power and reasons to do it, he just couldn't bring himself to do it.

"Ok Anton, let's talk, I will try to get some sleep after that," Nick replied.

Anton sat down opposite Nick and leaned forward onto the table between them.

"Right, sir. You should always expect the unexpected. To be fair, the initial victim was in a popular suicide area with local volunteers on hand to help. What made the event interesting, however, was your offer to cure her cancer."

"I don't regret it," Nick snapped.

"I know, that's fine, but I didn't foresee her seizing that chance so easily. Did you notice how at the point when you offered her this, how she didn't even think about saying no to you? How taking another life was not even a worry? I think she was already broken at that point."

"That is why she was there though, surely?"

"This was good for you to see, just how willing humans can be to commit the worst sin to get something they want. Now even though Clive saved the night by dying, there is just one thing that worries me – the damsel, this could turn on you. Keep your distance, forget about her."

"Ok, I will. I'm used to being alone." Nick hung his head.

"You need to take the next soul, sir. We now need to start to step things up. Get some sleep, and we will begin again tomorrow."

Nick stood up from the table, said goodnight to Anton and went to his room; he removed his clothes and climbed into bed. He was tired now, but his mind was still racing. All he could think of was the evening's events and how things didn't go according to plan.

Flashes of the night kept jumping into his mind, the rain, the mud, his nerves, Clive begging, Jennifer's eyes, her lips, her wet skin, her clothes soaked – stuck to her shapely figure. Her face looking up at him as he stroked her cold cheek, that moment when all the desire, hatred, fear, fight and evil in her emerged. He could see her eyes cloud over, the primal urge raging forward.

At that point, he knew she wasn't like anyone he had met before, but he was still young, still naive. Maybe most people were like this, and the raising of their own inner hell wouldn't take that much. He obviously knew that there were some people in this world who were evil and would kill for the pleasure, but he couldn't relate to this. He used to think he could, but not anymore. Yet, he knew he would have to become numb to this part; he had to build up his willingness to take a life he would need to if he wanted his own life back.

He let his eyes close and drift into sleep.

Every drop of rain seemed to cover the blade in his hands. He looked down at the object on the floor. Slivers of light highlighted the unconscious, naked girl's contours.

He lowered the blade toward her wrists and started to cut down, following the blue veins towards the inside of her elbow, and then the other arm, slowly watching the red ooze from her arms.

He lowed himself down over her blood, aching for the warmth to envelop his lips, he began to drink.

He could feel himself sink into her soul, devouring him, drowning him. He realised he couldn't breathe, he tried to pull back, gain control again, but he couldn't catch his breath and started to choke. Panic seized him, but it was too late; the picture in front of him started to fade until everything vanished.

He looked up again and strained his eyes to get accustomed to his new surroundings; he was in a coffee shop or a fifties American diner. Looking out across a parking lot, looking down realising he was stirring a cup of coffee. He looked up across the table to a young woman talking to him, not hearing what she was saying, he turned the napkin dispenser so he could see his reflection. He could see a young man with blonde short hair and a scruffy, wispy beard.

The reflection shocked him, slowly stroking the contours of his image it sickened him. He turned and looked back at the woman who was speaking to him with a concerned look on her face, her voice still in silence.

He looked down at his hands now dripping in blood. Nick looked back up to see the woman screaming, arms out in front of her dripping with blood. A river of red had now covered the floor where she stood, Nick looked down again and collapsed back into the blackness.

He was aware of something else now, an aroma, an acrid metal taste forming in his throat. The smell of rotting meat, a putrid smell. The room was in complete darkness; he kept blinking trying to focus in the dark.

He patted around with his palms to try and find clues to his location. He found something, something cold and wet. Pulling his hand back quickly, repulsed by the contact, it was then the smell hit him, this time bringing a lump to his throat, holding the vomit back, trying not to release.

He got to his feet and nearly fell over as the cold object dropped at his feet. Rebalancing himself, looking around, he spotted a crack of light. Carefully he stepped over to the light, trying not to step on anything that would take him down. He pushed the doors forward, the moonlight burst through the storm doors, blinding him.

Catching his breath and clearing the smell of rot from his

nose, he turned his head back into the darkness. That's when he caught the shape of a young girl, maybe thirteen-years-old but it wasn't completely clear, just lying there staring into the night sky -- cold, expressionless, colourless, rotting. The smell hit him again, this time he felt a powerful charge run through him like electricity. He closed the storm doors, padlocked them, slipped the key in his pocket, turned and stepped into the darkness.

♕

Nick sat up bolt right, sweating, breathless. He looked out over the ocean view, he was back in his bed and thankful. He could still smell the rot and taste the blood. He was wide awake and felt the fear racing through his thoughts, but it was clear in his mind what his next move had to be.

This vision was stronger and clearer than any he had previously experienced, so much so it confused him. Being in someone else's body and mind was a new experience for Nick; he didn't like not being in control; he was not a passenger. He knew the vision had announced his next soul; he was sure it was the monster that he had to destroy.

Nick was ready for this task, he was looking forward to punishing him. He was evil and how he made Nick feel – he never wanted to feel like that again. But, the vision also brought him pleasure and a strong dominating sense of power. Nick felt that he was ready to take the next step in his training. It was time to wake Anton.

Nick raced through the house towards the portal room; he called for Anton to meet him there. He had a lot to tell him and a lot to do. A few minutes later Anton stumbled into the room yawning.

"Sir? Is everything ok?"

Nick grabbed Anton by his shoulders and tightened his grip.

"I've had another vision, only this time it felt so real. I could feel, taste, smell, everything this bastard did. He's taken five already' he's looking for his next. I can stop him, Anton, I want to stop him!"

Nick positioned himself in the middle of the pentagram and prepared himself for the jump.

"Sir, are you sure it's him that you are meant to kill? It might be the next victim you want," said Anton, half asleep and struggling to keep his eyes open.

"Anton, wake up. I need you to be awake for this; don't let me down!"

Nick passed him the details of the location to which he needed to be sent.

"Get me to him. Now!" demanded Nick.

He braced himself ready for the discombobulating jump.

"I'm taking this fucker out; he won't know what hit him!"

Nick concentrated on the face he had seen in the mirror in the diner, the hair, the beard, his eyes.

Anton started the process and the room filled with the strong smell of brimstone and smoke, then CRACK and Nick was gone.

"I hope you're right, sir, Serial killers are not that easy to close in on; they know how to stay hidden," Anton shouted as he faded.

Nick arrived in a children's playground, out of view. He looked around at his new surroundings. In the distance, he could see five teenagers sitting on a small kid's roundabout slowly spinning and talking loudly among themselves; now and then laughing would break out. Nick couldn't see anyone nearby who could be his man.

The playground was surrounded by a park, well-kept with plenty of low light over the pathways and trees. The time seemed to be early evening around five o'clock and the day was starting to give way to dusk; the sky had started to cloud over, and the lights in the playground had just come on. The teenagers decided it was time to leave and started to make their way out of the playground to head home.

Nick's eyes darted around everywhere trying to see the guy he was after; however, he wasn't lucky. He closed his eyes to try to sense him, to smell him, but nothing.

Nick decided to follow the kids, hoping that this was a prelude to the incident, keeping his distance so he wasn't seen. The teens split ahead of Nick, the two boys broke away to the left leaving the two girls and the remaining boy to continue ahead. Nick stopped and started to panic: Who was he supposed to follow? The two who broke away didn't give off any vibe, and he knew his target wasn't after boys.

They reached the end of the park and Nick watched the two girls hug goodbye, shouting their goodbyes at each other across the road as they parted. It was at this point Nick noticed the white Ford slowly pulling away from the side of the street heading towards the girl. Nick clicked his fingers to reposition himself closer; he could feel the excitement grow in his chest as he knew his target would be feeling the same levels at this moment.

6

VERMIN CHILD

Evening fell awakening the street lights hanging above. Shadows stretched in between the parked cars, and the streets were beginning to grow more quiet as Sunday night beckoned. The white Ford had been waiting outside the park, in silence, anticipating the departure of the youths. He watched, feeling the excitement grow and now his wait was over. He savoured each moment, watching his new obsession caress the trees that grew over the park wall as she walked home, grabbing the odd leaf, crunching it and dropping it to the pavement. He put the car into gear and slowly pulled out.

The white car crawled behind her. She heard the rumble of the engine and quickly looked back. Her heart started to quicken and so did her pace. The car matched the increase in her cadence. Quietly he pulled alongside her, his excitement growing; he rolled the window down slowly, soaking in her youthful beauty. Sarah's heart was racing in her chest; her pace increased again. She looked for someone she could run to, but there was no one around. The car matched her pace.

The smell from the car hit her, a mixture of tobacco,

alcohol and something else. It vaguely reminded her of the dead fox at the bottom of her garden she had found last year. Then the aroma of strong aftershave, sweet and cheap, hit her, and that was the smell that would last, curdling her stomach as the fear wrenched at her innards.

"Hey, excuse me? I wondered if you could help, I think I'm lost."

The man's voice made her skin crawl, but she didn't stop. She didn't know him and didn't want to; her pace was almost a run. She was scared if she did run, he would run her over.

He had bided his time, stalked her from the shadows for a week now waiting for the perfect time to make his move. It was just a matter of patience and calmness; she wasn't his first and wouldn't be his last.

"Hey, sorry, I don't mean to scare you. I just need a pointer at least. I'm sure I'm nearly there. Look why don't you get in and show me? It would only be 2 minutes, I promise," the man said leaning towards her whilst keeping one eye on the road ahead.

His southern accent was hidden under the gruffness of his voice. She thought it was a familiar voice, but she couldn't quite place it. She just wanted to be away from him, looking at him would slow her down.

Hearing his voice again, Sarah's pace turned into a run, her heart was trying to climb out of her chest. All she could think about was getting away, getting home to her family, anywhere but here.

"Hey, Missy, what the fuck do you think you're doing?!!"

He shouted after her. He knew he couldn't leave without her; he always got what he wanted.

Sarah started to cry as she ran as fast as she could; her legs ached in horror and she could hear him shout after her.

She was close to home and only had to cross the road, so close.

Seeing her opportunity, she ran in front of the car, as she dropped off the pavement to run across the road her foot landed wrong, and her ankle buckled under her.

Seeing her fall, he went to jump out of the car and grab her; however, the handle didn't work and the door wouldn't open. A tap on his shoulder and he turned to see someone in his car he didn't know. With the arrival of this new person, he never noticed the girl had scrambled away and into a house, safe from him.

Nick had placed himself into the stalker's car, stopping him from making his final, desperate move.

"What the fuck! How did you..." shouted the man.

"Magic!" Nick taunted the driver. "So sorry, did I stop you from doing something bad?"

"What, er no! I was er… lost… just trying…" the driver stumbled with his words trying to make sense of the sudden change in his plans.

"Is that right Ethan? Lost? T-t-t-t-trying to. Shut up! You see I know you, I've watched you; I've been you... and now Ethan, now, you're mine."

A sickly grin spread on Nick's face.

"Get the fuck out of my car, get out," Ethan screamed at Nick, slamming his hands onto the steering wheel.

Ethan shook the wheel as hard as he could and then started to try to shove Nick out of the car on to the road. Nick sat still, not moving, solid like a block of granite.

"Get your hands off me, Ethan." Nick said calmly, "Don't touch me, I know where your hands have been, vermin child." Nick looked at Ethan as though he had just scrapped him off his shoe with a stick.

Ethan grabbed the wheel again, deciding not to stick

around after his failed attempt at grabbing the girl; he set off in a hurry, the movement pushed him into his seat.

"Who the fuck are you and how did you get in my car?"

Ethan couldn't recall anyone getting in or even the door opening. The speed of the car increased as he tried to make his unwelcome guest feel scared.

"Oh Ethan, are you trying to frighten me by going faster?" Nick mocked.

Ethan was now heading towards a busy crossroads. As they approached the lights turned red, and Nick could see the traffic starting to pass in front. The car screamed to a sudden stop at the point of crossing. The jolt hurled Ethan forward into the steering wheel, and he crashed into the windscreen, not hard enough to break the glass but enough to spread Ethan's nose across his face. He slumped back into his seat in pain.

"Red light, Ethan," Nick said calmly pointing at the traffic lights, even with the sudden stop that had launched Ethan, Nick didn't move an inch from his seat. "You really should wear your seat belt."

"What the fuck are you?" Ethan demanded as he smudged the blood pouring from his nose with the back of his hand.

"How did you do that?" Ethan looked at Nick, in shock as he tried to comprehend what had just happened to him.

"Ethan, you're an evil, sadistic, murderer. Your victims have gone through hell before you kill them. Tonight Ethan, I am their fear, I am their hate, I am their rape, I am their repulsion, I am their death. Ethan. I am their revenge!" Nick sneered.

Ethan stared at Nick, his mouth open, blood ran from his broken nose, with his hand hovering over his mouth, then he started to laugh.

"You are fucking funny friend; that's some weird shit you

saying there!" Ethan said, his southern accent heavy on his speech.

Ethan tried to adjust his sitting position to start driving again. Nick leaned over to Ethan and grabbed his chin; he snapped his head round to face his.

"Ethan, I don't think you understand me, you fucking vermin child."

"What'cha say?" asked Ethan, tilting his head.

"Vermin child!" Nick said, this time venom spat from his tongue.

"You don't get to say that; no one gets to say that!" Ethan rasped and he went to grab Nick.

Nick clicked his fingers.

Ethan opened his eyes to find himself in his childhood bedroom, not as a man but a small boy again. The moonlight poured through the curtains making the shadows darker and the surfaces brighter.

Nick could see the instant confusion and fear in Ethan's eyes as he spun his head around in the darkness, realising where he was. He then heard the handle turn; his head spun to the door and Ethan started to shake with fear.

"Vermin child, you awake?" Ethan's older sister whispered as she closed his door quietly from the inside. Nick heard a faint whimper from Ethan.

Nick clicked his fingers and froze the personal horror that took place most nights. He placed himself between Ethan and his older sister.

"Ethan, you awake?" Nick asked.

Ethan raised his head from his pillow, sweating and with tears creeping from his eyes he pleaded.

"Make this stop, get me outta here."

"You scared?" Nick asked, "You scared of what comes

next?" Nick looked up at Ethan's paused sister, he walked over to her.

"She doesn't look like much. She really must have been pretty fucked up to create a fucked up cunt like you," Nick said, leaning close into Ethan's face.

He clicked his fingers and allowed the nightmare play out.

"Move up, vermin."

She climbed in and pushed his head against the wall that touched the side of his bed. For a slight girl, she was unusually strong. She squeezed up against him, spooning him. She could feel him shake, and she smiled.

Nick clicked his fingers again and everything paused.

"Bet you never thought you would have to live through this again, did you?" Nick said smiling.

Ethan slowly turned his head to Nick.

"Please, make this stop, please..." he begged, tears ran down his face.

"What? Like the way you stopped with your victims? The innocent lives those young girls lost, did you stop for them?" Nick snarled.

He held his fingers together and clicked them again.

Ethan's sister pushed his head against the wall again, this time harder. She was at least 5 years older than Ethan and had made Ethan's life hell for a few years; she controlled him in everything he did. It never ended; every day she would beat him, scare him, manipulate him and from time to time molest him.

With one hand she held his head against the wall and started to slip her other hand down the front of his pyjamas.

Nick clicked his fingers again, it stopped again.

Nick leaned in, "Even though I enjoy the fact that you're getting to relive a very bad moment in your life, I don't want to see a child go through this twisted fucked-up hell, even if it is you."

Nick clicked his fingers again and the room melted away.

👑

Ethan opened his wet eyes; he tried to focus in the dark around him, but couldn't make out his location.

"Where am I?" he asked Nick quietly almost a whisper.

"Don't you know? The remains of the rotting girl in the corner didn't spark your memory" Nick asked.

"It's the storm shelter you like, the one where you bring the girls after you kill them. Only one at a time though, you do like to give them your undivided attention, don't you?" Nick rasped, sickened by the horrible place.

Ethan sat in the darkness, quiet, scared.

"Who are you? How can you do this?" Ethan questioned.

He couldn't see anything still, but he knew this place like the back of his hand.

"Ethan, I am your hell, I am the one who will make you understand what you have done and that it's going to stop. I am going to make sure you don't hurt anyone else, ever. I am your death, Ethan," said Nick calmly.

Ethan made a bolt for the storm doors of the shelter, as he launched his body up the stairs he was stopped by the locked doors. He tried to force them open, but he couldn't even make them shake.

"Oh yeah, you can't open them, they're locked," Nick said with a grin, he switched on the light.

The light hadn't worked for years, Ethan hadn't minded as he liked to have the room dark as he didn't want to have to face his victims once they had started to rot.

"Let's put a little light on the subject at hand," Nick said.

The room flooded with light showing every corner, the old broken recliner chair in the corner, the small table with the cigarette butts, tiny pieces of burnt silver foil, old beer cans scattered about and the odd empty whiskey bottle.

Then there was the girl slumped against the wall by the chair, partially clothed, pale almost grey. The skin on her face had started to tighten back as the body decomposed.

"Ethan, do you see her? Is this ok?" Nick looked disgusted as he pointed out the corpse.

"She's fine. She won't hurt you," Ethan said with a loving smile looking at her with affection.

Nick noticed the way he was unshaken by the decomposing girl and walked over to her. He crouched near to her and whispered in her ear.

"Natalie, I want to talk to you."

Ethan laughed, "She won't hear you. Jesus man, she's dead!"

The girl's eyes opened and her mouth gasped for air; she panicked, and clawed at her throat as she tried to breathe.

"It's ok, stay calm, I won't keep you long," Nick calmly spoke.

She slowed her breathing down, whilst staring intensely at Nick.

"My name is Nick, I asked for you to return briefly so I can take revenge for you. Nothing can harm you now; he won't hurt you anymore."

Natalie looked around Nick to see Ethan, in shock, standing by the storm doors.

"It's him. He killed me!" she screamed in terror, trying to move back up the wall.

"It's ok, Natalie, he can't touch you."

"How the fuck did you do that? She's fucking dead, she's dead," Ethan yelled.

Again, he made a run for the storm doors only to bounce off them.

"Ethan, I am the King of Hell and tonight you have my FULL attention."

Nick turned to the girl, "Would you like to torture your killer with me? It's ok; he can't hurt you. Remember, I won't let him hurt you anymore, but we can hurt him!"

Natalie tried to stand up, but couldn't, looking down she realised that one of her hips was dislocated; she remembered why. She remembered the roughness, the violence of Ethan, as he forced his way onto her and into her, how he pushed her head against the floor as he took her innocence.

Natalie turned towards Nick "Yes, Nick I would like to hurt him, very much!"

Ethan retreated into the corner, he stumbled on an empty whiskey bottle and fell.

"Natalie, do you think you can tell me what he did to you? Tell me about the pain that you suffered? Tell me how he enjoyed it, so we can enjoy his pain as much."

With discomfort Natalie spoke of her torture.

"He grabbed me from the street near my home as I walked back from school. I had stopped to fasten my shoelace, and his car stopped at the side of me and he pulled me into his car. He covered my mouth with a rag and it went dark. When I woke up I was here, trapped. He had tied my hands and feet together."

Natalie wanted to cry but the rotting shell that she occupied didn't work as it would if she were alive. Nick raised a hand, from out of the ether two lengths of rope appeared and slid around Ethen's wrists and ankles tying them together, tightly. Ethan, unable to stop this from happening, started to shout at Nick to stop. Begging for forgiveness, pleading and when that didn't work, he began to threaten them. Nick clicked his fingers and Ethan was mute.

"Then what happened?" Nick asked.

"He cut off my clothes, then I remember him washing me. I couldn't move, I couldn't scream. I didn't want to die. I didn't want to die." Natalie seemed lost in the fear of the moment as she relived it.

Nick held up his hand again as he faced Ethan, like before a sharp utility knife appeared near Ethan and started to slowly cut through his clothes and into the top layer of his skin. This continued slowly from his neck down his arms and down his chest. With each cut Ethan screamed in silence, his face contorting as the blood soaked through his dirty white shirt. The knife then worked its way down each leg. In his mind, Ethan was crying, spitting, pleading for Nick to stop, but he was mute. Nick wasn't sure if Ethan even realised that they couldn't hear him.

"He didn't cut me, he just cut the clothes," Natalie said wincing as blood pooled the floor.

Nick looked back at her and shrugged.

"Ah well, never mind. Oh and I'm not washing him either"

He turned back to face Ethen again, the blood seeping through his cut clothes, pain searing through his now defaced body.

"Then what?" Nick asked Natalie.

Natalie was now looking uneasy and clearly sickened by what was happening. Even though she was dead, and rotting, she didn't want to be there. She started to move back to the corner where her cadaver once lay twisted and slumped.

"He now raped me, but I don't want to see that, I'm not sure I want to see this either."

Nick turned to Natalie, "Natalie, what's wrong don't you want him to suffer for what he did to you?"

Confused, Nick dropped Ethan from his agonising position, and he slumped in a bloody mess on the floor, not moving.

"Let me go back, please? I don't want to be here anymore." Natalie begged.

Nick clicked his fingers and the broken body collapsed to the floor. He stared at the vacant features of her face and the situation finally hit home. He had been so wrapped up in his revenge and justice that he had lost his direction. Nick quickly turned to the blood-covered body; he clicked his fingers and Ethan's screams shot out filling the room.

Nick stepped back, realising the mess he had created, and the moment caught him. Did this make him any different from the evil killer in front of him? He had no idea what to do next. He couldn't let him carry on, he couldn't let him go and he couldn't kill him.

With a quick hand gesture, Nick allowed Ethan to fall to the floor; he checked his body for blood with his hands. His screaming had stopped; shocked, he looked up at Nick.

"What happened? The blood, the cuts, the girl?" Ethan asked, pointing at the slumped shape in the corner.

"I thought I was going to die, you said..." he paused realising, "Hey, why didn't you kill me? You fucked me up pretty bad. What are you? Who the fuck are you?"

Nick looked at Ethan with a tired expression, still not sure what to do.

"Ethan, I have already told you who I am; I'm not saying it again. The police are on their way, and you're going to tell them everything, or I will return and trust me I will know. You're scum, and I don't want to waste my energy on you anymore."

"What? You fucking pussy; you ain't got the fucking balls to finish me. I'm untouchable; that's why the police have never caught me. I'm a fucking god, you prick!" Ethan got to his feet and rushed to the storm doors.

"Wrong Ethan, you're not."

Nick dropped his chin to his chest, lifted his open hand, closed his eyes and quickly clenched his hand into a fist, Ethan's neck snapped and he collapsed down the steps, the storm doors sat wide open waiting for the police.

Nick sighed and disappeared as the distant sound of sirens grew louder.

7

ABSORPTION

A loud crack filled the air, and Nick hit the cold stone of the basement floor. For a moment Nick remained on his hands and knees, breathing heavily, straining to catch his breath, as though the floor were sucking him down.

"Well, at least there's no vomit this time, sir. I think it must have been that first jump that affected you," Anton guessed.

Nick slowly stood up, keeping his balance by placing his hands on his knees, his stomach swimming.

"What happened to me there? I lost control. Jesus, Anton, I even scared a corpse! I killed him!"

Nick stumbled slightly to one side as his equilibrium returned to normal. Both arms out wide for balance, he took a deep breath in and then he was sick.

"Ah, there it is! Lovely," Anton said with a grimace as he watched vomit spray the wall at the side of the portal.

Anton waited for Nick to finish before continuing.

"Look, sir, you control the event. You just invited a little too much evil to the party I guess, or is it a little too much human? Not sure? But, sir, you're going to have to get used to this. The routine is simple, you know this. You get the vision, absorb the host, hunt and kill."

"I know Anton, I get it. I think it's the absorption that's the hard part, having their memories swimming around in my head as well as my own. Having their personality in there battling with mine; it's not easy to control how that feels. One minute you want to kill, next minute you want to run. I was just recovering from Clive being killed and then having a serial killer bouncing about in there, I wanted that out immediately." Nick rubbed his head in his hands trying to erase Ethan's presence.

"I understand, sir. But this is the way it has to be. Soon you won't be able to tell if someone else is in there or not; and if there is, you will be able to control it. By the way, impressive neck break for your first time. I did feel a lot of resentfulness on that snap, why? You had to stop him from doing it again."

Anton wrung out the mop and started to clean up Nick's sick.

"I had to stop him, I saw no choice." Nick walked out of the room leaving Anton to his cleaning, "I had no choice!"

"Of course, sir"

Nick entered the kitchen and grabbed a coffee. He was still shaking from the night's events. He had taken someone's life, and he felt the regret cutting at his soul. If only he had stayed calm and focused on stopping him from leaving in time for the police. He banged his head with his hands hard in frustration, realising that he didn't need to kill, just maim, leave him to the police.

Stupid! Stupid!

Anton walked into the kitchen, "You feeling any better, sir? Hitting your head won't help."

He washed his hands and leant against the kitchen island.

Nick looked up surprised that he hadn't heard him approach.

"Sort of, I think I have control of the situation and then, like tonight, I take it too far. I don't want to become a killer; I don't want to do bad things to people. I need to get my head around this; I need to become stronger. I need to get my life back."

Nick walked over to the sliding doors that led out to the veranda.

"You're still learning, sir. Don't be hard on yourself; keep focused on your mother. You did well tonight. It may not feel like it right now, but it will get easier." Anton followed Nick outside.

"Would you prefer to go through today's analysis in the morning?" Anton asked.

"Please, not sure I can concentrate at the moment."

"Is that everything for tonight, sir?" Anton asked.

"Yeah, I won't be long now, I have a few things to work out in my head. Thanks." Nick put down his empty coffee cup on the table and stared out into the night sky.

"Goodnight, sir." Anton walked off to his bedroom, leaving Nick to his thoughts.

Nick stood up and walked over to the balcony and looked out over the calm ocean. His mind was racing with the events of the day and then he remembered Jennifer, the kiss. Then the sickness of Ethan's dream, stopping him from getting another victim, the rotting, living corpse of Natalie. The stench of that room still lingered, wafting through his nostrils.

Sighing, he sat back down and conjured up a stronger drink, after all, he was eighteen now, and after the day he had had, he needed it. With a smile on his face and the shot of whisky in a sipping glass, he relaxed back in his chair. Nick took a swallow, coughed, then took another sip, swirled the liquid around the sides and downed the rest.

The slight warm breeze over his now tingling face relaxed him as the whisky eased down his throat, warming his chest and stomach as it worked its way down. He put the glass down. His body relaxed and his eyes closed. He was exhausted and slowly he slipped into sleep.

♔

Blurred flashing blue and red lights faded into view. Torrential rain raged down, as thunder rumbled in the distance. Police sirens cried out as a voice over the two-way radio pierced through the wind.

"RTA, assistance required, motorcycle rider collision, code red, still breathing but critical; car driver, code white. Assistance urgent."

The reply from control faded, drowned by the rain and the wind.

His eyes opened slowly, the taste of blood in his mouth, choking. He felt the intense pain rush through his body. Looking down, he tried to reach for the phone; it sat on someone's lap. He tried stretching out, but the more he strained, the worse the pain, the worse the pain, the more he chocked. He felt like he was drowning – taking on water, but thick, metallic-tasting water. His consciousness went dark.

The images of the scene faded out; in the distance he heard a baby cry, feeling his heart tear, his soul sink; he was left with the sickening feeling of loss.

Just when things seemed darkest, a bright, warm light came through some curtains, filling the room with happiness that surrounded him. The cries from the baby were louder now, from the cot in the room. However it wasn't only the cries from the baby – a young woman slumped in the corner was also sobbing hysterically. The tears streamed out, staining the sunny room with desperation as she raged at the child's cot, the tears of attention from the baby suffocated the young woman.

"SHUT UP!" She screamed, "FOR GOD'S SAKE, SHUT UP!"

Her hands wrapped around her head like a child's security blanket.

He reached out a hand to touch her shoulder in comfort, but she always seemed too far away. All he wanted to do was hold her, but he choked on the metallic taste swilling in his mouth.

The heat of the morning sun on Nick's face surprised him. As he opened his eyes, he realised he had slept outside on the large seating area. Stretching and yawning, he caught a glimpse of dried blood on his hands. Nick stood up and looked around, checking the immediate area for the source of the blood, but nothing.

Anton walked over.

"Good morning sir, How was your sleep?" He asked.

"I'm, er, not really sure," Nick replied, still puzzled.

"I have blood on my hands, I'm not sure where from though."

"Oh, so you have, it's on your mouth and chin too." Anton pointed, as he laid Nick's breakfast out.

"What?"

Nick patted his chin and rushed off to the bathroom.

He stared at his face in the mirror, he saw the blood around his mouth and chin; he washed off the blood and checked for cuts. Then the vision hit him again. The choking, searching for breath as he felt as though he had drowned.

Nick washed his hands and rubbed water over his face trying to splash himself awake.

"Hi!"

An unexpected voice announced itself behind him.

Nick spun round to stare at a young man whom he had not seen before.

"Er, Hi?"

Nick was now frozen, water dripped to the floor.

"You're not Lucifer. I was expecting to see Lucifer! What's going on?"

The young man looked confused and left the bathroom.

Nick dried off quickly and rushed after him.

"Anton, where's Lucifer?" the man shouted.

"Oh yes, Sorry, my mistake. I forgot to mention, he's no longer here. This is Nick; he is the new King of Hell." Anton apologised and introduced Nick.

"Sir, this is Steve Harper. He has requested a meeting with you to discuss an urgent matter that he has been told you might be able to help with. If that will be all, I shall leave you two to it."

Nick sat down and Steve sat opposite to him in silence.

Nick sat starring at Steve.

"Have we met?"

Nick had a very strong gut feeling that their paths had crossed, but his face wasn't familiar at all.

"No, we haven't. Look can you help me?" Steve asked.

Still staring at Nick, he finished stirring his coffee and placed his teaspoon at the side of his coffee.

It hit home, and Nick banged the table.

"It's you, the accident, the bike, you were in the car; you drowned though; I definitely felt you drown, like you swallowed a lot of your own blood. How are you here? I was covered in your blood this morning, why?"

"I... I didn't. At least I don't think so anyway. Hang on, how did you know about my accident?" Steve asked puzzled as much as Nick was.

"I get... visions! They show me, people, what they went, or are going through." Nick explained, "Why are you here? I thought it was the woman who needed me?"

"Woman? You saw a woman?"

"Yes, she needed help."

"Well yes and no, it was me. Someone told me that the King of Hell had changed from killing people to helping people, is that true? Are you good now?"

"I don't know; I am trying to do what is right, if that is good or bad I don't know. Who was the woman? There was a woman and her baby in my vision, she seemed distressed, so did the baby." Nick asked.

"That sounds like my wife and child. She's better; she's not like that anymore, but I fear that she might slip and do something bad." Steve hung his head down, whilst brushing his hair down with his hand.

"So my vision wasn't from her but you? But you're dead, why do you care?" Nick asked Steve.

"Jesus, I care, that's my kid and wife. But if she's going to do something stupid, I need to stop her. Can you help me?" Steve asked again.

"Yes, well I think so, anything to get the taste of blood out of my mouth. It's not nice. Do you still get that?"

"Oh yes, would like to get rid of it too."

Nick finished his coffee and told Steve to follow him.

"Anton?" Nick shouted.

Anton appeared, "You called for me sir?"

"Can I take Steve through the portal? The vision I had last

and the blood this morning were from Steve, nice gift eh?" Nick turned to Steve to see him shrug.

"Not normally, but Steve is dead, so he can get where ever he needs as long as he has a connection. That's how he got here, his blood carried him."

"Do you want to go now? Do you need the portal prepared?" Anton asked Nick.

"Yes, let's do this quick. Steve, I will meet you there; I need to get changed first, slept in my clothes from yesterday."

Nick shot Steve a smile, a nod, and he left the kitchen and headed towards his room.

Steve turned towards Anton.

"Is he any good? I mean, he seems a little young?"

"He's no Lucifer, but you will be glad he's not. Personally, I wish he were."

Anton walked towards the portal room and Steve vanished.

8

FABRICATED

J ane stood looking out her kitchen window. She watched her six-year-old son run around the garden, whilst their small black Italian greyhound, Jack, gave chase. Tommy was energetic, inquisitive and very happy; he was a typical little boy. The bond between him and his dog was so strong, they were practically inseparable.

Tommy's father, Steve, had left six years ago on the day Tommy was born. Jane and Steve had been married for five years and had loved every moment; they spent all their time together and wanted nothing more than a child that they could shower with love and attention.

On the day Jane went into labour, Steve was at work. When he got the call, he immediately left, strapped on his helmet and climbed onto his bike.

As he turned the last corner before the hospital, the driver of the oncoming car reached for his phone and accidentally turned his wheel, with his knee, into the wrong lane. Steve hit the car square on and was sent through the windscreen, crushing the drivers head with his helmet. The impact pushed

Steve's helmet and his head sideways, breaking his collar bone and forcing it through his skin and into his neck, slicing his trachea and damaging his carotid artery. The blood quickly filled the wound in his trachea, with every panicked breath, the blood filled his lungs, drowning him within minutes. Steve didn't die on impact, and tried to reach for the phone on his victim's knee to ring for help before he suffocated to death.

After Steve's funeral, Jane was flooded with help from everyone. Not a day went by that family or friends hadn't visited and helped her with raising Tommy; Jane had not dealt with her loss well at all. She struggled to bond with Tommy, even to the point of leaving him in a store on one of the very few trips she made out of the house.

Jane needed help.

For the next several years, Jane had help in every aspect of her life. Her parents had dedicated their lives to be on hand as much as possible, and over time, Jane learned to deal with the loss of her soul mate.

Inside her head, the connection between the death of Steve and the birth of Tommy collided, blurring the loving instincts of a mother and the regret that if he had not been born, Steve would still be alive.

Jane, for the first few years, had battled the two extreme feelings constantly and found herself screaming at Tommy, which obviously would upset Tommy more; and the vicious cycle would escalate until either her father or mother would remove her from the room.

It took her years to become independent, and in time her love developed for Tommy. The last six months had been a lot better. She had managed to find herself a part-time job and was finally building a strong future for them both.

Steve stood in the kitchen behind Jane, watching her

watch Tommy. He had spent years just watching, knowing he wasn't Patrick Swayze and this wasn't "Ghost." Of course, he had tried everything to get her attention, even seeking out a clairvoyant, but everyone he found just turned out to be a fraud.

Steve had come to embrace the fact that no-one would help him to make contact, to tell her that she was not alone, that he had watched her, and how proud he was of both of them.

But, Steve had his fears too. He noticed from time to time a drop in Tommy's health. Over the past week, he had seen a drop again, maybe it was just a virus, but the boy wasn't as active as normal. This was the most active he had seen him in the last week. Perhaps, he had nothing to worry about, and Steve's concerns were just his dead brain starting to disappear.

"Hey, Steve." a voice from behind him broke his trance. Nick was stood there looking more awake.

"She can't see or hear you can she?" Steve asked.

"No, totally invisible to her, like yourself."

Nick started to look around to sink into his surroundings. As he watched, Jane bolted out of the door screaming Tommy's name. They both followed at pace.

Tommy had collapsed on the grass, and Jack was barking at Jane repeatedly. She pushed him out of the way to get to Tommy. She crouched down at Tommy's side, checked his breathing, and gently she picked him up and carried him into the house.

Tommy slowly moved when Jane put him down on the sofa, but his movements were lethargic and small. He was still breathing and alive. Jack stood at his side, resting his head on the cushions placed against him.

"See, Nick? Something is wrong, she's calm. Why is she

calm? Tommy has just collapsed, and she's ok with it!" He gestured with his arms.

"I don't see anything bad here; he fainted, she checked him, he's alive. Why am I here?" Nick stood watching Steve who was monitoring his son closely.

Jane picked up the phone in a relaxed fashion, as though she were going to ring her mother to discuss a program on TV. She dialed for an ambulance.

"Help me please; my son has collapsed!" Then suddenly becoming hysterical, Jane continued to give details.

Steve and Nick stood there, their mouths open, not expecting the total change in her mannerisms.

"Ok Steve, I get your concerns. That was not normal."

Jane in a flood of tears completed her call and hung up the phone. Wiping the tears and mucus from her face, she stood at the end of the sofa watching Tommy breathe, smiling to herself.

Nick turned to Steve, "I will meet you at the hospital. It seems pointless me waiting here for the ambulance when I won't be taking it. Keep an eye on her; God knows what's going on in her head."

"Of course. Glad it wasn't just me seeing that happen." Steve crouched at the side of Tommy, "It's going to be ok, Tommy; we will get you through this."

Nick snapped his fingers and disappeared.

Nick arrived at the hospital before Steve and Jane. As soon as he appeared in the emergency room's waiting area, he immediately had a strange pulling sensation in the pit of his stomach. It felt as though he were being directed somewhere; the sensation was so strong he had to follow it.

As Nick walked through the corridors of the hospital, the feeling grew, steering him towards a ward on the third floor. Nick opened the swing doors and walked on to the ward. He walked past each room and stopped outside the sixth room on the left; the name on the door was Ms. J Clarke. Nick looked through the small window on the door and could see a young woman in the bed. As he looked at her, she snapped her head around and the pulling in his stomach stopped.

Nick flinched and tried to move his head away quickly so she didn't see him. Unfortunately, he wasn't fast enough and she recognised him immediately.

"Nick?" Jennifer cried.

She tried to get out of her bed to get to the door, but multitudes of cables attached to her, monitoring her condition, restrained her.

"NICK!" She shouted.

Nick paused behind the door, out of sight.

"NICK!" Jennifer screamed, pulling at the cables attached to her, the cannula tubes tensing, stinging her arm.

"Jesus, fucking cables!"

Jennifer tugged at them again, only triggering the alarms on the machines.

"No, No, NICK!" Jennifer panicked and continued to disconnect herself; leaving cables trailing on the floor.

Nick couldn't walk away when she was clearly in such distress. But then his guilt got the better of him and he opened the door and walked in.

"OK, OK, calm down, I'm here!"

Nick's focus was on Jennifer and the bandages around her wrists, with the addition of the cables partially attached to her, and a weeping cannula.

"Jennifer, what the hell happened to you? I left you to go live your life; you were free of your cancer."

"I'm sorry, after what happened that night I couldn't rest. I got home and I couldn't sleep. I was awake all night, the images and feelings wouldn't stop!" Jennifer got back on her bed.

A nurse rushed into the room and stopped the alarms from the heart monitoring machines attached to Jennifer, leaving the room in uncomfortable silence.

"Are you ok Ms. Clarke? Why are all your cables out? Look, your cannula's bleeding! What have you been doing?"

The nurse reattached the monitoring cables and reset the needle in her arm. "You need to stay in bed, did you fall out?"

"No, I saw Nick; he's come to visit me," Jennifer said with a smile on her face.

"She can't see me." Nick said whilst shaking his head.

"Couldn't he stay?" asked Nurse Sanderson, as she started the fluid drip going again.

"Clearly not," she said confused whilst starring at Nick.

"Now don't do that again; you need to get better," Nurse Sanderson instructed her as she walked away.

Once the nurse had left the room Jen turned to Nick, "What do you mean she couldn't see you?"

"I am only visible to people by whom I want to be seen," Nick explained, "Anyway, regarding what you said before the nurse came in, I expected you to have problems at first, but it should have eased off."

"No, It didn't ease; things got worse. It was you; I couldn't think of anything else. I could still feel you; I sensed you when you entered the hospital. I just couldn't get to you." Jennifer was crying again. "I can't believe you're here; I hoped you would come."

"I was here for someone else; I'm not here for you. I had this feeling something was pulling me here, but I didn't know it was you."

Nick worried that this had happened. He remembered the words that Anton had said about getting involved but this was unavoidable; for some reason she could see him whilst others couldn't.

"Nick, this was fate. You had to come and save me; otherwise, why would you be here?" Jennifer urged forwards towards Nick.

Nick backed away a couple of steps, keeping her at arm's reach.

"Jen, what did you do to your wrists?"

"I needed to see you again. I didn't know what else to do; you didn't hear me when I called, screamed, begged, so I tried to kill myself again. But you didn't come, you weren't there. Why?" She started to sob in anguish.

"Why would you even do this to yourself? I gave you what you wanted, I gave you your life. Clean, cancer-free."

Nick felt Jen's pain, but he tried to hide the concern. He felt that if he let anything out, she would never let him go.

"I needed to see you again. That kiss, I can still feel it. Please, I need you with me." Jennifer tried to reach for Nick again, tightening the monitor cables.

"Listen, Jen, you can't have me. My life is way too hard to deal with by myself, never mind with another person. Besides, you have your son and Chris? They need you; don't throw it all away!" Nick turned to look at the room doors.

"No, Nick, it's you I need. I don't need them. When you're here with me, I feel whole; I'm soulless without you. Don't you feel this too? Please?" She begged, sobbing.

"You need to stop; we can never be together. Listen, you need to get sorted, get home, live your life. Don't you fucking dare waste it after taking Clive's life," Nick warned her, "I have to go; you have to forget me. Think of your son."

Nick walked towards the room doors. Jennifer stood up

and tried to follow, but the cables restricted her and she dropped to her knees.

Nick left her screaming, pleading for him to return. The pulling in his stomach started again as he walked out the door. He hoped that would be their last meeting, but he knew it wouldn't be.

ꙮ

Nick refocused on locating Steve and Jane, and learning if they had arrived yet. During the time he was scanning for them, the pulling in his gut was getting strong again. The feeling made him sick. He located where they were and snapped his fingers; he appeared outside the room where Tommy had just arrived. Keeping a distance Nick watched Steve and Jane; they stood outside Tommy's room, one oblivious to the fact that the other was there.

Jane stood talking to a nurse, listening intently, whilst wiping tears from her face.

Nick passed by them, keeping his presence invisible to all of them including Steve. He walked into the room and up to Tommy, watched him for a while sleeping. It was peaceful, and apart from the sounds of the corridors outside, it was relaxing.

Nick wondered just what had happened. Had Jane done something to him? Her mood swing was shocking to watch and hear. Was it planned?

He hadn't seen anything like it before, but Nick then remembered a kid he once knew in high school. He had been there for about six months, but during that time everyone had thought was crazy. He would lash out at someone or something, shouting or hitting, then when the teacher came to sort out the chaos, he would deny it. Six months later he left and the rumour was he had schizophrenia. Jane just didn't seem like that; it seemed more controlled.

She walked into the room and let the door close behind her. Steve passed through the door seconds after.

⚊

"Tommy?" She whispered as she leaned over her son, straightening his bedclothes.

Tommy opened his eyes and looked up at his mother, "Mummy?" Tommy's voice was weak and cracked.

"Do you know where you are?" Jane asked.

"No, I don't feel well, mummy." Tommy croaked.

"It's ok, the doctors are here to help us," Jane said in a calm voice still tucking his covers in.

"Are you going to give me some more medicine?" Tommy asked, "I don't like it; it tastes funny."

"No, not now Tommy. If the doctors ask if you have swallowed anything that you shouldn't have, don't tell them about the medicine. That is only between me and you. If they knew we had it, they would take it from us. Don't forget Daddy told me to give it to you to make you big and strong."

Jane stopped tucking in Tommy's covers and looked at him. "You don't want to upset Daddy do you?"

"No. I won't say anything," Tommy promised.

"What medicine are they talking about, Steve?" Nick demanded.

"I don't know? Why would she say that? What is she giving him?"

Steve turned to Jane, "What are you doing to our son, you evil bitch?" He cursed.

"Give me a few minutes." Nick snapped his fingers and he was gone.

Steve watched Jane brush Tommy's hand with her fingers. "What have you done Jane?"

The room door opened and in walked Nick in a white coat and clipboard, "Mrs. Harper?" Nick asked.

"Yes?" Jane answered.

"Ah, this must be Tommy?" Nick gestured at Tommy.

"How are you feeling, Tommy?" Nick asked.

Tommy looked at his mother, she nodded her confirmation to answer the doctor's question, then back at Nick, "I'm feeling a bit sick."

"Ok Tommy, well I will ask one of the nurses to see if we can get anything to ease that for you?"

Nick turned to Jane, "Mrs. Harper, we found something unusual in his blood samples. Have you been giving him anything that isn't part of his normal diet?"

"No, why what did you find?" the colour drained from her cheeks.

"I think we need to discuss this in another room. Tommy, do you mind if I just borrow your mother for a moment?" Nick reassured him with a smile.

"Err... ok?" Tommy looked as worried at his mum.

As Jane left the room, Tommy started to drift back to sleep.

"Mrs. Harper, just through here, please." Nick held the door open for her as she walked through the hospital room door into her own kitchen.

Jane stopped, looked around, her kitchen. Nick's idea was to scare her; throw her off balance and have her reveal her secret.

She spun around, "What! Wait! What just happened? How am I in my kitchen?"

"What have you been giving Tommy, Jane?" Nick was not going to let her leave until the truth came out.

"Please, I don't understand, this is my kitchen, but the hospital is through there!" Jane was trying to understand what she had just experienced.

"What's going on? Who are you?" Jane wasn't listening to Nick; her confusion was controlling her fear.

"What have you been giving Tommy? I heard you ask Tommy not to tell the doctors what you had been giving him. So, I will ask you one more time; what have you been giving Tommy?"

Nick had thought that if he shocked her, she would be scared into saying what she had done, but even though she shook with fear, she still denied everything.

"Nothing, Nothing!" She screamed.

"Tell me now, or you can explain it all to Steve, He's not happy!"

"Steve? My husband? He's dead; he died years ago!"

Nick's idea hadn't worked, so reluctantly left it to Steve to sort things out, "Walk back through the doors."

Nick pointed to the double doors that had re-appeared behind him where there hadn't been any before.

She slowly passed Nick and creeped the doors open, not knowing what she would see next.

Sitting at the side of Tommy was Steve; he looked up at Jane entering the room. With tears in his eyes, he stood.

"Steve? Is that you?"

The sight of Steve after all these years flooded her with sorrow and happiness. Unable to restrain herself she ran for him, to embrace him. Steve, however, had other plans; he wanted to strangle her.

He launched himself at her and screamed, "You fucking bitch!"

9

LOVE HIM TO DEATH

The second Jane stepped through the doors into the hospital room, she was attacked by her dead husband who was screaming insults at her. In shock, she stumbled back into the wall behind her and collapsed into a heap on the floor. At the moment that Nick walked back into the room, Steve flew past him to grab his slumped wife on the floor.

"What did you do to…" Steve spun back round to see Nick, who was almost perched on his shoulder, "Wait, can she see me?"

Nick nodded.

"Hear me?" Asked Steve.

"Yes, Steve, yes I can, I can hear you!" Jane insisted as she pulled herself to her feet again in excitement to see Steve.

"Is it really you, Steve?"

Nick interrupted the question, "Yes, Steve, Jane, you can see and talk to each other, but you can't touch her, Steve, you're still dead."

Jane broke down crying again.

"Please don't cry again Jane; you know I hate it when you cry. I just need to know what you have done to Tommy?"

"How are you here?" Jane asked through sobbing and sudden intakes of breath as she tried to stop her tears.

"I can't believe you've come back to me!"

Jane tried to touch his face, but she only got cold fingers as her hand passed through his cheek. Steve tried to hold her hand in a natural response, but his spiritual body passed through her living flesh.

Steve dropped his hands to his side, and with a sigh he made a calmer approach; he looked into Janes' eyes. Her breathing was a heavy, borderline panic attack.

"What was the medicine you talked to Tommy about earlier?" Steve asked.

"You heard that? But you weren't here. I didn't see you!" Jane's breathing got heavier and the panic in her voice grew now the crying had stopped.

Nick was getting impatient with her, and the tugging in his stomach was still causing him discomfort. His thoughts drifted, and the images of Jennifer crying were vivid and starting to make him feel sick. The longer he stayed here, the more the pulling in his stomach would take over and drive him back to her.

"For God sake Jane, tell us. If you don't your son will die."

"No, he will be fine, he won't die; I only gave him enough to make him ill. Didn't I?" Jane looked at Nick, then back to Steve, "I wouldn't hurt him, I just needed you; I needed help!" She started to cry again.

"Jane, what the fuck did you give him?" Steve snapped with his impatience. He tried to grab her by the shoulders to shake her into telling him, but again his hands only slipped through the muscle and bone.

Jane looked around scared, "Arsenic. It was arsenic, it was only a small amount. Just enough to make him ill, I read it somewhere how people could consume it for years and not die; they only got ill. Is he going to die?" Steve stood up and darted to Tommy. Jane grimaced and stared at Nick, "Is he going to die?"

"Not if you tell the doctor or nurses now. I am sure he will be ok, but you need to say something," Nick urged her, "Why have you poisoned your own son? He's your child; he's part of you."

"You need to tell the doctor, Jane, tell them now!" Steve shouted at her.

"Are you not a doctor?" Jane asked as she looked at Nick confused.

Nick waved his hand in front of him and his normal clothes were back on, "I am afraid not. I'm someone who wants to make sure this stops, and Tommy is ok."

Jane was confused and scared; her dead husband was here with someone who could change the perception of his surroundings. Jane did the only thing that anyone would do. She made a grab for Tommy, who was now unconscious. As she started to lift him and unplug the cables that were attached to the machines that monitored his condition, the alarms rang out. The doors swung open and two nurses ran in.

"Mrs. Harper, what are you doing? Why are you moving him?" The nurses both tried to stop Jane from running with Tommy.

"They want to hurt him!" Jane screamed.

"Who wants to hurt him?" One of the nurses asked in surprise.

"Them!" Jane pointed to Nick and Steve as she continued to unplug cables that the nurses had plugged back in.

Nick started to find the situation funny and sniggered at the panic in the room.

"Jane, they can't see us; they will think you're crazy. You better tell them what you have given Tommy, or I will and that will be so much worse for you. You will be locked up, and Tommy will die without the care that he needs." Nick threatened.

Steve got up close to Jane and pleaded, "Do this for me and you, and Tommy; he needs help. Please?"

"I… I… I gave him arsenic." She sobbed, "I'm sorry, I… I gave him arsenic."

Jane passed Tommy back to one of the nurses, who placed him back on the bed, whilst the other rushed out of the room to find a doctor.

The nurse walked up to Jane and took both her hands, "It's ok we will save him, I think you need to talk to someone though. Don't be afraid; it's ok; we can help you too. Do you know why you gave your son what you did?"

Jane knew why she had given her son arsenic, "I needed help, I can't do this by myself." Jane looked up at Steve, then stared back down to her knees.

"I have seen this kind of behaviour before, Jane. It's ok. Have you done anything like this to your son or yourself before?" The nurse asked.

Jane nodded, accepting her problem, she began to cry into her hands again.

The nurse looked at Jane with compassion, "You have made a huge step today by telling us. I will let the doctor know what you have told me, and we will help you both."

The other nurse returned with the doctor.

"Mrs. Harper, you need to tell us exactly what you gave him and how much. We will deal with the why after."

Jane handed the doctor a small bottle of arsenic from her

bag, "I gave him a few drops of that over a month, only enough to make him ill. I don't want to kill him. I... I just wanted help."

"I will get this off to the lab and start treating Tommy, immediately. He will be ok, but you will have to speak to one of our child care workers, she is on her way now. I'm sorry but we will need to get them involved." The doctor left the room along with both the nurses.

"Thank you for telling them, Jane. I'm sorry for leaving you. I should never have bought that bike. Tommy will be ok, and so will you. Tell them everything and why you needed to do it, please? They will help you." Steve passed his hand through her face again forgetting he couldn't touch her.

"Why have you come back, Steve?" Jane asked wiping her tears away.

"To save you and Tommy. I begged them to let me help you, I watch over you both all the time. You just don't know that I am there."

Steve knelt down in front of Jane. "I love you both very much, but you need to get better, get help, move on, find someone else. Don't do this all alone. Please?"

"I'm sorry. I just wanted you back, even though I knew I couldn't have you." Jane leaned forward and tried to kiss Steve. Steve leant in and even though they didn't touch, they could still feel the electricity they once had.

"If I know you are watching over me, I know I can do this. You give me strength" Jane smiled.

"Steve, we have to go," Nick said, as the room started to fill with nurses, doctors and the social worker. The pulling in his stomach was now unbearable, and he had to go, with or without Steve.

"Jane, I will be in your heart forever, but be free. I will

always love you." Steve said as Jane stood up to go with the social worker.

"I will never love anyone as I loved you, ever," Jane shouted through the tears to her dead husband, leaving the staff to look around puzzled.

"Who are you talking to Mrs. Harper?" asked the social worker.

Jane turned back, "My son."

The social worker looked confused, "If you would come with me Mrs. Harper, I think we need a chat."

Jane nodded and left the room.

Steve walked over to the bed and kissed Tommy on his cheek before walking back to Nick.

"Stay strong little soldier, for Daddy."

Nick clicked his fingers and they both disappeared.

They returned to Jane's house. Furniture was strewn about the living room from the rushing of the paramedics moving Tommy from the sofa to the ambulance.

"Well Steve, this is where I leave you. I presume you're going back to keep an eye on things?"

"I think so, I was told I would be here only for a short period, just enough time to make sure Tommy is safe and Jane gets help. I will head back to the hospital, and watch over them until I can't." Steve said.

"Listen, Nick, I know it's not the norm for you to help people, but today you did, and if, at any point, I can help you, let me know."

Nick shook Steve's hand, "I don't know what the norm is yet. I know I have to be evil, but as you can see, I am not. As for your family, I am sure everything will be ok." He smiled at Steve, "Listen, answer me this question, I know when I pass a soul over they go to Hades, what then?"

"When I first got to Hades I was assessed, most souls are. Hades knows if your heart is true, then he will select you to pass to Heaven. I was chosen to go to Heaven, and I was there for a few years, flitting between Jane's and heaven before I was given the chance to stay and help my family. I miss Heaven, everything seems pale compared to it."

"Thank you, Steve, and good luck." Nick smiled and clicked his fingers again and he was gone.

Nick reappeared in the portal room back at the retreat. As Nick flashed back into existence, he caught sight of Anton standing at the rim of the seal with a mop and bucket, waiting for the introduction of the contents of Nicks stomach across the stone floor. Nick straightened up from his landing and walked out of the room without saying anything or even looking at Anton.

"Well done, sir. You seem to be mastering control of your gut," said Anton as he placed the bucket and mop to one side and walked out of the chamber.

Nick was upstairs, and as usual, was standing with the fridge door open.

"Everything ok, sir?"

"Why am I doing that kind of shit? I was happy for the kid, but that was some weird family crap! I mean, how am I going to get the power I need to take on Lucifer, if all I am doing is being a child's nanny?" Nick slammed the fridge door and walked to his favourite spot, the veranda.

Anton followed him out, "You had an option, sir. You

could have killed the kid, the mother, even both - but you didn't. Your job is to take souls not save souls."

Anton was clearly disappointed that the task hadn't resulted in someone's death, "Look, get some rest, hopefully, the next one will be better."

Nick sat, looking out over the beautiful blue ocean that spread out in front of him; it seemed like a never-ending watercolour. He got to thinking about the tasks he had undertaken thus far and that he only managed to take two souls out of a possible seven. Nick knew he needed to be stronger and not let his weaknesses get in his way. There would be no way of him dominating Lucifer's powers, if all that Nick could do was party tricks. If only he could disconnect from his feelings, things would be easier and he could get home quicker.

His thoughts went back to his encounter with Jennifer, the pulling in his stomach that took him to her, and the feeling of calmness when he saw her again. That wasn't right; did his body know something he didn't? Was it his soul guiding him? Why her? She was older than he; she still looked good though, but she had a child and another man.

Whatever he said, he couldn't take his mind off Jen. All he could think of was when he was with her in the hospital, how much he wanted to grab her and rip off her gown. But the same thought kept coming back, if only he weren't so weak. He knew that the right thing was to try to make her see sense, to go back to her normal life and live it for her son.

The early evening air was, as always here, warm with a slight breeze. The fact that the climate never changed was starting to get to Nick – not enough to want to change it, but, enough to notice it. He started to feel a bit trapped. At least when he was at home, he could go out, stretch his legs and enjoy his life. But not here, every day was starting to feel the same.

Nick realised he hadn't checked up on home for a few days. He clicked his fingers and a drink appeared in his hand, another click and a small screen sat in front of him, floating in the air, showing him his home.

He watched his mother busy herself around the kitchen, cooking and cleaning. But he couldn't see Lucifer; he wasn't there! Where was he? He scanned the rooms again, nothing, then he realised that there was an additional section to the house that he couldn't see properly. Every time he moved to the new section of the house, it blinked back to the kitchen area. Nick repeated this over and over again trying to catch an image or an idea of what was going on. What was this area? Had Lucifer created it? Was he planning something? Was he even starting to grow weaker as Anton said he would do?

Nick motioned his hand in a swipe motion in front of the screen and it vanished.

Lucifer was up to something. Why would he say he wanted to have a normal life and then use magic to build another section to the house? Did Nick's mother know? Had she seen it? Nick decided he would confront Anton in the morning, to see if he could explain it.

However, right now Nick was dead on his feet. He was desperately hoping for no more visions, and a night of peaceful sleep.

He stood up, finished his drink and headed to bed. Still thinking about Jen, the image of her screaming for him. But even with the bandages and cables hanging from her, there was still something about her that caused his stomach to pull. He knew he would see her again, and it wasn't a matter of if, but when.

10

DECEPTION

Nick opened his eyes to the same spectacular view he had seen every morning since his arrival – the same deep blue ocean, the same sparkling white sands of the beach, presaging yet another gloriously vivid blue, cloudless sky.

He got up, showered, dressed and sauntered out of the bedroom, through the living room and over to the kitchen, where Anton was preparing breakfast.

Nick had only one question on his mind: What was Lucifer doing?

He had decided that he wasn't going to accept any more bullshit from Anton. He felt as though he were being lied to, and today was the day that he faced him. Just who did Anton work for? Nick had heard the little quips that he had spilt from time to time about not being evil enough, and Lucifer would have done it a different way. He was sick of his "yes sir, no sir, of course, sir." every time he interacted with him. Today was the day the weather was going to change.

"Morning, Anton, another sunny day, for a change?" Nick said, his tone dripping with sarcasm.

"Absolutely, sir. Good morning, looks like you had a clear night's sleep, no visions?" he asked as he placed Nick's breakfast on the kitchen counter.

"No, it was nice, I feel like myself today, clear-headed and wide awake."

Nick grabbed his breakfast and walked onto the veranda into yet another sun-drenched day. Anton followed him outside.

Anton watched over Nick as he ate.

"Seeing that you don't seem to have any particular distractions today, would you like to work on any magic or skills you are having any issues with?"

Nick paused for a moment thinking, "Actually yes, two things have entered my thoughts today. First of all, I would like to understand how I can change or randomise the weather to make it more, erm, normal? And secondly, can you show me how to hide things from people? I want to know how to hide things that are small, like a ring or large, as well as larger things, like a house, for example."

Anton looked puzzled at Nick, "Do you not like the beautiful sunny weather, sir?"

"I do Anton, I really do, but not every bleeding day. I need rain, snow, wind and fog. Jesus, Anton, even mild weather would be amazing." Nick's frustration with his situation was beginning to show.

"Of course, sir, follow me. I will show you the climate control panel."

Anton left the veranda and led Nick back into the kitchen. As he walked through the doors, he turned right to a panel on the wall.

"This, sir, is the climate control panel. From here you can set any weather you like." He paused and looked at Nick,

"I'm sure I showed you this before?" Anton said with a confused look on his face.

Nick stared at it, then looked at Anton, "That's new!" He pointed at it. "How long has that been there? You have never shown me this before."

"Are you sure, sir? It's been there all the time. What would you like it on?" Anton asked.

"Is there a random setting? Let's have some surprises, might as well, seems to be the topic of the day!"

Nick walked away and back to the veranda, only to be greeted with heavy grey fog. "Jesus, that was quick!" He grabbed his breakfast and took it back into the kitchen.

"Better, sir?" Anton said with a grin.

"Yes, thank you." Nick sat down to eat his food.

"That, Anton, is exactly what I mean by hiding things. I know that wasn't there before, and you defiantly haven't pointed it out before," he said in between mouthfuls of food.

"Sorry, sir, I must have been mistaken then. But I am not sure what you mean by hiding things. This is your place, and I am here only to serve you." Anton seemed to be sincere in his reply.

"Ok, let's say I want to hide something from you. Like, an object, how would I do that?" Nick asked, folding his arms across his body waiting for a reply.

"Well, it's easy, like what?" Anton asked. Nick noticed he looked worried.

"Now Anton, I'm not going to tell you as I don't know if it has worked then, do I? But just for an example the climate control panel!" Nick pointed at the device on the wall, knowing that is what had happened.

"Sir, is there a problem? You seem to be annoyed about something, I'm here only to help you."

"Maybe you can tell me why, when I was looking at my

home last night, checking in on Lucifer and how my mum was, I noticed multiple additional rooms in the house? Actually, more like an additional fucking house!" shouted Nick. "And, why, when I tried to look at the additional rooms, I couldn't! I would move to the new room, there would be a flicker and I would be looking at the kitchen again, every fucking time!"

Anton looked at Nick, confused, "Has Lucifer been building an extension? Is that what you're saying? He might have; overall, he does like to build. And as for not being able to see them, I don't know. Maybe you were tired?"

"What! Tired? Really? Is that the best you have? Right, let me show you!" Nick clicked his fingers and brought up a screen in front of them. He focused the image onto the area where the new rooms had been. There was nothing there, no new rooms, just how it had always been. He wiped back and forwards, trying to make the display change to see what he had seen the night before. Still nothing.

"They've gone, I swear they were there yesterday!"

"Sir, as I said, perhaps you were tired?" Anton commented.

Nick continued to change angles, he swiped backwards, forwards, left, right, closed it down, brought it back up again. Nothing he did changed the fact that the alterations to his home were gone.

"How did that happen? I saw the changes, Anton. Do you think Lucifer knew I had seen what he had done?"

Nick started to look around for cameras, or something that resembled camera equipment, or anything that he thought might be spy equipment. He then refocused on Anton.

"It's you, you're telling him; you're spying on me and telling HIM!" Nick made a move towards Anton; as he did, Anton moved back.

"Sir, please calm down. I haven't been spying on you for 'HIM'. I am here to help you. When you're tired, magic can get a little weird if you're not focused. It could have easily been that. Lucifer has no desire to watch you, he has his own life now."

"Bullshit! He has MY life now."

"Well, quite. But you know what I mean. Nick, you need to relax, no one is out to get you. Get yourself focused." Anton stopped moving backwards.

Nick paused and looked at Anton puzzled.

"You just called me by my name; you never call me by my name, always sir! Why did you just do that?"

"I did that to try to reach you, to see me as a friend not just as your butler. I'm sorry it won't happen again. I just don't want you to become weak and blinded by your paranoia. This can happen from time to time to people with great power," Anton explained.

"Ok, well if that is the case, then why do you make so many comments under your breath at me and ridicule the decisions that I make during assignments, and don't say you don't, I hear you. I heard you say to Steve that you wish I was more like Lucifer." Nick looked at Anton, waiting for some sign of reaction.

"Ah, you heard that. I'm very sorry, I spoke out of line. I just think you need to be more ruthless, to improve your closure skills and not to give in to your human traits. In the end, this will make you stronger in the field and help you beat Lucifer. At the moment you wouldn't win; he would take advantage of your weak human feelings as he did with your mother."

"Don't you talk shit about my mother. She did what she believed was right," Nick yelled.

Anton kept his calm, "Again, I am sorry, sir. I am just

trying to make you understand how far you need to go to be able to at least challenge Lucifer. Don't forget he gets weaker the stronger you get; you need to be more ruthless.

"I am not about to become evil because Lucifer wants it; not every situation must bring death, and not every solution must end in blood."

Nick's temper was rising and the fact that Anton was staying relaxed annoyed Nick even more.

"You have to stop thinking with your heart and think with your head. Your job is to harvest their souls, not be their Samaritan. You are the King of Hell; you are Death!" Anton got lost in the mention of Hell and death, throwing his hands up in prayer.

"No Anton, I am not. I am an eighteen-year-old fuck up, who just wants to get home. I am not one of the four horsemen."

Anton laughed, "However, sir, that is exactly what you are. You don't have a choice and the sooner you realise that, the easier this will be. You can't leave. You can't walk away. You sealed your fate when you signed the contract."

Nick stopped pacing; he felt a slight coldness flash through his body. His eyesight seemed a bit hazy for a couple of seconds and just as quickly as it came, it passed. He shook his head and continued to pace.

"That's another thing, that fucking contract. I know I have read it hundreds of times, trying to find a loophole in it, but hours later I can't remember it, even when I talk about it…"

Nick stopped and rubbed his forehead. "Look, just because I have to do this, doesn't mean I must be evil. I can't change. To be honest, I won't change!"

Nick felt dizzy and a coldness flashed through his chest. Feeling light-headed he grabbed a stool and sat. He put his head in his hands and rubbed his temples. Closing his eyes he could feel the coldness return; only this time with a feeling of sickness.

"I… I am what I am, you can't change me."

"Sir, are you feeling ok?" Anton made his way quickly to Nick, "you don't look so good."

Nick's vision became hazy and Anton's voice seemed to fade further away. As the cold flash grew stronger, Nick felt his body begin to feel really heavy and within seconds he had slumped down off the seat and blacked out, collapsing in a heap, face down on the floor. Anton tried to grab him before he hit the ground, but he wasn't quick enough.

"Sir? SIR?" Anton shouted at Nick. When Nick didn't respond, Anton slapped the boy's face; again no response. Anton shook him, but nothing. Anton dropped him back to the floor, without a care for his safety.

Anton smiled.

"Thank fuck for that; he lasted longer than I thought he would. Probably need to up the dosage next time."

Anton grabbed Nick's hand and dragged his unconscious body, across the kitchen floor, through the living room, and through the long hallway to his bedroom. He threw Nick on to the bed like a marionette puppet, his limbs limp.

Anton removed Nick's clothes and redressed him in his pyjamas.

He left Nick's room, closed the door and walked towards the kitchen. He stopped and tidied up Nick's breakfast dishes, wiped the sides down and walked over towards the climate control panel, turning the controls back to summer evening again.

He walked out of the kitchen and onto the veranda.

A figure stood looking out onto the beach soaking in the warm sun on his face.

"I have missed this view Anton, so very much." he turned around to the butler.

"Not as much as you though."

Anton smiled and blushed slightly.

"How is the Prince of Darkness? Is he counting slaughtered lambs?"

"Well, he's out cold and should be for a long time, sir."

11

HOLLOW

Lucifer turned, smiled, and strolled over to Anton. He stopped, grabbed him by his shoulders and held him at arm's length, absorbing his presence; he then pulled him in close and gave him a lingering hug.

He then sat down in the seating area on the sun-drenched veranda and pulled a large whisky out of the air. The last time Nick had seen him, he had stolen his face, size, weight and mannerisms; he had become Nick. But today, Lucifer looked like Lucifer, the tall, well-built cocky angel. He was an insanely confident man, but with a dramatic, thespian flair.

"Oh Anton, this whole experience has been vile! I don't think I will ever wash the Nick off of me, but it's all for the greater good." Lucifer shook his head in disgust of the thought of staying the same for eons; he steadied himself and took a large swig from his glass.

"Damn, that always tastes best with this view." He smiled at Anton.

"Anyway, how is he doing?" he asked.

"Apart from him being heavily drugged?" Anton asked as

he sat down beside him, "He's onto you about the changes to the house."

"I know, I got the alert last night. I cleared up the spell; he shouldn't be able to view it now," Lucifer said.

"He can't, he tried again today, just before he became a drooling mess."

They both laughed.

"He is developing his skills, but his human soul is holding him back. At this rate, it's going to take forever for him to be able to reach the level you need him to be at."

Lucifer sat back, took another drink and stroked his neatly trimmed beard. As he stared out over the crystal blue ocean, a thought came to his evil mind.

"I wonder if it's his soul that is getting in the way, mmm. What would happen if we took it away from him?" A grin spread across his face, "Surely, no soul, no remorse?"

"Would it kill him?" Anton asked.

"I don't think so; he might be a bit strange for a few days. All we are doing is speeding up the process by removing his buffer."

Anton looked confused, "How are you going to store it? Obviously, you need to keep hold of it. This one is not for Hades. You can't let it escape; otherwise, your plan won't work."

"Anton, it's fine, I will keep his soul secure and locked up in me. It won't be pleasant for him, but I don't really care about that." Lucifer laughed, taking another drink.

"As long as it won't hurt you, and we can get him to the point where we need him, then ok. But if either is in jeopardy then don't risk it; it's not worth losing you," Anton said, a concerned look on his face.

"I will be just fine. Don't worry, this will work." Lucifer

stood up, he finished his drink and threw the glass off into the distance, miles out into the ocean.

"Let's go rip this boy's soul out!" With a cool swagger, Lucifer headed towards Nick's room and Anton followed.

Nick had not moved from the position into which Anton had thrown him. He was still breathing; his pulse was slower than normal, and he looked as if he were in a coma. The deep sleep spell that Anton had used earlier in order for Lucifer to visit had worked so well that Nick's body couldn't even reposition itself when in an awkward position.

"Jesus Anton! How much did you give him? He's totally fucked!" Lucifer gasped.

Anton shrugged his shoulders, "Enough, he kept fighting it. He started to blame me for spying, you for planning something; even accused me of hiding the climate control panel," snapped Anton.

"He's not dumb then? He's got us nailed down to a tee."

Anton smiled and lifted Nick's arm up and dropped it again; it fell like a marionette. Then Anton punched him in the face, hard. Nick didn't flinch apart from his head jolting to one side from the blow.

Lucifer nodded and set his position at the bottom of the bed. He began to chant. Nick rose off the bed in unison with Lucifer's arms as they rose, they stopped in front of him. Nick slowly started to glow in a pale blue light, Lucifer lifted his left arm above his right and clenched his fist. With a loud crack, he smashed his left hand into his right, and Nick smashed into the bed. The glowing outline stayed floating in the air above Nick. Lucifer pulled both hands to his chest and passed the blue glow into his own body.

With a loud cry of ecstasy, Lucifer dropped to one knee, breathing heavily.

"Oh crap! That was a lot harder than usual. Who the hell

is he?" Lucifer gathered himself and left the room still holding his chest as the new soul settled into its new home.

"Right, hopefully, there shouldn't be any more delays. I don't know how much longer I can go on dealing with that fucking witch. Honestly, I can't understand how the hell Nick didn't leave her before now." Lucifer shook as if someone had walked over his grave.

"Anyway, I better go. Push him hard; he might be more pliable now." Lucifer hugged Anton; he released and held his face, lost in his eyes. He leaned in and kissed him. They tasted each other, held together with passion from thousands of years.

Lucifer stepped back from Anton reluctantly, "I fucking love you, Anton. Make this work; it's hard being away from you."

Anton smiled, "I know, but it will all be worth it in the end."

Lucifer winked and with a loud crack, he was gone.

♔

He opened his eyes, the taste of alcohol tightened his throat, and he choked on the cigarettes that lingered on his palate. His head was pounding, and the lights hurt his eyes. With a push, he stood up and felt the sway of the room.

He staggered to the toilet and grabbed the sink to balance himself. Looking up he saw a shell of a man, thinning hair and long stubble. He ran the tap and looked down to his hands. As the water ran over them, cooling them down with the ice-cold water, he watched the dried blood run from them and into the sink. He splashed the freezing water over his face, but the shock of the coldness only seemed to affect him for a few seconds before he began feeling drowsy again. He looked into the mirror, into his bloodshot, empty eyes. The light faded into darkness.

The door handle formed in his vision. Turning it, he watched the door swing open and the smell of raw meat hit his nostrils. As the room filled with the light of the corridor behind him, he saw the start of the massacre. Crimson splashes cascaded across the walls and ceiling. Two limp, slashed, beaten bodies lay on the bed holding each other. He smiled as he embraced the knowledge of finally gaining his freedom – no more nagging, no more problems. He had finally done it and the blood-splattered sheets were the last "fuck you" to a woman and daughter who had stolen his youth. He closed the door behind him, and the light faded.

He felt the rain slowly soak through his slippers as he dragged the refuse bags towards the garage where he kept the new wood chipper. With the warm rain pounding down on his back, he couldn't help but smile, knowing he only had this last job to do before he could leave and live his new life. He could feel the excitement pounding in his chest.

Nick sat bolt upright, sweating and out of breath. He calmed himself down quickly and rubbed his jaw. Where had that pain come from? He rubbed his eyes and realised he was in bed. He didn't remember going to bed. He vaguely remembered getting up yesterday, never mind actually going back to bed. The last real memory he had was with Steve Harper in the hospital.

At that moment Anton walked through the door.

"Oh, thank God, sir, you're awake. You passed out a day ago, slumped straight down off the stool in the kitchen and crashed onto the floor, I was very worried."

"Really? My jaw, why does my jaw hurt so much?" Nick asked rubbing his jaw.

"Ah, you hit it on the way down onto the floor. I tried to grab you, but you fell fast," explained Anton. "By the time I got to you, it was too late; you had hit the floor. I wasn't sure what had happened, so I just got you into bed and kept an eye on you. I made the presumption it was down to your body still getting used to the portal."

Nick slowly dropped his legs out of bed and stood up.

"Fuck, I feel like I have been in a fight. My limbs ache, and my head is pounding. I ache so much I'm expecting something to fall off."

"You took a heavy fall, sir. I'm surprised you're wanting to get out of bed at all today," Anton said.

"Well I had a pretty grotesque vision, so I think I better get myself sorted and get back out there." Nick slowly walked to the bathroom rubbing his back, "I won't be long, can you sort me some food out?" asked Nick.

"Of course, sir. But what about the vision?" Anton shouted.

"It's fine; it can wait. Food first," replied Nick.

Anton left Nick's room, leaving Nick to get himself ready. Thirty minutes later Nick arrived in the kitchen.

Anton asked as soon as Nick pull up a chair at the counter, "Sir, the vision, what was it?"

"Drunk Dad killed his family, " Nick poked at his food, " We got any bacon with this?" he asked.

Anton looked surprised, "A drunk father killing his family? And you're still here asking about bacon?"

"Yeah, why?" Nick asked whilst eating.

"Don't you think you should be trying to get there soon and help them?" Anton said with a slight shiver.

"Yeah, and I will. I just want some bacon." Nick walked

to the fridge and looked inside. "Jesus, I'm so hungry, how long was I out for?" he asked as he rummaged through the fridge.

"A day, just a day. Aren't you worried about the family?" Anton asked trying to get more of a reply than food-related answers.

"It's fine, there's no rush; he's already killed them. Bacon?" Nick waved the empty plate in the direction of Anton.

Anton fried him some bacon and pushed it under his nose.

Nick finished his bacon and walked off to the portal room, Anton hurried behind.

"How are you feeling, sir?" Anton asked, surprised that the removal of Nick's soul would affect him so quickly.

"I feel good Anton, kind of light. It seems like my mind isn't as confused today; things seem clear and simple. I find the guy, choke him out, and the job's done. Why hasn't it been this simple before?"

Anton cut his hand and held it over the basin that controlled the portal and with a bang and a cloud of sulphur, Nick was gone.

♔

Nick arrived in a large, dark outbuilding. The rain outside hit the corrugated metal roof like tiny ball bearings. Then he heard the dragging on the gravel outside, just beyond the barn doors. He knew from his vision what that noise was, and what was about to happen.

He braced himself for what was to come, he didn't feel sick with the anticipation; in fact, he felt excited about what was going to happen.

The barn door opened slowly and the moonlight

illuminated the contents of the barn highlighting all the machinery, tools and Nick. Danny didn't see him at first. Danny didn't see him until he spoke.

It wasn't until he had dragged the bloodied lumps of his family into the barn and switched the light on. Nick sat on the corroded tractor, the one Danny had promised to repair and sell seven years ago. There were several vehicles in here like that. His wife had given up asking him about them, years ago.

Nick watched Danny drag the sacks in through the barn doors and close them behind him. He switched the light on and stood, hands on his hips looking at the sacks in front of him.

"Now then my darlings, I think it's about time I introduced you to the wood chipper. You know the one, you told me was a waste of money to buy. You pointed out that we didn't have any trees. Well, I didn't buy it for that, I bought it for you; it was all part of the plan, sweetheart!"

"Really! You had a plan, Danny?" Nick scoffed, "You couldn't plan shit. Your wife knew that; your daughter knew that. Christ Danny, I have only known you for a few hours, and I know you couldn't plan shit!"

Nick jumped down to confront Danny who stood there. Mouth open, speechless. Nick pushed Danny's bloodstained chin shut with his finger.

"Who?... What?" Danny stood shocked. This was not part of his plan.

"I'm here to help you get away with the massacre that had just taken place in your loving, family home." Nick bent down to open the refuse sacks that he stood over.

As Nick bent over, Danny reached for a crowbar that leaned against the tractor and brought it down hard across the back of Nick's head.

12

VOICES

Danny stood with the crowbar in his hands; he stared at Nick waiting for him to go down. When he didn't, he swung the crowbar again.

Same response.

When the second blow hit Nick's back, he stood and turned to face Danny.

"Seriously Danny? Do you deal with all your problems with violence?"

Danny went for another swing with the crowbar, this time though, Nick grabbed it. He tried to wrestle it from Nick's grasp but embarrassingly failed. He pulled at the bar with all his strength, as he did so the tool disappeared and he went flying back onto the dusty floor. Pulling himself up quickly and trying to shake off the fall, Danny made a dash for the doors.

"Danny!" Nick shouted, "Danny? Don't you want to introduce me to your family? They seem nice! Hey, Danny?"

Danny grabbed the door handle and pushed, but the doors didn't move. He rattled them back and forth to try and work them loose, but the doors remained static, confusing him. He turned to Nick with fear and confusion racing through his head.

"Who are you?"

"Oh, hi Danny, I'm Nick," Nick said waving his hand like a children's television presenter.

Then he looked back at Danny's bags containing his chopped-up family.

"I'm guessing this isn't just a normal Wednesday for you? I mean, slice and dice isn't a weekly family game, is it?"

Nick gritted his teeth in disgust at the bags as he tapped them with his foot, then Nick turned to Danny. He stuck his arm out in the direction of the man and with a magical force dragged him to where Nick stood.

"Get the fuck off me! Don't fucking touch me!" Danny screamed, petrified. All he wanted to do was escape.

"Can't do Danny boy. You see, you've been a bad, bad man, and I have come to punish you."

"Wh.. what do you mean? I haven't done anything!" Danny protested.

"You haven't?" Nick said sarcastically, "Mrs. Danny, er… your husband said he shouldn't be punished, is he right?" Nick pointed an imaginary microphone to the refuge sacks. "Well, Danny, she found that funny! Look, she's in bits!"

"She had it coming; that bitch ruined my life. Thirty-two years of nagging, complaining; she made my life fucking hell," Danny spat.

"I see. Oh, I'm with you, I mean you're such a catch too! Look at you. What a man! You don't look a day over twenty!" Nick continued to mock.

"Shut up!" Danny vented, "What are you anyway? A pig?"

"Oh Dan, you fucking wish I was the police, I'm going to fuck you up so bad that you will be begging to be locked up!"

Nick calmed himself. He readied himself to get revenge for Danny's family and take his soul, but not without making him feel it first.

"Jesus man, if you're not the police, who are you? How are you holding me?" He tried to wriggle free. "Let me go, you're making my fucking skin crawl!"

Nick listened to Danny's rantings and a grin spread across his face.

"Danny, that hurts me; it really does. I make your skin crawl?" Nick's expression morphed from joking to deadly serious, "Would you like me to make your skin crawl?"

Danny looked down at his blood-stained hands and could see small lumps starting to appear under the skin on his fingertips. They crawled up his fingers at first, then began to grow in size, throbbing. Worming their way to the back of his hands. Danny could see cockroach sized shapes slowly crawling up under his skin, ripping his flesh beneath whilst staying embedded under the surface.

Danny screamed in pain as the insects continued to carve through the muscle tissue in his arm. He watched the movement of the legs crawling and heading towards his face. Danny's screams got louder. Blood was now starting to seep through his skin as the insects burrowed a route to his neck. They dug through his throat and swarmed his mouth, making him gag. Danny had stopped screaming because he was now choking as the insects streamed out of his mouth and scattered across the floor.

Nick decided to stop the ordeal. He didn't want to kill him yet; he wanted to play.

Danny vomited a mixture of blood and dirt that the insects had dragged up on their journey through his shredded limbs.

He then dropped onto the ground as Nick released his hold.

He grabbed his head, crying, pleading for Nick to stop.

"You're right, Danny, I do make your skin crawl. Word of advice, don't give me ideas!" Nick turned back to the refuse sacks on the floor, "So, what exactly are you going to do to your loved ones?"

Nick was calm and controlled; his sarcastic mocking had stopped.

Danny couldn't talk; the cockroaches had caused serious damage to his mouth and throat, and he was still spitting out blood. Nick clicked his fingers and the damage was gone.

Danny grabbed his throat, coughed as to test its reaction. He couldn't feel any pain. When he looked down at his arms, there was no blood or scarring.

"How did you do that? Are you a wizard?" Danny spluttered in surprise.

"Yes Danny. I'm a wizard and I'm here to collect you and take you to Hogwarts," Nick mocked.

"Really? Don't you think I'm a bit too old?" Danny struggled with Nick's dry delivery.

"Fuck sake! I was being sarcastic!"

Nick was now starting to get impatient with Danny's stupidity, and just wanted to speed things up.

"I'm the King of Hell. I'm here for your soul. You piece of shit!"

"Why? For that?" Danny pointed at the bloodied bags on the floor.

"Danny, you killed your family. You hacked, smashed and chopped them up. That's not normal, There is no equivalent punishment for that. Danny, you're a monster."

"No, no I'm not. I did this because if I didn't, she would have killed me. She tried to poison me with that slop she called food. She drove me to do this. She… she asked for this." Danny grabbed his head again, "Shut up!" he yelled.

"What?" Nick was taken aback, "Are you telling me to shut up?"

"No, I won't, I can't; he's stronger, SHUT UP!" Danny squeezed his head tighter and began to sob again.

Nick looked at Danny and walked over to him as he cowered on the floor.

"Danny, how many people are here in this room or in your head?"

He crouched down at Danny's side and tapped him on his head, "How many are there in there?"

"Err… I don't know, two. They keep telling me that you're not real, and you don't exist."

Danny had stopped crying and looked up to him, "So, I'm going to ignore you and continue doing what I planned to do."

Danny stood up and started to walk to the sacks on the floor.

Nick watched him, as he opened one sack and watched him power up the wood chipper. Danny had planned to dispose of the family's remains this way and had bought a large chipper; he would then scatter the remains across the local fields.

He had built up to this night over the last few months and wasn't going to change the plan now. Danny walked back to the bags and crouched down; he stuck his hand in and pulled out a foot. The limb was grey and covered in semi-dried blood; he stopped and looked at it, turning it round in his hand. Danny examined the hacked mess of the tibia – the blood had not quite dried yet – or it could have been blood from another body part in the sack. He flicked the switch to start up the machine and tossed the foot into the opening.

Before the limb made contact with the blades, it stopped in mid-air. Nick switched off the machine and grabbed the hovering foot, feeling the cold, almost-hardened skin in his fingers. It left a cold touch lingering on his fingertips.

"Oh! Getting rid of the evidence? Sorry, chief, no can do. Don't you think you've done enough?" Nick said with disgust in his voice.

Danny continued grabbing severed body parts and throwing them into the chipper's mouth. Each time, Nick stopped the limb before it dropped into the opening, Danny, unaware of the continued resistance or the fact that the machine wasn't running, had warmed to his task. He seemed to be blocking out Nick and anything he was doing. Danny was in a trance, like someone else was at the wheel.

"Danny?" Nick shouted, then gave him a heavy smack across the back of his head; Danny's head jolted forward, snapping him out of the trance.

Danny turned around and looked up at Nick.

"You're back? I thought you had gone like they said you would." He switched the wood chipper back on.

"This wood ain't going to chip itself!" he said in a happy voice as he bent down to the mess of body parts scattered on the dusty floor.

Nick switched it off.

"That isn't wood!" he said pointing at the macabre floor covering.

Danny switched the machine back on, "Of course it's wood. What else would it be?" he scoffed. "I have to get this done before they arrive; they don't want this lying about, where would they park?"

"Fuck sake, Danny, it's your wife and daughter you're trying to shred. You're starting to really fucking irritate me now. Put the body parts back in the bag, or you're going in the fucking wood chipper instead."

Nick's patience was running thin and he was very close to killing Danny now.

Danny stood up and walked to one of the shelves on the wall where a rusty axe lay. It wasn't like the heavy, long-handled new one that lay on his bedroom floor, covered in blood and torn skin. This one was small and ideal for throwing – which is what he did, aiming straight at Nick's head. The blade made contact, but it bounced off with a thud sound and spun across the floor.

"Right, Danny. I've had enough; get in the fucking shredder!" Nick pointed at the wood chipper.

Danny slowly slid across the concrete floor towards the machine's gaping mouth, its teeth yearning for food. Danny's face suddenly came to life as though someone had turned a light on.

"Stop! What the fuck are you doing? Please stop you're going to kill me!" Danny screamed, waking to the instant nightmare.

"Please, I have a family; they need me!"

Nick stopped, "Wait, What? You mean, you HAD a Family! Had!"

Danny looked down at the open bags on the floor, surrounded by his family's remains. "Oh God! What's that?"

Nick stared in disbelief.

"Really? It's your loving family that you slaughtered, with an axe and a knife. Then you bagged and dragged them from the house…"

"No! No! I wouldn't. Oh my God, no, my daughter? No!"

Danny became hysterical; he started screaming and crying. He looked at his hands as he pulled them to his face and realised they were covered in blood.

"NO! NO!"

Nick released his hold on Danny. As soon his invisible grip was removed, Danny's eyes glazed over again and he bolted for the door.

Nick threw his hands to the sky in disbelief.

Danny got to the door and had it opened when a force slammed it shut in his face. He tried pulling on the handle with all his strength but it was solid in its resistance.

Nick raised his hand towards Danny and lifted him into the air once more. The glaze in his eyes dispersed, and the uncontrollable screaming started again. It seemed as if he were being possessed, and as soon as Danny's life was in danger the possessor left.

Danny hovered in the air screaming. Nick moved him above the wood chipper and dropped him feet first, into the man-size shaft. His screams were now reaching a manic level; he couldn't move apart from his head. Nick watched Danny pass out as his shoes started to hit the blades. The peace from the screaming was a blessing but not the crunching, or the sound of ripping flesh as Danny slowly churned through the blades.

The pile of warm, red mulch gradually built up at the other end across the concrete flooring, the steam rising in the evening's cold air.

Once the wood chipper's victim had finally passed through, Nick stopped the machine and there was silence in the barn, apart from the blood dripping onto the wet mound of fresh, shredded flesh and bone.

Nick stood and looked at the violence in front of him; he wiped a splash of blood off his cheek and took a deep breath. He had just ground a clearly very ill man into sludge and didn't feel bad or ill about it. He just knew that was the job, kill and take the soul. It seemed so simple now, no confusion.

There seemed to be something strange about Danny, apart from what was quite obviously schizophrenia. It was almost as if another entity were jumping in and out of him, controlling him like a puppet.

Nick took one last look around the barn and the horrific massacre, then he clicked his fingers and disappeared.

He returned, standing in the middle of the portal room. Calm and relaxed, he smiled at Anton.

"Well, that was a fucking bloodbath. I'm glad I don't see that every day." He then strolled towards the kitchen; Anton silently cheered to himself and punched the air.

When they reached the kitchen, Nick rummaged through the fridge, closed the door and turned to Anton.

"I need food, quick. I'm starving," He snapped his fingers and a large pepperoni pizza appeared on the side.

"Did you get there in time, sir?" Asked Anton.

"Nah! He had already butchered them before I arrived. Strange thing though, he looked like he was possessed, controlled somehow." Nick rammed another slice into his mouth, catching the cheese dripping off the pizza onto his hand as it dragged sauce with it.

"Wouldn't like to be the one who finds that mess. Seriously, he had them sliced and diced and bagged when I arrived. Fucking mayhem, man."

"So, you took his soul, sir?"

"Yep, shredded the crazy fucker, put him through his new wood chipper." Nick stuffed the remaining pizza slice into his mouth and shut the box lid.

Anton smiled, "That's not like you, sir. Didn't you feel the desire to help him?"

"Nope, no saving him. He was a mess. Anyway, I think I'm gonna go down to the beach."

Nick stood up and walked out of the kitchen. As he

disappeared through the doors leading to the beach, Anton waited a few minutes. After a while, Anton smiled.

"Think the removal of his soul worked a treat, Lucifer. We are back on with the plan."

Lucifer leaned back in his chair, in his room, surrounded by screens.

"We are, Anton. I did lose control of that idiot a few times, but we got the ending we wanted, so that's all that matters. It looked like Nick noticed something, so we can't use the possession trick again." He smiled and spun around once in his chair. "Not long now."

Anton stood outside, on the veranda, watching Nick walk down to the beach, and out to the sea for a swim.

"Enjoy it whilst you can, boy, because this won't last forever. And the world you know will come crashing down worse than what it is now."

13

CONTACT

When Nick returned from his swim, he was invigorated and for the first time since being here, relaxed. He grabbed more food from the fridge, and he sat out in the radiance of the sun.

He relished the fact that the weather never changed here; he remembered a vague memory that he had wanted a change from the sun. But right now it seemed the furthest thing from his mind.

One thing he had noticed today, however, was his hunger. It seemed to be a non-stop emptiness that just couldn't be filled, a bottomless void.

Nick still couldn't remember anything from the last few days too. He had slivers of memory regarding Steve Harper and his kid, but nothing of detail. He seemed to have vague patches that drifted in and out; the more he thought about it the more he realised there was a gap of time missing. But then he realised he didn't care enough about to let it worry him.

The only thing that was prominent in his mind was the hunger, and how his limbs and jaw still ached. He leaned back and stretched out in the large L-shaped seating area and looked up at the clear uranian blue sky. Nick was completely relaxed and happy; it had been a while since he had felt at peace.

The constant underlying emotional pain about being away from his mother, from his home, had been a burden he had carried with him since being here. He didn't feel that now, or the hatred for Lucifer, a being who had turned his life upside down and ripped his heart out. Today, he didn't feel the hatred, the anguish, just the emptiness.

Nick closed his eyes and felt the heat from the sun beat down warming his face, not a burning heat, just comfortably warm. He smiled and enjoyed the feeling.

Anton stood in the doorway watching Nick. Lucifer's plan had worked extremely well, no more emotionally charged adolescent demanding how things should be. Anton liked the new Nick, carefree and happy, not miserable and full of holier than thou attitude.

Nick rubbed his jaw again, and Anton smiled; he felt a warm pleasure in having caused him pain.

"It's for the best Jen; he can't keep seeing you like this. You're a mess."her father said as they left with her son. As she watched the door slam shut, she looked at her scarred arms, the deep cuts grooved in her skin, the lighter scar tissue. No one knew why, or just how much the constant yearning and need charged through her. That kiss still on her lips, on her soul, chewing through every sinew in her body.

She started to cry again, not for the loss of her son, but the pain in her chest from the aching, the desire. The wanting of just one more kiss, one more touch.

She knew one day it would happen, and she was happy to lose everything for it. One more chance was all she needed and she wouldn't waste it. What would happen if she took another life? Would he come again, be with her, touch her like he did that time? She was willing to do anything it took.

She felt the excitement race through her now; her skin felt electric. The thought of being near him again aroused her. She could feel her nipples stiffen at the thought of tasting his lips again. The image of her arms faded to black.

As the image sharpened, she saw the nightclub in the distance. She felt the rain hit her face like hail, there was only one thing on her mind though, a victim, and HIM.

She could see his youthful face, his shoulder-length hair, trench coat hanging from his shoulders, like a dark dream. He was her craving. She paced with a purpose to The Dimebar, ignoring the persistent rain pounding through her clothes.

She knew she could take a naive, weak man from this place and kill him. She had developed strength from the kiss that had surprised her; she wasn't scared of hurting or being hurt as Chris, her ex- had found out.

Her craving blurred her clarity between right and what was wrong. Things she wouldn't have even thought of before, she found herself doing just to get what she must have.

The bouncers let her in without queuing; they knew her well, the drinking, the fights. She had earned total respect from them over the months of trying to kill her desires. She smiled at them as she walked past; they responded likewise and said, "Behave tonight!"

The music grew louder as she walked into the main bar, the baseline pounding on her chest, the screaming guitars blasting out of the speakers that surrounded the open dance floor. She headed towards the bar to begin the ritual of the numbing that the alcohol brought. The bar faded into black.

The cold night air bit into her skin as she left a few hours late. She turned and pulled his arm with her. He staggered out into the street following, looking confident and excited to be leaving with someone.

Both way too drunk to be able to walk in a straight line they leaned on each other to stop from falling over. They walked to a flat that she had rented nearby, and as she closed the door behind them, she slid the bolts and locked them in. She walked into the room behind her guest, extremely drunk and ready to commit murder. She closed the door behind her, and the scene faded into black.

Feeling a cool breeze brush across his face, he stirred awake. The early evening had started to steal the sunlight from the sky, and Nick wiped the drool from the side of his mouth and sat up. He felt a tug on the neck of his t-shirt; he relaxed and tried to sit up again, this time there were no problems. He rubbed his head and looked around the veranda where he had fallen asleep; he was alone.

"Crap, I guess I'm going out tonight."

Nick stood up and walked through the kitchen to his room to grab a shower.

He had decided to sort this out, not only had it fucked her life up, but he now knew how she felt and what she had lost.

He owed her something, even if it was just to try to fix what he had done.

Nick decided that he was not going to tell Anton about this trip; he knew the butler would not approve. He had already warned him about getting too close, but Nick knew that the obsession wasn't just one way; he felt the same yearning.

Nick showered, dressed and headed to the portal room. He had watched Anton enough to understand the basics, fingers crossed he didn't die trying.

Rushing down to the room he made sure the route was clear. Careful not to disturb Anton, he couldn't be arsed with the lecture. He slipped into the portal room, activated the portal and disappeared.

Nick arrived in the street outside Jennifer's flat. Immediately he felt the strange sensation of the pulling in his stomach. He knew where to find her; she was close and it was just a case of following the pull. He waited outside looking up at the flat window that he could sense was hers. The curtain twitched, and he felt an excitement that wasn't his. Nick knew that the pulling in her stomach was happening, and she knew he was close.

He made his way inside to Jennifer's flat. He stood by the door, pausing, thinking. He could just walk straight in, but he wanted to feel the anticipation. He knew she stood at the other side of the door, waiting, thinking. He heard the door unlock, and she stood there, her hands covered in blood.

"I knew you would come, I told Dave you would come; he begged for you to come too!"

Jennifer looked down at her hands and put them behind her back, hiding them in shame. She realised she should have cleaned them before she answered the door.

"What have you done, Jen?" Nick pushed past her, shoving her into the wall; she closed the door behind him and locked it.

Nick walked into a room and he was greeted with Dave, tied to the bed and bleeding from several places.

Jen walked in behind Nick and walked to Dave; she dragged her bloodied hands along his semi-naked torso and turned to look at Nick.

"He's still alive; he's just passed out. Do you want to finish him off?"

With the smell of fear and blood in the air, Jen was thriving off the excitement. Nick, however, wasn't.

"Get rid of him," Nick insisted.

"Why? I did this for you. To bring you here. Haven't you come for him?"

"I'm not here for him; it's you I'm here for."

Jen moved to Nick; then a moan came from the bed. The young man was becoming conscious again. Nick pushed Jen to one side and made his way to the bed.

Nick touched the bleeding man's forehead with a finger, and he passed out again.

"What was the plan? What if I hadn't come? What were you going to do with a corpse?"

Jen had not thought that far ahead. In her fantasy, she would hurt someone, and Nick would arrive and finish the person's life. He would have her, and they would fall to the bed and have sweaty, bloody sex.

"I don't know, dump him somewhere? I did this for you, I've tried everything else. I thought you would come, and you would snap your fingers and he would be gone, or whatever it is that you do."

"And if I hadn't come? Jesus Jen, you need to start thinking about what you're doing."

Nick, frustrated at her recklessness, squeezed his head with his hand, "Right, let's sort this out first."

Nick slowly moved his hand from head to toe over Dave's

body and healed his cuts. He snapped his fingers, and the man was gone.

Jen dropped to her knees and wrapped her head in her hands and started to cry. Nick walked over to her and crouched at her side; he touched her hair, softly.

"He's gone, no wounds, no memory of tonight. He's just passed out in the bar down the road where you found him."

He grabbed her and held her close.

"Have you got anything to drink?" he asked.

Jen wiped her tears with her hands, "There is some whisky in the cupboard to the right. I don't have any glasses, sorry."

Nick stood up, got the whiskey from the cupboard and snapped his fingers; two glasses appeared.

"Ice?"

"No, straight. Is there anything you can't do?" she asked getting herself off the floor and sitting on the bed.

"Yeah, get my real life back. But at least till then, I can do what the fuck I want." Nick smiled.

"What do you mean? Is this not your life?"

"God no, well yes, but no. It's a shit story, and I would rather leave that for another time," Nick said.

He downed his drink and poured another, gesturing to Jen if she wanted a top-up. She looked at Nick; he could see her hand shaking slightly as she held her glass out.

"Another time?" Jen questioned, "You're not here to kill me?"

"Fuck no, I've seen how much you have lost, and how much I have wrecked your life."

"You haven't; I have. I have this constant nervous sick feeling when I feel as though I'm close to you. In the hospital I had this pulling in my stomach, pulling me to you. You won't understand." Jen felt stupid trying to explain this to Nick.

"I know, I feel it too."

Jen looked up, "Really, no fucking way! So why tonight? Why not in the hospital? Why didn't you say something then?" she asked grabbing his hand.

"Things have changed, I don't want to just do what's right anymore. If this is my life, then I want control of it and not to be told what I can or can't do."

Nick stroked the back of Jen's hand; she felt her whole body charge with excitement and the tiny hairs on her neck stood on end.

Nick stood, "I'm not sure I should be here. I am getting thoughts in my head that I know I shouldn't act upon."

"Why?"

Jen walked over to Nick as he held the door handle, deciding on his next action. She slid her hand over the back of his.

"Don't you want me?"

Nick looked at her trying to find the voice inside that told him, no. He knew it should be there, but it wasn't. This wasn't the first time he'd noticed this over the last few days, no inner voice. It was as though it had been gagged. He turned the handle, then he felt Jen wrap her arms around him. Her hands reached under his shirt and across his naked stomach up towards his chest.

She slowly began to pull them back out, dragging her blood-stained nails, lightly, across his skin and out of his shirt. Nick turned to face her and she shoved him against the door. He was surprised by her strength, holding his arms up as far as she could.

"You're not going anywhere, I have you now and unless

you snap your fingers and disappear then that tells me you want this too."

Nick paused, spun her around, forcing her against the wall. He pushed himself against her, feeling her body against his.

He leaned into her ear and spoke softly, "Is this what you want? If I took this further, this could send you insane. The craving you feel now is nothing. Look at the mess one kiss made."

Nick slowly licked the side of her neck, and Jen let out a restricted moan.

She pushed him back onto the bed, climbed on top and straddled him, holding his arms down again.

"Don't fuck with me. I've given up too much to be here. I want this with all my soul, and I will have this one way or another."

Nick felt her hands tighten around his wrists and her legs tighten on his waist as she pushed herself down onto him. Jennifer learned forwards to kiss Nick, but he pulled back and turned his head away. She leaned in and bit his neck, hard. She expected blood but was disappointed and surprised when she looked down and saw she had left no mark. She bit him harder, still nothing.

"You can't hurt me. I can feel it, but you can't hurt me."

Nick stood, lifting Jen with him. She kept a tight hold and he pulled her in even tighter. He pushed his face into her cleavage, kissing the visible skin that pushed through her buttoned shirt. He traced her chest up to her neck with his tongue, then stopped. Nick turned and threw her onto the bed.

"I have to go; this is fucking crazy!"

Nick grabbed his face and dragged his hands down off his chin, searching for the voice, the common sense. But the voice was silent, muted, and without the voice, nothing was stopping him. She wanted this, he wanted this. Then the switch in his brain tripped; Stop thinking, just do – as he had done in the barn.

Now all he was left with was want, and nothing was stopping him with taking what he wanted.

"You know what Jen? I do fucking want you, and I'm going to have you. I'm sick of listening to everyone else."

Jen jumped off the bed and launched herself onto him, wrapping her legs around him. Grabbing his face and kissing him. She immediately felt the strength in her rage, and Nick lifted her. With one hand he held her arse, while the other hand ventured under her loose-fitting top, running slowly up her naked spine under her bra, and unhooked the fastener.

Jen pushed his jacket down off his shoulders, he dropped it as she clung to him. She noticed how thin his arms seemed compared to the strength that he was using to hold her up. Nick walked to the bed and dropped her on it. He took off his T-shirt and he pulled her legs towards him.

She ripped her top off, buttons popping everywhere. Jen pulled off her bra and flung it across the room. Nick dropped onto her, as their kisses deepened, Jen felt his hardness through his jeans. She rolled herself back on top into a more dominant position; she took control and guided him as they continued to explore each other's bodies.

This was a night that Nick would never forget and a night that would create an addiction inside Jennifer that would grow stronger with every touch. This drug didn't destroy the mind – it destroyed the soul.

14

FRICTION

Nick woke and rubbed his eyes, expecting dazzling sunshine and a glorious view of the ocean, then he realised he was still at Jen's. He must have fallen asleep after their night of passion. He turned to feel Jen's naked skin at his side; after he kissed the back of her neck he climbed out of bed.

Ten minutes later Jennifer stirred; she let out a groan, remembering the amount of alcohol she had consumed and patted the empty space beside her. Realising her visitor was not there, she turned quickly and squinted in the dark.

"Nick? Nick?" she jumped out of bed and ran into the living room. Nick sat looking out the window in just his jeans, a cup of coffee in his hand.

"Sorry, I didn't want to wake you," Nick said.

"It's fine, I thought you had gone." Jen walked over to Nick and sat at his side, wrapping her arms around him. "Do you have to go?"

"No, not yet. Don't you have work or something to go to?"

"Not anymore, I had more important things to concentrate

on than working in a supermarket."

She grabbed Nick's coffee and placed it on the floor. She pushed him back into the chair and sat on his lap, facing him.

"What happens now?"

Nick opened her shirt, cupped under her breasts and licked each nipple slowly. "More of this I guess."

Jen groaned and pushed herself down on Nick; she slowly rotated her hips, enjoying the control she had over him.

Suddenly there was a loud crack and Nick disappeared. Jen fell off the chair and collapsed onto the floor. She looked around in panic and screamed for Nick, but he was gone.

♔

A flash of light and Nick arrived in the portal room, in a pile, on the cold concrete floor. Shirtless and shoeless, he looked up at Anton,.

"Thank god, sir, you're ok! I have been worried sick about you. I checked on you this morning, and you weren't in your room. I checked on the beach, and I couldn't see you anywhere." Anton was clearly concerned, and the panic in his voice was obvious.

"What the fuck man! I was fine. Why did you bring me back?" yelled Nick.

"As I said, sir, you weren't here."

Nick stood up and left the room. Anton followed behind.

"Sir, where are your shoes and shirt?"

"On someone's bedroom floor, exactly where I should be." Nick stormed off to the kitchen; the hunger was dominating his thoughts again.

"What happened? Where did you go? Sorry, whose bedroom floor? And why didn't you wake me if you had another vision?" Anton followed closely behind.

"Fuck off Anton, I don't need to tell you everywhere I go or what I do! You're not my fucking mother!"

"I'm sorry, sir, but I thought you had been taken. Or even worse, you had decided to take on Lucifer." Anton quickly walked to Nick's bedroom to get him some clothes.

Nick pulled himself out of the fridge he had been leaning into.

"Taken? By who? Who the fuck is going to take me?" He shouted, spitting bits of chewed chicken into the air.

Anton came quickly back into the kitchen area carrying some clothes for Nick. "Here, sir, put these on. What is wrong with your back? Why are there scratches across your back?"

Nick grabbed a plate of food and headed outside.

"My kidnappers liked it rough. Taken! Jesus, get a grip, Anton."

Anton followed Nick out onto the veranda and stood by him as he sat in the warm sunshine, still in his socks and jeans that he had worn the previous night.

"What happened last night, sir?" Anton asked.

"I went out to see an old friend, I didn't want to disturb you, so I used the portal myself. It's not hard."

"It is dangerous, one wrong setting and it could turn you into spaghetti, very fine spaghetti, and you couldn't come back from that. And with you dead, I would hate to think what Lucifer would do to your mother."

"You don't get to talk about my mother and him in the same sentence." Nick threw his plate at the wall, "This food is shit! You're feeding me shit food. Why is this stuff not filling me? It doesn't matter what I eat; I am never full!"

"Very good, sir, I will get you better food." Anton started to clean up the mess, "What did you do last night, sir?"

"I decided to let off some much-needed steam; that's all

you need to know. I'm going down to the beach." Nick stood up and headed down to the beach.

Anton picked up the mess left by Nick's outburst.

"Little shit!" Anton mumbled, as he stood up, turned and walked straight into the ghost of Steve Harper.

"Holy crap!" Anton blurted out as he dropped the smashed plate again.

"Hello, Anton. How are you?"

"I'm very sorry, Mr. Harper, you startled me."

"Yeah, sorry about that. I have a tendency to do that; no footsteps you see." Steve pointed down to the transparent view through his feet to the floor below.

"I wondered if Nick was around?"

"Yes, he's on the beach."

Steve said thank you and floated down to the beach, leaving Anton to complain to himself. He could see a shirtless Nick staring out to the ocean, watching the sea stroke the white sand with every gentle wave.

"Hey Nick, how's it going?"

Nick spun around quickly in surprise. "Steve! Jesus, you made me jump!"

"Yeah! No footsteps…" Steve gestured to his feet again.

"What's wrong? What's your crazy wife been doing this time?"

"She's doing well; she's seeing someone to resolve the disorder, and Tommy is doing a lot better too. She has her family back helping again, not as much, but they are keeping a close watch on her."

Steve paused and looked at Nick as though something were wrong.

"Are you ok?"

"Me?" Nick said puzzled pointing to himself, "I'm fine, mate, why do you ask?"

"You feel different. I can't put my figure on it, but it's almost like you're not yourself."

"It's this place. I need to get away from here." Nick said.

"Why? This place is amazing. You have your own beach, man! Your own beach!"

"I know, but I feel trapped, as though I'm being watched constantly. I'm young, I need to be out."

Nick shifted his weight where he sat and leaned to Steve, looking around making sure Anton wasn't close by.

"I sneaked out last night; I went to see a friend. I needed to see someone. I really shouldn't have done it, but it was amazing."

"Did Anton try to stop you?"

"I didn't tell him; like I said I escaped. I was free, well till this morning when he dragged me back." Nick pointed up to the house.

"Who did you go see?"

"A woman. We met a while ago, I was supposed to persuade her to jump off a cliff, but instead, I saved her. I removed her cancer, and now she craves me." Nick looked pleased with himself as he explained to Steve.

"Craves you?" Steve seemed confused by this statement. "What? Like a drug?"

"Yep, I think it has something to do with how I removed her cancer. I may have touched her soul in the process. Well, that's what Anton said, but it wasn't like that last night. It was amazing. In fact, I need you to do me a favour."

"Ok, what?"

"If I give you an address, can you get there? I need you to pass a message on to her. I got pulled back here this morning, but to her, I just disappeared. She isn't stable, so I don't know what state she will be in"

"I don't know, Nick. This doesn't sound like a healthy

relationship. This could make things worse for you," Steve said apprehensively.

"Steve, I helped you, you owe me this much. Just tell her, I'm ok and that I will get back to her as soon as I can."

"I don't know if I can do it though; I think I need like anchor points to get to these places I go. Like a loved one or an object that I owned."

"Fuck sake Steve, who told you that shit?"

"I saw it in a film once, or read it in a book, not sure."

"Steve, you can go anywhere you want; you just need to know where." Nick turned and watched the ocean again.

"Read it in a book! This ain't Harry fucking Potter you know. Just do this for me and any debt you owe me will be scratched."

"Debt?"

"Yes, Steve. I helped you when you needed it; you now help me when I need it. I'm not running a charity, I'm not helping people for fun."

Nick stood up, "Do this one thing and you can return to the other side. If not, you're going to be at my beck and call forever." Nick left Steve standing on the beach as he headed back to the house.

Steve watched the ocean, trying to work out how he was going to do what Nick had asked for. He saw a small amount of steam raise from his palm, and within seconds an address was carved into his hand. No pain, no blood, as though it had always been there. He stood up and slowly faded into nothing as he glided along the beach.

Nick climbed the stairs, back up at the house and walked into the kitchen where Anton stood.

"You need to give me some freedom. I bet HE wasn't locked up all the time, so why am I?"

"No HE wasn't. sir, but HE wasn't new to this world and

He understood his place in it. You still have a long way to go. You're also going to have to trust me, sir. You need someone here in the portal room; you need to be able to return; otherwise, you will be stuck in the physical plane and you don't belong there now," Anton warned Nick with a tone Nick hadn't heard from Anton before.

"I don't belong here either, I have nothing I want here; it doesn't even feel like mine. I know it sounds weird but I still think he's watching me, and I hate that."

"Sir, this place is yours. Lucifer will not be returning at any point. He has moved on and you need to as well, it's for your own good."

"I will never move on. I will never give up. I will get back what is mine, Anton. And on that day, all this will be gone from my life. This is only temporary." Nick stormed off to his room, slamming the door behind himself.

Anton did his best to keep his anger in, but he let out a very quiet growl as he squeezed the edge of the kitchens work surface.

"Can't we just kill him now? He's getting on my fucking nerves," he said under his breath.

"Patience Anton, you know we need to stick to the plan. We can't fuck this up again. And listen to you, potty-mouth. Don't let him hear you swear; that's twice today you slipped. Keep it together," Lucifer's voice whispered in Anton's head.

"I just want this over with, I want us back together again; I miss you." Anton was calming down after hearing Lucifer's voice.

"We will be together again, soon. We just need to push him along now. Leave it with me," and with that Lucifer left Anton's head.

👑

Jennifer had spent most of the morning bouncing between anger, crying and reliving every second of last night to try to get the feeling of his skin on her back inside her head. She had found his shirt on the floor and put it on, breathing in his scent. She knew that there was so much she wanted to know about him, who was he? Where did he come from? How did he appear and disappear? Why did she need him so much?

She had realised after a few hours that he wasn't coming back. He had used her for what he had wanted and gone, leaving her alone. The pain inside hurt more than the craving had done before, but that had returned too. The fact that he wasn't fully dressed and that he seemed to be enjoying himself when he left, did spark some questions. It was as if he had been suddenly pulled back to wherever he came from against his will. If that were the case, would she see him again? Had someone pulled him back to hurt him? This whole circle of anger, hatred, concern and loss just kept looping through her head and eventually, she fell asleep.

After three hours Jennifer woke up; she wiped the slight drool from the side of her mouth and rubbed her sore eyes. The crying had taken its toll. As she sat up, she was aware of another presence in the room with her. She turned her head and saw a man standing, facing the window, watching the passers-by outside.

He was silent and still, and in her flat. He hadn't noticed her waking up, and rather than waiting around to find out why he was there, she decided to run. Nick had gone suddenly; she wasn't taking any chances. Jen slowly raised off the sofa and made a dash for the door.

"Jennifer? Wait, I need to talk to you."

The stranger yelled to get her attention before she forced him into a chase.

"It's about Nick!"

Jennifer stopped as she was about to slam the outside door shut. She paused for a moment to take in Nick's name, turned and stuck her head around the door, trying not to look at him. She wasn't willing to acknowledge what she had just seen, a ghost was just too much for her, at the moment.

"You know Nick?" she asked.

"Yes, please come back in, I'm not here to hurt you. To be honest, I don't think I could hurt you, or anything." Steve floated from the window and centralised himself near the sofa in the room.

Jen's heart was racing, she had been through a lot recently, and now seeing ghosts was just added pressure on her already frayed nerves.

"Is he ok? He suddenly left this morning without saying anything. I thought I had done something wrong."

"No, he thought last night was amazing, but he can't return at the moment. He told me to tell you he will be back as soon as he can."

"What is he? When I first met him, he told me he was Death? But I don't think that is the case. And who are you? And, this is going to sound silly, I know, but are you a ghost?" She tried to focus on his eyes without looking through him.

"Sorry, my name is Steve. Yes, I am a ghost, and I owed Nick a favour. As for Nick, I'm not really sure to be fair. What I am told and what I see are two different things," Steve explained.

"Steve, since meeting Nick, losing my family, losing myself, I'm just accepting weird on face value. I've done some bad shit over this last six months, just to get Nick to see me. I don't want to not see him again, but I don't understand why? Is he what he says he is? Death?" Jen seemed easier now, especially since she knew Nick would be back, that panic had subsided.

"Ok, so, he is supposed to be Lucifer's replacement, so he is Death to some."

"Lucifer? Is Nick evil?" Jen seemed shocked by this.

"No, not really. He has changed since I met him, but I'm not sure why."

Steve seemed to drift thinking about what he had seen while talking to Nick earlier, "He's a good guy, a little distant, but I wouldn't say he's evil."

"So why can't he come back here now?" Jen asked.

"He has a job to do, it could be days or weeks before he can get back. I don't know the full story behind how Nick has become what he is, but I'm sure he will tell you at some point. Anyway, I have passed you the message, so I'm going to go."

Steve moved to the window and passed through as though it weren't there.

Jen's stomach dropped as he disappeared through the wall; she jumped to try to make a grab for him so he didn't fall. Then she realised he had gone. She looked down to the street, but there was no sign of him.

Jen sat back down, shocked by the fact she had just seen a ghost; beaten cancer; committed murder; tried suicide, twice; lost her son and her family; and had sex with Lucifer's replacement.

Her year wasn't going well, and she was hoping things would improve. The craving had started to kick in again, but now she knew it could be a while before he would be back. She reached for the whisky, unscrewed the top, and drank from the bottle. Drowning the pain and hunger was the only thing that seemed to help.

15

THE SLIP

Nick woke up, tired, thirsty, hungry and smelling from the madness of the last two days. He had crashed in his room like a thirteen-year-old throwing a tantrum. He remembered the argument he had with Anton and how the butler had taken HIS side again, or that's how Nick thought it had gone.

He dragged himself out of bed and into the bathroom, knowing even a perfect shower wouldn't make him feel any better.

Nick still had this hollow feeling in his body, and it was now gnawing at his brain. He couldn't shake the feeling that there was something seriously wrong, and he needed to find what it was. It was as though his mind were leaving him, not his brain because that was letting him know this, but his mind, which seemed to be on holiday.

Nick got dressed and felt a bit fresher, not better, just a bit more awake. He left his room to be met by a happy, singing Anton where he usually was, in the kitchen.

"Good Morning, sir. How are you feeling today? Better I hope?"

"Not really. Why are you so happy?" Nick snarled as he sat down at one of the kitchen barstools.

"It's another glorious day and I have a very good feeling today will be lovely!"

"I don't think so. I need some food; I feel like I haven't eaten for weeks. I have this weird empty feeling, I can't work out why or what it is." Nick rubbed his chest where he felt the hollowness the most.

Anton paused and looked at him with a slight panic in his eyes; Nick saw this.

"You just need some food, I have cooked you a plate of fresh bacon, eggs and toast." He turned his back on Nick, hoping to hide the stress in his face.

"What was that Anton? You looked guilty about something; what is it? Why am I feeling this way?" Nick got up and started to move towards Anton.

"Sir, I promise you I didn't look at you in any way different. I just worry about how all of this is affecting you. You need to take things easy for a few days and try to relax." He placed the plate on the counter.

"I saw something in your eyes, Anton. You know, sometimes, I wonder just whose side you're on?"

Hunger had distracted Nick enough for his stomach to take priority, and he sat back down to eat his breakfast.

"Sir, I am on your side; I always will be. You are tired and need rest."

Nick ate quickly as if this were the first food he had tasted for weeks. He was trying to fill the hole, but failing. He started to feel tired, slightly dizzy and then the feeling that the floor was falling away happened again. Then there was a familiar cracking noise and a familiar voice.

"For fuck sake Anton, WHY!! You're going to fuck the plan up again!"

Then Nick hit the floor and everything went black.

⚜

Nick opened his eyes, stared into the dark, and blinked a few times to get accustomed to the blackness. He recognised the contours of his room, but there was a different shape in the room that wasn't normally there. He sat up quickly trying to bring the unknown shape to life, then it moved.

"Hello?" Nick nervously asked.

The shape stirred and awoke.

"Sir, you're awake. It seemed you had another incident; it must be the teleporter. I think we will need to think seriously about recalibrating the device. I would hate to think what it is doing to your head." Anton stood up and moved toward Nick who sat up holding his head.

"What happened? How long this time?"

"Only about twelve hours this time. I think you might need some more rest. I will go make you some food, sir. Why not go relax on the beach? I know you enjoy the ocean."

"No! I'm not hungry. Please, leave me." Nick was hungry, but he was starting not to trust Anton; he couldn't remember what had happened, but he knew something felt wrong about him.

"Of course, sir" Anton left the room leaving Nick holding his head.

He dragged himself out of bed and into the shower; everything now had a feeling of *deja vu*. It seemed only two minutes ago he had got up feeling like crap, showered and got dressed. Yet here he was the next day again feeling like crap, heading to the shower. What happened to yesterday?

He let the hot water wash over his body, invigorating his muscles and aching joints. He stood head down leaning with his hand against the wall. He was trying to remember what had occurred. Did he actually pass out? Did he remember anything? Anything?

Then, suddenly, as though someone had connected the shower to the mains electricity supply, he had a sharp shock charge through his brain and it hit him hard. He stood up straight, and, without slipping, ran from the shower, through the bedroom and straight out into the living room area. Standing, naked, dripping wet Nick threw his accusation.

"He was HERE!"

Anton looked up in surprise, shocked and slightly aroused seeing Nick's young naked body wet from the shower.

"I'm sorry, sir, who? Sir, you're dripping all over the floor." Anton moved quickly towards Nick.

"HIM! I saw him, standing, shouting at you!"

"Are you sure? Are you referring to Lucifer, sir?" Anton asked placing his hand on Nick's shoulder and suggesting with his other hand that he guide Nick back to his bedroom for a towel.

"Yes, Lucifer! He was here. Why was he here? Is he causing these blackouts? I bet he is; he's killing me! He wants me dead, out of the picture." Nick wrapped himself in the towel from Anton.

"Sir, yes he was here, only because he is worried about your blackouts. You see if anything happens to you, the contract is void, so I guess he was checking on his investment."

"What? How did he know? I saw him for a split second then I lost consciousness, but he was here as soon as I started to go. I remember."

"I informed him of what was happening and about the time before. We were both worried; as I explained if you die, the contract is void. So, he gave me a device to press when it happened again. I saw you were starting to pass out, and I pressed it. He came to make sure you were all right." Anton walked towards the door.

"Why did you tell him?"

"I panicked and asked him if it could be the portal causing this; he confirmed what I thought and left. He explained how to recalibrate the portal." Anton turned to leave, "Is that all, sir?"

"For now."

Anton shut the door, and Nick dried himself off. He didn't believe a single thing Anton had said. He knew what he had seen and heard; he was being lied to and he knew it now. He didn't understand why this felt very familiar, almost as if this conversation had happened before. It felt like an itch on the brain that he couldn't scratch.

Nick got dressed and headed for the beach; he ignored Anton as the butler tidied up an already tidy kitchen area. He could feel the glare on the back of his head as he left for the sun-drenched beach. Anton asked Nick if he wanted anything brought to him, but Nick just shook his head and continued his walk.

As soon as he left the steps and felt the warm, white sand, Nick raced to the water and swam out enough so he could submerge himself in the clear blue ocean. This place was becoming his salvation, his retreat away from Anton and all the confusion he was feeling with his position in life – or was it his afterlife?

He still couldn't work out what he was anymore; he had started to feel that the Nick he knew had begun to fade or even die, as he felt less and less humanity towards other people. He took a deep breath and held it, then lowered his head under the water. Nick stayed still, floating under the surface, in a vast world of blue. Lost in his thoughts he remembered where he was and panicked. He accidentally swallowed some water and expected to choke, but he didn't. He took another quick swallow, but nothing.

Nick tried to choke himself deliberately. He opened his mouth wide and swallowed, but the massive gulp did nothing. He dragged his open fingers through the water to test it again and he felt the fluid pull through his fingers as he swung his arms around. It felt like water, it looked like water – but he couldn't drown.

The thought of suicide had crawled through his mind; he felt desperately empty and lonely. The only time he had felt something recently was when he was with Jen, and now he couldn't get back to her without Anton trying to stop him. Now knowing that if he died, the contract with Lucifer was over was making him think maybe he should find a way to end it all.

He slowly let himself drop to the bottom of the ocean, he hadn't gone out enough for a long drop. He sank in the silence, slowly; it seemed to be forever before he hit the ocean bed. And there he stood deflated, his hands limp at his side. The water pressure hugged him like a long-lost friend, and slowly he walked back to the shore.

Standing, waiting for him on the beach was Steve, pale in the sunshine. He looked worried, then once he saw Nick leave the water, he smiled.

"I thought you were a dead man! I saw you go under, and there was a bit of splashing then nothing. I was going to jump in, but then I realised I wouldn't be able to do anything anyway, not solid you see." Steve gestured to his torso and placed his hands inside his chest.

"Its fine Steve. I can't die, this fucking deal won't let me." Nick sat down and faced the sea again, "Did you do it? What I asked you to do?"

"Absolutely. I found her place, I told her. She asked some questions about you. It seems you two haven't really talked about each other much. Considering she has given up a lot just to be with you, I told her very little, but she seems to know nothing about you or what you do. You need to tell her, you owe her that."

"Don't you think I know that? I will one day. As long as those two don't kill me first."

"Who? Who wants to kill you?"

"Lucifer and Anton, they're planning something. I have passed out twice, for a day or two over the past week. When it happened last time, I saw Lucifer here before I blacked out. I have asked Anton about it, and he's sketchy as hell with me. I'm telling you they want me dead." Nick picked up a handful of sand and emptied it through his fingers watching it fall into his other hand.

"Why would they want to kill you? I thought Lucifer had done this so he could have a normal life? Surely that would destroy his chances?"

"I don't know, I think it's time I spoke to Lucifer, face to face."

Nick pulled himself up and took one last look out at the ripples of the ocean. He looked down at Steve and kicked some sand lightly in Steve's direction, watching it cascade through his ethereal body.

"Thanks, Steve, one last thing. Do you know if it is possible for Lucifer to appear places without using some sort of portal device? I mean, how did you manage to get to Jen's place to speak to her?"

"I knew I had to get there, so I just concentrated on the address you had kindly burned on my palm and closed my eyes and when I opened them, I was there. I didn't realise it at first until Jen started to run out of the door. Why do you ask?"

"I wonder if it's possible for me to do it? If Lucifer appeared here, how would he manage to do it? I know there is no portal room at my actual home, so?" Nick shrugged.

"He's Lucifer, I'm pretty sure it would be easy for him."

"Then I should be able to do it. I am supposed to have the same powers. Anyway, Steve, thank you again; I have no need for you now; go and enjoy your death." Nick started to walk up to the cliff.

"Take care Nick, don't get yourself killed. You're worth more alive than dead."

They said their farewells and Steve disappeared along the beach, fading into the flickering heatwave from the hot sands.

Nick ascended the steps and stepped on to the overlooking veranda. Anton was relaxing outside in the seating area. Nick ignored Anton and walked past without saying a word. Anton stood and followed Nick.

"How was your swim, sir? Would you like anything to eat or drink?" Anton asked.

"No, I'm fine."

"Sir, you haven't eaten in days. You must be famished?"

Nick stopped and turned on Anton.

"Look, I am starving. Honestly, I could eat a fucking horse. But, I don't trust you. Each time I have collapsed, it has been at the kitchen counter whilst shovelling food into my mouth – food that you cooked."

"Your episodes have nothing to do with my cooking; there is no reason for you to think that. I want to help you. I am here to make sure you have everything you need; you have to trust me." Anton begged.

"Well, I don't. There are too many things that I have seen and heard, that make me not trust you. I think you and 'HIM' want me dead!"

"Absolutely not! Lucifer needs you alive; he would never want you dead"

"And you Anton? What do you want?" Nick pointed at Anton aggressively, "You think by poisoning me, I won't notice? I don't know why you want to kill me. Am I not the Lucifer you both wanted? Am I not evil enough?"

"Sir, I do not want you dead. You are doing fine. You have to believe me!"

"Why? Why do I have to believe you?"

"Because.. because…" Anton struggled to find a good reason, "without you I don't exist. There is no reason for me to be here… alive."

"So, without me, you're dead?" Nick stopped and looked at Anton, searching for the slightest twitch, the slightest hint of a lie.

"Yes," Anton's left eye flicked nervously.

"There… you're fucking lying. I might only be eighteen, but I can sniff a lie out. My mates used to call me the human lie detector. I have this knack for spotting when people lie, and you're lying." Nick walked off towards his room.

Anton grabbed his shoulder and Nick turned. He brought his clenched fist round and smashed it into Anton's jaw. Anton stumbled back in horror as he grabbed his jaw in shock.

Then Nick heard the familiar sound of a loud crack, and suddenly Lucifer was standing between Nick and Anton.

"What the FUCK do you think you're doing? How dare you hit Anton?" Lucifer spun round to see Anton holding his jaw.

"He hit me!" Anton squealed in shock.

"Did he hurt you? Are you ok?" Lucifer held Anton's chin and turned his head around to make sure there were no bruising or cuts. He spun on Nick, who was now smiling, knowing he had done what he had intended to do and attracted the attention of Lucifer.

"What is wrong with you?"

"How did you know? How did you get here so quick?" Nick asked, now feeling smug and in control.

"You hurt him and I know. You don't spend thousands of years with someone without forming a connection, a connection beyond anything mortals will ever know."

Lucifer let go of Anton and walked towards Nick.

"So what happens now, Nick? How does this play out? I wonder what kind of beating your mortal mother would take from something like me. How many seconds will she take before her delicate face would become a mushy, bloody mess?"

"You wouldn't dare! This contract means way too much to you to break it."

Lucifer stood staring down Nick, anger on his face as he formed his next course of action.

"Nick, you are a very foolish little boy; you are poking a tiger with a twig. I haven't eaten for months and your twig is about to snap – and so is your mother!"

16

CONFRONTATION

The whole room was suddenly silent as Nick realised what Lucifer was saying. He had stepped over the line, and now he knew there was going to be a knock-on effect. Only the dominoes would not fall in his favour. Lucifer had the upper hand here, and he knew it. The smile started to spread across his face which made Nick very uneasy. He expected Lucifer to disappear, to take revenge on his mother.

Even though Nick didn't feel the fear for his mother that he knew he should, his brain told him that no good could come of this for him or his mother; after all, this was Lucifer, a fallen angel.

"Do you want me to hit your mother, Nick? Fair warning, I don't hit like a child. I hit hard, hard like a fucking battering ram!"

Lucifer was now up close to him; he was taller than Nick, and he used this to his advantage, looking down on him, making him feel inferior.

Trying not to back down and show weakness Nick moved in closer.

"Why did I see you here when I passed out the other night?" Nick demanded.

Lucifer looked confused by this then remembered the conversation between Nick and Anton, "…I was concerned, I don't want anything to happen that would change our deal."

"This isn't our deal; this was yours and my mother's deal. It had nothing to do with me, remember?"

"Oh Nick, you signed the contract; it's your deal, not ours," Lucifer said in a sickly, matter-of-fact way. He then turned to Anton who was just watching now but still holding his jaw. "Did you ever finish reading your contract, Nick?" Lucifer asked as he winked at Anton.

"Yes…. I think so. No, I definitely did… I remember reading it."

"Are you sure? You don't seem sure. You seem confused by my simple question. Did you or didn't you?"

Lucifer turned his right hand to ice and held it to Anton's face to ease any swelling. Nick couldn't see Lucifer's face, and Anton tried to keep his face straight.

"Because if you had read it, you would know what happens in situations like this, where harm has come to your mother or to Anton."

Nick knew he had read the contract countless times, but he couldn't remember anything that was on it, not a word. He remembered days of trying to get through it. He remembered this, but it seemed as if he had only dreamed it now. The more he tried to remember, to focus, the more it seemed further away.

"Err…. No, I don't remember, I don't know why though; I have read it, a lot," Nick mumbled.

Lucifer turned away from Anton, shook his hand and watched it turned back to soft flesh from the frozen block it had been.

"Well we have two options now, Nick. I could go and do the same to your mother. As I explained before, that could be pretty messy, physically and mentally for her, or I can do it to you. Which one?"

Nick thought for a moment. His head was saying you have to do what you know to be right, and his heart was saying nothing as it had done for the past few weeks. In the absence of his heart, he decided it would be wrong for his mum to be punished for something he had done.

"Hello… Nick, this shouldn't be a hard one to decide! My god man, don't you have a soul? Do you want me to smack your whore of a mother around or not?" Lucifer held up his hand with his fingers splayed in front of Nick, "I'm giving you five seconds to decide then I'm gone. Five.."

Nick was still trying to choose – pain or no pain, right and wrong. This seemed so confusing yet so simple.

"Four…"

Nick stood staring at Lucifer and his slowly closing fingers.

"Three…"

"Ok, Ok, me, it's me; I hit him. I will take the punishment."

Nick's plan to find out what was going on had taken a very bad turn, and now was heading in a direction he knew he might not come out well at all.

"Nick, two seconds and I would be pounding on your mother's face. Well done, you made the right decision."

Lucifer smirked, his cock-eyed grin and charged at Nick. He picked up Nick and threw him against the wall, Nick bounced off the wall and crashed onto the floor.

Nick stood up and braced himself for another attack as Lucifer's clenched left hand struck his jaw. The force from the punch snapped his head to the right so fast and hard that

Nick was lifted off his feet. He spun and collided with the wall he had just ricocheted off a few seconds before. He collapsed to the floor. Scraping himself up off the floor, he waited for the next attack.

"Are you not going to fight back?" Lucifer said surprisingly, readying himself again.

Nick realised at this point, he wasn't in pain. There was no blood, and as he was about to say something before another clenched fist hit him clean in the middle of the nose. This sent him back flying through the air, landing he glided across the room into the wall. Nick's reaction was to stand up again and check his nose, realising again there was no blood – and no pain.

"Why am I not in pain? Where's the blood?" Nick looked up and Lucifer was gone and within a split second an arm was around his neck pulling in tight, choking him.

"Are you enjoying this Nick? I could go on all day! Do you want the pain? The blood? Would that make it easier to sink in your tiny brain?" Lucifer pulled tighter.

"...No...stop..." Nick started to feel the restricting arm around his throat, he started to feel pain. Nick squirmed in Lucifer's grasp and released his right elbow; he slammed it backwards and into Lucifer's ribs. Nick repeated this until the choke hold relaxed slightly, enough to get out.

"So you can hurt me, how? How did I hurt you? How did you get behind me like that? I didn't see you move!" Nick was confused and had more questions than ever now, he held his throat and coughed trying to ease the pain.

Lucifer grabbed his side in discomfort, "Questions, questions, why so many questions? You felt pain because I wanted you to feel pain; you did not hurt me, and I moved behind you because that was my wish too."

Lucifer stood tall again and put his arm out in front of

him, pointing in Nick's direction and with an unseen force lifted him in the air. Frozen, Nick was unable to move.

"Just like now, this is my desire to lift you up and rip you to bits."

Anton caught Lucifer's eye and he shook his head. He looked worried. Lucifer lowered Nick down slowly and physically grabbed him by his throat, lifting him again.

"I don't have to answer any of your questions! I don't have to tell you everything! I am and will always be your superior!" Lucifer let go of Nick, and he dropped to the floor choking.

Nick grabbed his throat and looked up at Lucifer, "Are you just playing with me? Why won't you do something that is really going to hurt me? I hurt him and clearly, you're close, like you say thousands of years. Surely, you would really want me to be hurt too?"

"Just because I haven't killed you, doesn't mean I won't or can't, I just choose not to; you are too important to the life I want."

Lucifer returned to Anton's side; he had stopped holding his jaw now. It was still aching but no damage had been done.

"I don't understand why you clearly have this link still with Anton yet you choose another life away from him, my life. Why would anyone want to do that?"

"I told you before. I have done this for thousands of years; I am sick of it, I just want a normal life."

"That still makes no sense. Why didn't you just leave and go live somewhere as normal people, together? I am sure your magic would keep you invisible to the human eye forever."

"Stop with the questions Nick. This is my choice, and it's what I want. I don't want to be myself; I want to be someone else; I want to be something else. To escape slaughter after slaughter, there are only so many people you can kill before you're bored, only so many ways to kill before it becomes mundane." Lucifer looked at Nick with a beaten expression, "The thrill of the kill is gone, you know?"

Nick didn't know because he couldn't relate. Each kill for him made him feel nothing. He knew he shouldn't be doing it, but he couldn't stop as he knew this was how this job worked.

"I don't want to know that; I don't want to know murder is acceptable, because it's not."

"It didn't stop you from killing that poor schizophrenic with the wood chipper."

"He was a killer; he murdered his family. It seemed logical he would kill again. He was brutal." Nick reared up to defend himself.

"And then there is that young man whom you and your crazy girlfriend hacked up!"

"We didn't kill him, she didn't, I didn't... wait how do you know about that?" Nick was now starting to get angry again.

"Oh, Anton mentioned it when I was here when you last collapsed." Lucifer winked at Anton, but Nick didn't see it.

"I didn't tell Anton anything about that. Are you spying on me?"

"Well no, not really, we still have to monitor you, just in case you need help or you mess things up. I find it very important to keep an eye on my investments."

"Your investments? I am not your fucking investment! You might have my life but I am not yours! I need to have some sort of life; am I a prisoner here?"

"Being King of Hell is a privilege, you need people around you to help you, to steer you. To be fair, there have been a few times where you have coloured outside the lines. I mean, helping people instead of doing your job. We don't help, Nick, we end," Lucifer insisted.

"Why are you smiling, are you laughing at me? Are you playing with me?" Nick went to grab Lucifer. Nick was at his boiling point, and it seemed Lucifer knew exactly how to push Nick's buttons.

Lucifer sidestepped Nick in a blink of an eye and grabbed the back of his neck as he stumbled past him. Again Lucifer lifted him up in the air. This time Nick could move a bit but not easily. His limbs felt like lead, and struggled to lift them and fight back.

"Don't you ever learn? I can do things to you Nick that can't be taught. I can throw you around like a rag doll, but it doesn't help me." Lucifer turned Nick around with one arm outstretched in front of him so he was still dangling, but facing Lucifer, as he struggled to breathe.

Nick could feel the pain being slowly turned up. Lucifer's smile began to widen as the pain raced through his body. Nick started to bleed from his nose, and no matter how much he tried to lift his arms to stop him, they were too heavy. His limbs felt as if they were flooded with concrete. The pain grew in Nick; tears trickled down his cheeks and he began to pass out from the anguish, and Lucifer's smile grew even broader.

"Stop, stop this; you're going to kill him! This is not what you want; you need him to be alive. Drop him, for me? Please?" Anton pleaded with Lucifer.

Lucifer dropped Nick, whose knees buckled under him as he slammed into the floor face down.

"Don't touch Anton again, or worse will happen. Next time it won't be you. Understand?"

Nick nodded because he couldn't speak. He could move his arms again and the pain started to pass. He slowly opened his eyes and he saw the blood from his nose, mouth and eyes pool in front of his face. Nick coughed and spat some more blood out.

Nick pushed himself up into a sitting position and looked up at Lucifer who was towering over him. Wiping his face, he swiped his bloody hand on his jeans.

"Anton, I'm sorry, I shouldn't have hit you," Nick said with a croaky voice, "I don't know what's wrong with me recently; I haven't been my usual self."

"It's fine, sir. I'm just glad we could get this sorted without any real damage done." Lucifer cringed at Anton calling Nick "sir."

Lucifer turned to Anton, hugged him and whispered in his ear, "Are you ok? Do you need me to stay?"

"No, I am fine; you better go. I will clean this mess up." Anton smiled at Lucifer, who smiled back, winked and disappeared.

Nick coughed again and spat out the last of the blood.

"Thank you for stopping him, I thought I was going to die. I felt my insides starting to tear. I can't explain it. But I feel Ok now, no more pain." Nick still found it hard to speak, his whole neck was calming down.

"That went way too far; he gets like that from time to time. I think you now understand how hard it is for me and him. But this is the right move for him. It's time he started to feel like a human; it will be good for his temper, hopefully."

"I still don't understand, I have more questions now than I had before." Nick stood up and walked to the veranda doors, "But I guess I will learn more when I deserve to."

Anton watched Nick disappear outside. He prepared a drink for Nick and followed him into the sunshine. "I thought you would like a drink, sir."

Nick lifted the drink off the tray and smiled at Anton,

"Thank you. I think we need to have a chat about your relationship and how that will affect our future."

"Sorry, sir, I don't understand?"

"Don't worry, it's not a chat for today. I think there has been too much excitement for one day, don't you agree?" Nick took a sip of his drink.

"Of course, sir. Is that all for now?" Anton waited for Nick's nod and he left for the kitchen. He placed the tray down and walked towards his quarters.

Nick's head was racing. He was being spied on twenty-four/seven. Lucifer could control Nick's body. He could do things Nick couldn't. He needed to know how to do all of them quickly. He couldn't afford to do anything stupid again. This time he had been lucky.

17

MELINA

As the distant shapes in the blackness began to take form, she could sense her next prey.

She could hear her soon-to-be victim's heart beating, racing, and she faded into the undergrowth again.

Her victim's pace increased, as did her pulse. She got closer, next to the prey. Waiting for that moment to appear, to attack, to tear, to feed.

She could hear the blood racing through her victim's veins; she could almost taste the, soon-to-be, feast in her mind, making her mouth salivate.

Her victim started to run, sensing something bad was about to happen.

The time was right! The blood was now racing, feeding every vein, every muscle.

Then she pounced.

Her victim fell, and she forced her onto her back, as the feast tried to stop the inevitable.

The uncontrollable yearning to rip and feed, her nails tearing into her victim's shirt, ripping her clothes open. Face to face with naked flesh, she smiled; her victim screamed as *she tried to fight back, but the creature on top was too dominant.*

She ripped open her chest and fed in a bloody, frenzied rage.

She tore, and forced her hands into the exposed ribcage, breaking her bones quickly to get to her still-beating heart. She ripped it out, cupped it in her hands and as it raced to a sudden stop, she sank her teeth into the warm muscle. She sucked, drained. She sat on her victim for a few seconds looking at the shredded, gaping hole, then up to the victim's young, horrified face.

She smiled with sympathy, thanked her and kissed her forehead gently. She dragged the remaining, tattered corpse into the undergrowth and then she ran.

With the new life pumping through her, intensified with the excitement of the kill, she howled, laughing to the moon.

Blackness enveloped her, and she was gone.

⚝

Nick bolted up straight, heart racing, grasping at his chest and his mouth. Choking, Nick spat out blood and tiny bits of bones. He felt a strange heightening of energy racing through him; his heart was still racing, not from fear but from excitement.

He sat on his sweat-soaked bedding, feeling this strange euphoria, then after a few minutes, it slowly stopped and his heart settled.

What was he going to be dealing with next? The creature in his vision felt like an animal, like a werewolf, but the bloodlust had him thinking more like a vampire. He stopped and laughed to himself. Nick knew these were only creatures of a writer's imagination or some form of ancient myth.

Whatever it was it couldn't continue to kill as it was doing, so brutal and without a care.

He wasn't looking forward to the next soul to take. Was it going to be some kind of animal or magical creature? The way she had ripped the girl's chest open had made him feel uneasy, even though he knew he couldn't be killed or even hurt. Nick got ready quickly and left his room.

As usual, Anton was pottering around the kitchen looking busy, but Nick sensed he hadn't been there for long. He thought he had been instructed to be ready for him when he left his room, knowing Lucifer was now watching and would have seen him wake up.

"Good morning, sir. Did you have a good sleep?" Anton asked.

"Not bad, until I ended up ripping someone's heart out!"

Anton stopped what he was doing and looked at Nick, smiling. "Vision?"

"Yeah. How's the jaw?"

"It's fine, sir. I just hope that it's all behind us now. So the vision? Heart's being ripped out? Sounds very interesting."

"Not when you're sucking it dry, it's not. The attack was brutal!"

"Werewolf?" Anton keenly asked.

Nick snorted to himself, "Yeah, a werewolf, or a vampire, or a pixie, or Santa!"

"Oh, I see. You don't think they're real?"

"Err... No..." Nick looked at Anton with suspicion.

"Well, they are!"

Nick smiled, "Santa?"

"Yes. Well, not nowadays though, but Santa, Father Christmas, he did exist. But he was hanged, then drawn and quartered when he was found with two young boys' bodies in his sleigh, very nasty man. We had dinner with him once, him and his wife. We thought they were odd then."

"What?" Nick was waiting for the punchline to drop, but it didn't drop, and Anton's face didn't change.

"So, what are your first feelings, werewolf or vampire?"

"Neither, just an animal or a crazy woman."

Anton looked disappointed, but he gazed at Nick, smiled and crossed his fingers and said, "Well, here's hoping it's not Santa!"

"Right. Anyway, I think we better get ready to go look for this creature then." Nick started to head towards the portal room.

"No food this morning, Sir?" Anton asked.

"No, I don't think I can eat after what I experienced before with this animal."

Anton followed Nick towards the portal room. Nick kept the lead and his mind was only on one thing, and that was how was he going to beat this beast? She seemed to be a large, powerful, focused killing machine, but for some reason, he also sensed a gentle feminine side. Nick was hoping for the latter when they were face to face.

He stepped into the portal and Anton stood by.

"I don't know what I'm facing, I will only need help if something goes wrong; don't try to do anything. I need the illusion that I am not scared. This one frightens me, but I don't want it to think I am afraid. I have a feeling she will sense fear."

The portal started, followed by the familiar loud crack, and Nick was gone leaving smoke and sulphur filling the room.

It was midday and Nick stood on a street overlooking a harbour, with what seemed to be a church and a deserted abbey on the opposite side of the bay. His attention was drawn to a thin, tall woman who sat on a bench looking down onto the seaside town. Nick knew from the feeling that this was his monster.

He followed the pathway round to the end bench, and before he sat down, Nick read the plaque on the bench:

The view from this spot inspired
Bram Stoker (1847 - 1912)
To use Whitby as the setting of part of his
World-Famous novel
DRACULA
This seat was erected by Scarborough borough council
And the Dracula Society to mark the 68th Anniversary
Of Stoker's death - April 20th, 1980

Nick now knew what he was dealing with.

"Little cliche, don't you think?"

The woman didn't move her head, just kept staring into the bay.

"Every day for the past thirty-five years I have sat here, looking for answers."

"To what?"

"The why?" She looked at Nick who had sat down and was staring at the same view, "Thirty-five years! And nothing."

"I'm sorry, I'm not with you?"

"This!" She said gesturing to her being, "I never asked for this; I didn't want it. Is that why you're here? To end it?"

"Well, mainly yes, but... I'm sorry, do you know who I am?" Nick looked confused.

"I knew you were coming; I sensed you at my last kill, probably the only gift I have with this curse. Spidey sense!"

"Are you actually, well I feel stupid saying this, this is not how these things normally go... are you actually a... a vampire?"

"Vampire? Jesus, no... I'm a regular person, apart from the bloodlust and destructive urges." She smiled and looked back at the bay. "Yes, I think what you would call me is a daughter of Cain."

Nick smiled, "I thought vampires were just a myth created by people like Mr. Stoker. Do you have all the powers you read about? Like being able to fly, transform, persuade the opposite sex to succumb to your wiles?"

She looked down and shook her head.

"Nope, not me anyway, nothing, just the senses. Like an animal."

"You must have the retractable teeth? The speed?" Nick smiled, "The twinkling in the sun..."

"Shut the fuck up! None of that, and look at me; do I fucking sparkle?" She smiled.

"Oh yeah! It's daytime! Clearly, you don't crumble in the sun?"

"I'm fine, as long as I put suntan lotion on, factor 100!"

Nick laughed. How could she be the same thing that ripped a hole in the girl's chest? He actually liked her. She was funny, a break from the horror show his life had become.

"Melina, you know why I'm here? Right?" Nick asked

"I presume you're here to end me? To make sure I stop feeding? You know I don't want to do what I do, don't you?"

"Really? So you don't enjoy it?"

"Absolutely not, but it's the craving, it won't stop. I can feed, and a week later I need to kill again." Melina looked at Nick with a pleading face, like a puppy being told off.

Nick looked at her in disbelief.

"Lying bitch! I saw and felt just how much you loved the kill; you howled at the fucking moon like a wolf!"

Melina laughed, "Yeah, you're right! Mind you the last one was fucking stunning, I was so close not to eating her, I think I paused for a split second once I ripped her shirt off, just to adore her, but the heart was already in my hands before I could stop." Melina shrugged.

"Why do you go for the heart? Why not the neck like everyone is led to believe?"

Melina showed Nick her teeth, "See normal canines. When I was made, my sire showed me how to feed, 'straight for the jugular,' he would say, but he had needle-sharp canines; it was easy for him. I tried, but I would just hack and make a mess that started to congeal every time. After a decade, my strength had improved enough to overpower my victims. So I started to just rip the throat out, but there was too much in the way. Then, I decided to go for the heart. I did my research and learned which ribs were the weakest, and how to get to the heart while it was still beating. I had a few problems at first, but after a couple of years and disasters, I got it down to a professional smash and grab. Get them scared and the heart is racing, the blood just gushes down your throat."

"Oh, I thought there was a more symbolic reason behind it. Thanks for the life story though." Nick stared back at the bay with a disappointed look on his face. "So you have no magic at all?"

"No, my sire tried to teach me the ways, the 'tricks of the trade,' but nothing."

"What did he try to teach you?"

"Flight, hypnosis, possession, teeth retraction, teleportation, transformation. You know the usual." The silence fell on their conversation and Melina stood up, "Anyway. I will be off; I should be sleeping really, big feed last night." She slapped her thin, rock hard, stomach and went to walk past Nick.

Nick stood up at the same time to face her. Melina was at least a foot taller than Nick and looked in her early twenties, even though he knew she was in her forties.

"I don't think so; you're not going anywhere else, apart from with me." Nick made a grab for her arm.

She looked down at his hand and immediately made a grab for his throat.

"I don't give a fuck who you are, no-one touches me unless I want them to!" Melina's demeanour changed instantly, and she lifted Nick up in the air.

Nick looked down and smiled; he spoke in a voice that didn't sound like he was choking. With her grip on his throat, he should have been and this surprised Melina.

"You can't hurt me, but if you want to take this down the violent route, I'm pretty sure you will end up getting the ending you deeply crave."

Melina dropped him, "What do you want from me?"

"I'm here to take your soul, which really does surprise me seeing as you're a vamp, you shouldn't have one. Am I right?"

An elderly couple walked past them; all four made eye contact and smiled as they passed by. Nick looked back at Melina who was now looking for a way out without looking too conspicuous.

"Look, I don't know, all these years, and I still don't understand the majority of this." She looked at Nick trying to read his next move, "Are you going to let me pass, or are we going to go beast mode in front of these passersby?"

"You say the vampire that made you tried to train you? Didn't he tell you anything to help you gain your abilities or explain why you still have a soul?"

"Look, if you're wanting to share stories, then this is not the place for it; you're going to have to come with me." Nick stepped back and let Melina past and followed her down towards the bay.

"So, where are taking me? Your lair?" Nick mocked.

"Funny bastard! I rent a small flat down on Church Street. I'm not a fucking animal!"

The route to Melina's place was a busy one. The area was full of visitors, and Nick started to wonder just how many people around them would have been there only because of the legends of Dracula? How many secretly would have given themselves to Melina if they knew what she was? But also just how many would have run if they knew who he was.

A small child pushed in between Nick and Melina getting to her father, who was crossing the bridge at the same time. She looked up at Nick and stuck her tongue out at him. Nick did the same but split his tongue at the same time, she screamed and ran into her dad's legs, crying. Nick smiled as they passed.

Melina talked to Nick over her shoulder as she led the way.

"Are you scaring kids now?"

"Listen, this is the first time in a while I have been around a lot of people, and besides which she stuck her tongue out at me first!"

She stopped and turned face to face with Nick, "How old are you?"

"Eighteen"

"Eighteen? Who exactly are you?"

"The truth or the spiel?"

"Truth"

"My name's Nick. I was tricked into a contract with Lucifer, where I do his fucking job while he lives my life! Now, I go around taking people's souls in order to keep the good and evil balanced, or something like that."

"And I thought my life was fucked!"

They reached the place and mounted the stairs into the small flat. As Melina put the key into the lock, she noticed the door was ajar slightly. She pushed the door open slowly looking around into the flat and came face to face with a bearded man. He made a quick dash for the door barging past Melina.

Nick clicked his fingers and the man stopped moving.

"You know him?" Nick asked Melina.

"How did you do that? Can he see and hear us?"

"It's magic! He can if I want him to." Nick asked again, "Do you know him?"

"I have seen him from time to time but didn't realise he was following me. But no, I don't 'know' him."

"Ok, let's find out who he is and why he's snooping around your flat."

Nick clicked his fingers and the man disappeared and reappeared in the centre of the room, tied to a kitchen chair.

Nick clicked his fingers and the man could move his head again.

"I'm going to smash this fucking chair and ram it's leg straight into your heart you fucking bitch!" The man tried to struggle loose, but he was paralysed from his neck down, "What the fuck have you done to me?"

"Hi. Are you comfy?"

"No, now let me loose so I can kill this whore!"

Nick looked at Melina, "Are you sure you don't know him? He seems to know you."

"You killed my fucking wife!"

At the same time, the door swung open and a young man crashed through, straight into Melina's hand. She picked him up and dangled him by his throat.

Melina turned to the bearded man, "This yours?"

SECRETS AND LIES

Melina stood in the doorway to her small flat while a man sat shouting obscenities at her, whilst being tied to a chair and paralysed from the neck down. She also held a younger man by his throat, dangling with his legs kicking, and turning pale.

She tightened her grip and the man swung at her arm, weakening with every movement.

Melina looked back at the man in the chair, "Does this belong to you?"

"Yes, put him down, don't kill him. Please, don't kill him!" The bearded man pleaded.

Nick motioned to Melina to put him down; he then clicked his fingers and he suddenly appeared next to the first man in the middle of the room. He was tied with something, but he was still coughing trying to get his breath back.

"What? How? Who are you? I thought she was alone." The intruder flustered his questions.

"I tied you to a chair and paralysed you from the neck down, magic, Nick, and no, you were wrong. Also, your timing is shit; I really could have done without you being here. Instead, I am going to have to deal with you two."

"What?"

"Jesus, you're stupid too. Why are you chasing a vampire?"

Melina sat down and watched her visitors' faces looking in disbelief and surprise.

"Vampire? You're as crazy as she is!" The man laughed.

"No, I wish it were just a case of mental stability, but it's not. She's a vampire and I'm actually Lucifer's replacement!"

"Is this a joke? Do you think she's actually a vampire? And you're Lucifer? You're nuts!" The man looked down and shook his head.

"No, I'm his replacement, not actually him. And this is not a joke. If you don't believe me, do you remember sitting down and being tied up?"

"I err... well... I don't know."

Nick turned to Melina, "You're quiet; don't fancy sharing?"

"No, I'm good, besides you seem to have this under control."

"Right, so you're here to get revenge on Melina for killing your wife? Is that it?"

The intruder nodded, "She did kill her, and I will get my revenge!"

"Ok, so shall we take a trip down memory lane?" Nick turned to the visitors, "If this is your son, you might want him to close his eyes, no one wants to see their mother murdered." Nick crouched in front of the two tied up men, "What you're going to see is Melina's memories of what happened with your wife. I'm going to have to get some details from your memories first, so I will need to touch your head."

Nick went to touch the man's head, but he jerked it back.

"I'm not asking; I am doing it anyway! I'm going to show you what actually happened." Nick touched the side of the man's head and closed his eyes for a few seconds.

Nick then walked over to Melina and did the same to her. Nick stood still with his eyes shut and clicked his fingers.

The small flat disappeared into the darkness, and the four of them were transported into a cramped back alley where the smell of alcohol filled their nostrils. A middle-aged women left via a side door of a pub; she said goodnight to her work colleagues as she left.

The seaside air filled the woman's lungs, and a chill ran down her spine. She pulled her coat tighter to keep the heat inside and walked along the cobbled street, down towards the bridge that connected the old town with the new town.

A sea mist quickly rolled in and with the soft yellow glow of the street lights, the visibility was extremely poor. As midnight hit, the bells could be heard from the church at the top of the hill and the streets were very quiet.

The street would be still busy during the summer months at this time of the night, but it was late winter and mid-week, so only the odd person or two could be seen staggering home.

She began to cross the bridge when a car appeared from nowhere and hit her side on, crushing her hip and snapping her left femur; her body twisted with the force of the car and her head hit the bonnet, rendering her immediately unconscious.

The driver slammed on the brakes, throwing the woman spinning to the side of the road. As she lay there unconscious another woman appeared out of the fog and watched the car accelerate away.

Melina reached down and felt for a pulse on the woman's neck, it was faint. She paused, considered her next action for a moment, looking down on the still body. Melina looked around, then back at the motionless body and ran to the nearest building with lights on and banged on the door.

A young man answered the door, Melina explained what had happened and how the car had hit the woman, leaving her for dead, and she needed an ambulance quickly. The man reached for his mobile phone from the sideboard behind and turned back, but Melina had fled.

The scene collapsed into blackness. Slowly the daylight broke through the blackness, bringing the four back into the small room of Melina's flat.

Nick clapped his hands and turned to the two intruders tied up in the chairs.

"Questions, boys?"

The two men sat in shocked silence; the older one of the two slowly looked up at Nick with tears rolling down his face, "… It was a car accident … it wasn't you … but … why did you run?"

Melina looked to be in shock too, "What? I … er … it wasn't a good time for me … I just wanted her to be OK … I'm sorry."

Nick winked at Melina as she looked up at the man, tears in his eyes.

"You see guys? She looks shocked still by the incident and what happened. You can clearly see she didn't kill your wife, she tried to save her. Don't you think it would probably be for the best that you stop this witch hunt and try to get past this accident?"

"Who are you?" asked the older man again, looking up at Nick.

"We have already gone through this. I'm the man whom you don't want to meet again. I am not here for you two, but I am going to release you and I expect you to walk out of here quietly and apologise to this lady. If you don't, I will take your son's life." Nick smiled and clicked his fingers.

The two men felt the bonds release from round them and they ran for the door, in fear and sorrow, apologising to Melina and Nick. As he closed the door behind them, Nick watched them climb into their car and drive away. He sat on one of the now-vacant chairs, facing Melina and smiled.

"What the fuck was that? You lied to them!"

"I did; do you know why?"

"It wasn't a car that hit her; it was me, I killed her. That was one of my experiments. I figured if I snapped a limb and the skin was pierced, then the rush of blood to that location would mean a faster flow, but that wasn't the case. It took me three kills to realise that. But, that was impressive how you made them believe – you had me questioning it too."

"I still don't realise why you went for help though, that was really risky," Nick asked.

"It was early days; I was still getting used to the emotional separation you need to survive. After a few years, you learn to detach yourself from the task at hand. But why did you lie to them?"

"Did you want me to tell them it was you? Would you have felt better? Did you want me to leave them to attack you instead?"

"You knew if they tried to attack me, I would have ripped them to shreds?"

"Look, you said something earlier that interested me, and I think we could help each other out. You mentioned that your sire had taught you various tricks, you mentioned teleportation. I think you can help me."

"I told you that I couldn't do it, I couldn't do anything. I'm a dud!"

Nick leaned forward in his chair, "I don't need you to do

it. I need you to remember how to do it and tell me. It's something that I want. I don't like relying on people. I know it's possible; I have seen someone do it."

Melina rubbed her forehead, "I'm not sure, wait a minute."

She stood up and walked to the kitchen, opened a small cupboard and lifted a floorboard up from inside. She then lifted out a leather-bound, black journal and unwrapped the ties around it. She blew some of the dust off the cover and started to flick through the pages.

"Here, it's here." Melina handed the book to Nick.

Nick read the pages and understood them completely; he had gone through similar processes when he used the time jump trick on Ethan when he showed him his past. But he had been told that this would only work if it was between using the portal.

This had been a lie, if a vampire could do it, surely he could do it too. He read it again, just in case he hadn't missed any of it, and stood up.

"This reads as though you can teleport anywhere as long as you have something there, a connection to the place? Like what?"

"I'm pretty sure it could be anything, an object, a memory, a person even. As long as you have had contact with the item then you're fine."

"Could it be a picture? Like if I saw a map, would that work?"

"No, that's why a vampire needs some kind of contact with its victim, a scent, a touch, anything but has to be physical. Maps or pictures don't work."

Nick thought about this and shut the book, as it was closing, his eyes caught something scribbled at the bottom he hadn't noticed. It was a spell on how to block people from teleporting near him. He opened the book back open and looked up at Melina.

"I think I love you! This? Does this work?" Nick pointed out the scribble at the bottom of the page.

"Oh yes, that works well. That is a way we protect ourselves from other vamps. I wouldn't think you would need that though!"

"For that not only will I not be leaving here today with your soul, but, I will protect you if you ever need me. Thank you for this."

Nick waved his hand over the page and created a fresh piece of paper out of the air and pocketed it. He passed the book back to Melina.

Nick made a point, however, of touching her finger during the transaction for future connections.

Melina felt his finger touch hers, and she immediately looked up at him, "Why did you touch me? Do you think I am some kind of lending library, you can just turn up whenever you need something?"

"Listen, if I want something, I'm going to take it. It's like you explained, this way we have a connection that we could both find helpful."

Melina stood up, her tall, toned frame looked as if it weren't capable of the power and force that she used to devour her victims. Nick stood up as she approached him; she stopped an inch away from him and looked down at him.

"You won't take anything from me. I don't care who you are, I don't break easy!" Melina threatened gently and stroked his cheek with the back of her fingers.

Nick grabbed her arm and twisted it, Melina buckled under Nick's strength but she was determined not to show any weakness.

"Melina, neither do I! Do you want to fuck up this friendship that could be what we both need?"

Nick held her arm in a very painful position, smiled and let go.

"I don't want a friendship. I work alone. And unless you can switch on the vampire powers that I should have, then there is nothing I need from you." Melina rubbed her arm.

"Leave that with me; they might be something I can do yet. Who did you say your sire was? Maybe there is something I can look into with him."

"I didn't say who he was, and I don't want to ever meet him again, he's gone." Melina walked over to the door and opened it. "I think it's time you left."

Nick walked to the door and turned to her, "Melina, I mean no harm. I can help you as you have helped me. I just need you to understand I am not weak and I am not your prey!"

Nick stopped at the door and looked at Melina, "You ever need me, just call." Nick smiled, clicked his fingers and disappeared.

Melina slammed the door shut and collapsed on the floor and began to sob. She had lived a lot of her life controlled by men, and now this. Twenty years free, by herself, no one controlling her life and now this, another man. It was time to hide again.

♛

The portal room came into focus, and Nick landed on his feet and walked past Anton who was silent. Anton followed Nick out back to the kitchen.

"What happened, sir?" Anton asked holding his arms out at his side in disbelief.

"Nothing happened Anton, nothing. I think I got that one wrong."

"Wrong? What do you mean wrong?"

"Look, there was no reason for me to take any souls today, maybe next time."

"Sir, you can't keep walking away from your responsibilities. I mean, how are you going to grow your power and defeat Lucifer, when you're scared to take the evil souls?" Anton's voice started to rise with anger.

Nick stopped walking and turned to Anton, "Don't say that to me anymore. I know and you know, that I would not be able to beat Lucifer. I know that you and he are still as tight as you have ever been. So, how can you say anything like that? What is your plan? What is this all about really?"

"Sir, why do we have to go through this again? You already know why you are here and what you have to do. There really is no underlying evil plan. Lucifer just wants a normal life; he is very envious of humans having normal lifestyles, and he's spent the last 200 or so years watching and yearning for it."

"Look, I can't see any way around this, other than finding a loophole in the contract, and that will never happen due to the contract being some kind of bewitched object. So, please stop pretending as though you're on my side or you only want what is best for me, because this is getting as old as you."

Nick left Anton speechless and walked to the kitchen, grabbing a drink from the fridge, he went out to the veranda.

Anton, shortly after, joined him.

"Sir, we still need to discuss why you didn't take the soul. If you don't start to take souls, there will be an imbalance. We need to keep up the tally. We do not want an imbalance; otherwise, there will need to be a massacre or worse a pandemic."

"Honestly, Anton, I don't think I need you anymore. I think I have reached a point now where I have all the knowledge I need to continue by myself."

Nick lifted his glass and looked through the liquid at the clear blue sky.

"I learned something today. I don't need anyone to guide me. I actually have this shit all figured out." Nick put his glass down and stood up, "In fact, if anything, I really do think it is you who needs me."

Nick walked off leaving Anton in silence staring at the glass that was glinting in the bright sunshine.

19

PUNISHMENT DUE

Nick sat on the bed in his room, and he pulled out the piece of paper with a simple hand gesture. It appeared, floating in mid-air then he snatched it. He read the protection spell section again, making sure that he re-read it several times to get it right; Nick knew he couldn't make a mistake; this was the key that would stop Lucifer from suddenly appearing, and that meant he could hurt Anton and find out what their plan was. Nick would love to hurt Lucifer, and hurting Anton would be a perfect way to do that. This also put him in the winning position, for a change.

Nick closed his eyes and recited the spell making sure not to make any mistakes; the problem now was how could he test it? Should he attack Anton immediately, hoping the spell had worked, or build up to it slowly? He felt the latter would be the ideal way; the last thing he wanted was for Lucifer to turn up and kick his arse again.

What did Anton and Lucifer know about what had just happened with Melina? Did they know about the teleportation spell or the protection spell? He just assumed that if they had have known about the spells they would have been waiting for him on his return.

Nick left his room and walked back to the kitchen. Surprisingly, there was no Anton. He walked out to the veranda, again, no Anton. He walked over to the railings overlooking the beach, still no Anton. He turned around to go back to the kitchen and standing in the doorway was Anton, looking shocked and worried.

"What have you done?" Anton asked nervously.

Nick smiled knowing exactly what he was nervous about.

"What do you mean?"

Anton looked back in the kitchen as though he were waiting for something to happen. "I er… I mean did you… er… notice anything change about five minutes ago?"

Nick looked around and shook his head, "No, you mean the weather? Never changes, Anton, never changes."

"No, it doesn't matter; just thought I felt something change, forget it." And he left through the doorway into the kitchen.

Nick calmly followed, "Hey Anton, what do you mean something changed?"

"Sir, forget I mentioned it. Please." Anton was visibly panicking.

Nick turned into the kitchen and grabbed a drink out of the fridge, as he turned to Anton to say something, he noticed something on the wall that he hadn't noticed before. He walked over to it and felt a shudder down his spine. He turned to Anton.

"What the fuck is this?" And pointed to the unit on the wall by the door.

Anton looked at the unit that was usually hidden by Lucifer's magic. "Sir, that is the climate control for the retreat; it's always been there." Anton's eye's darted around as though he were expecting a visitor.

"Climate control? I haven't seen this before. Does this control the weather? Really, you mean it doesn't have to be sunny all the time? I can have whatever weather I want?" Anton nodded, "Wow, that's incredible, it really is, shame it's never been there before!"

"Sir, I think I am going to have a lie-down. I'm not feeling very well. If you will excuse me?" Anton started to leave the room.

"Anton, wait, what's wrong? You look pale."

"Sir, I don't feel well at all. I will be fine; I think I just need some sleep." Anton started to leave again.

"Just one minute. Why does the climate control panel suddenly appearing seem, er… familiar? Why does it feel as though this conversation has happened before?"

Anton stood there with his back to Nick, thinking, "I believe I mentioned it on the first day you arrived."

"No. I would have definitely remembered that. Come on, every day sunny, if I could have changed it, I would have. No, this feels recent."

Nick pointed to the kitchen, "I was sitting on the stool there," He then pointed at the fridge, "and you were over there."

Nick's memory was starting to return and as each second passed, he recalled more. He stood in silence as he relived his flashback until he had passed out. "Anton? What did you do?"

Anton froze.

"Nick, you have to understand that was for your own good. We thought you had worked too hard and needed a rest. You weren't harmed; you needed the rest."

"We? Of course, Lucifer! Always fucking Lucifer! I knew

he would have been behind it; in fact; I'm really surprised that he's not here now, or is he?" Nick started to look around, "Lucifer, come out and play! Oh Lucifer, where are you?" Nick shouted mockingly.

Anton sighed placing his hands on Nick's shoulders in comfort.

"Well, yes, he knew you were struggling to deal with everything that you were going through. He had to deal with the same at first, and the only way he got through it was by having a few days with a sleeping potion. Even he couldn't get through all the hell he created without it. He couldn't sleep. Magic can only keep you going for so long."

Nick looked at Anton closely, he watched his eye's dart between Nick's eyes. He pushed Anton's hands off his shoulders.

"Don't touch me. You two are killing me. I don't feel like I used to anymore; I feel constantly empty like I'm missing something, and I am betting that shit is down to you two."

Anton looking around, frantically, "Lucifer!" Anton shouted. "Lucifer!"

Nick opened his mouth and slapped his forehead, "Oh shit! Anton! I don't think he's coming back, well not right now! You see I found something that stops him from just popping up and being the big man. Looks like his magic can't get here either!"

"How? I fucking knew you had done something!"

"Anton! You swore!"

"Shut up you little shit! What did you do? Are you fucking stupid? What do you think will happen when he realises something is going on? What about your mother?"

"I don't know, but I don't think he will do anything until he knows for sure, until he knows you're OK."

Nick turned around and walked out to the veranda and looked into the distance.

"So, Anton, what's the plan? Why am I really here?"

Anton sat down, looking very pale and scared. "The plan is what it has always been, you here, him there. I really don't know why you think it would be any different." he looked up at Nick with pleading eyes, "Please, Nick, stop this."

Nick returned to the kitchen.

"If that's true, then why are you so scared? I mean, you have magic, don't you? Or is it the fact that you can't use magic without Lucifer's connection?"

Anton's poker face was now gone, "Nick, please just let me go; this is between you and him."

Nick stood next to a very weary-looking Anton and placed a hand on his shoulder.

"That's it, isn't it? You need his connection to have magic? Oh my God, and he's left you with me, and now I know how to block him."

Nick smiled, held Anton by the chin and bent slightly to be his height and said, "And now I'm going to kill you."

Anton pushed Nicks hand off his face, stood up and started to run. As he ran, Nick raised his arms and stopped Anton in his tracks; he lifted him and turned him slowly so he was facing Nick.

"You're going to regret this! When he finds out, he's going to kill you and your bitch of a mother!"

"Anton, Anton, I don't think you're in a position to get angry with me right now. After all, your life is in my hands, and I'm feeling itchy to do some damage to you. After all the shit you have both put me through, I think it's time to turn the tables. Don't you?"

Nick pulled a stool away from the kitchen island and set it

in front of Anton who was motionless, hanging in midair in a Jesus Christ pose, head slightly tilted forward.

Nick pushed himself up on to the stool and looked up at Anton.

"It's funny to see you like this, Anton, arms out wide, Christ-like, and yet you and your lover are as far away from him as anyone could be. What do you get from this? I mean, whilst he is out there doing whatever, you're here babysitting. This must really piss you off; it must really get to you?"

Anton looked down at Nick.

"What do I get? I get to do my God's bidding. His work continues and I am still a big part of it. I have dedicated my life to him and it will continue to be his servant. I will do whatever he asks of me, nothing will stop that."

"Nothing? What about pain?"

Nick turned a hand and Anton's limbs started to stretch out, Anton closed his eyes, gritted his teeth in agony and grunted as he felt his muscles tighten. Nick smiled and relaxed the pulling slightly.

"Is that it? Is that all you have?" taunted Anton.

Nick twisted his hand again, as though he were turning up a dial. Anton winced at first then as Nick's hand continued to turn, Anton started to crease with pain as his limbs were being pulled in each direction. They heard the first pop as one of Anton's shoulders dislocated; Nick turned back the other way, relaxing the pulling again, he waited for Anton's next comment.

Anton lifted his head up to face Nick again; then he spat some blood at Nick.

"Have we taught you nothing about pain and how to inflict it? I always knew you were weak, but this is fucking pathetic." Anton let out a snigger.

The pulling started again, only this time it was stronger,

faster. Anton gritted his teeth and let out a guttural wail as a couple more pops and cracks could be heard. Nick relaxed the pulling again and sat forward on his stool. "Is that any better for you?"

Anton groaned and coughed up more blood, this time not spitting it in Nick's direction, he moaned and looked up at Nick again.

"Better…" Anton got his breath back, "I still don't understand why you insist on fighting against us; you're never going to truly be everything you can be whilst you hold back. Why do you keep holding back?"

"For fuck sake, what do you want from me? I do what you want; I have changed a lot, too much really if you ask me. I have even started to become numb to the death I bestow, and yet you want more from me. When will it end? When will this nightmare end?"

Anton started to smile; he felt each of his limbs ache and pain shooting up his left leg from his broken ankle and dislocated knee.

"And there it is again, the 'why me?' 'You're so fucking weak!" Anton spat another mouthful of blood out.

Nick's frustrations were starting to rise to the surface as he stood up and kicked the stool away.

"Weak? Pathetic? Do you want more pain? Do you actually want me to kill you? You want me to rip you to pieces?"

"Ha! You don't have the balls, son!"

The butler persona that Anton had built up over the months of being with Nick, had disappeared in less than thirty minutes. Nick could see that this had all been a cover for something more. He didn't know what, but he wasn't buying the story anymore of Anton's just wanting to help.

"What? You think I don't have the balls? Think again old

man; it's you that doesn't have the balls!" Using one hand Nick swiped his left hand down ripping Anton's trousers off and with his other hand clenched his fist and pulled down, Anton screamed in pain as Nick ripped his scrotum and testicles away from his body. Blood poured down his legs as Anton's body writhed in agony as it hung in midair tethered by Nick's invisible ropes.

Anton was crying in pain; he looked down to the blood oozing over his feet onto the floor.

Nick looked at his victim with no pity, "Doesn't look like your sweetheart is coming to rescue you, now, does it?"

Anton was gasping for breath in between the floods of pain shooting through his body. Whimpering now he lifted his head, "Please, stop…"

"Do you think this will break Lucifer's heart to see you die? Or do you think he will just move on to the next puppet? I mean it seems to me he has left you here to die as he starts a new life, without you."

"He will be back, and he will kill you… he will kill you!"

"Shut up; I have had enough of you, I think it's your time to die!"

Nick lifted his hands together above his head and quickly pulled them apart, Anton screamed in extreme pain as he was flayed; his skin ripped from every part of him, leaving his body a bloody, dripping, exposed, quivering mess. Nick lifted a hand made a fist and stopped Anton's heart with a single twist.

Anton hung motionless. Nick looked up and pondered his victim's vulnerability, his dead teacher. The one who had shown him how to lure, snare and kill his prey. Now he was caught in an unbreakable trap. Nick walked around his creation, thinking about what to do next. What would have the most effect on Lucifer when he could finally return here and save his lover.

He slowly levitated the limp, Anton through the open doors that led out to the veranda, and lifted him up to the side of the building, posed him into a crucified position and rammed four nails into him. One in his left wrist, one in his right, and one in each foot. Attaching him to the building that towered above him. He knew that Lucifer would wreak revenge on him as soon as he saw this atrocity. Nick knew his next move would have to be quick, and he had to get to his mother before Lucifer did.

Nick wasn't sure if the blocking magic on the retreat would lift when Nick left, or if there was a period of time before it dissipated. He was praying that it would leave him time to get to his mother and then Jennifer. He knew Lucifer would be going for them both.

He reviewed his piece of paper, which held the details of the magic he needed for teleportation, and clicked his fingers. Nick left and made his way to his mother.

Within seconds after Nick leaving, Lucifer arrived in a panicked state.

He landed near the kitchen area. Seeing the blood trail through the kitchen out towards the veranda, he ran, trying not to slip on the blood.

Lucifer looked up, and stared at Anton's corpse. He had only one place to go now - straight for revenge. Nick was going to pay, slowly and painfully, in as many different ways he could.

20

REVENGE

Friday nights had become movie night for Nick and Jude for the past six months; they had either gone to the cinema or watched a movie at home. Jude didn't care which film they watched just as long as they were together. Nick had been a different son for a while now; he stayed at home the majority of the time and wanted to be with her more. Until recently, Nick seemed to want to be more independent, but something had changed. She didn't care what it was but things were happier now.

The front door opened and Jude walked through carrying two pizzas for the evening's meal. She closed the door behind her and she shouted for Nick.

"Nick, I'm home."

There was no answer.

Jude took off her coat and hung it up; she put her work bag away in the cupboard and walked into the kitchen placing the two pizza boxes on the side.

"Mum!"

Jude turned to see her son in the kitchen doorway with blood dripping from his hands. She looked down onto the pools of red forming on the floor and back up to her son's face.

Grabbing her mouth in horror, she ran to her son, "Nick, what… what's happened?"

"Mum!" Nick threw his arms around her and pulled her in tight. "I'm so sorry!"

"Nick, where is this blood coming from? Have you cut yourself? Why is there so much blood?"

Jude pulled herself away from Nick, checking his wrists and arms.

"Is this your blood?"

"No, it's Anton's." Nick looked down at the blood, mesmerised.

Jude looked back up to Nick's face.

"Anton? Have you hurt someone?"

Nick raised his head back up, looked at Jude, and smiled.

"Not yet, but I think it's time I did."

He hit her across her face with the back of his hand sending her crashing into the table sending the pizza boxes flying off the table and on to the floor, cupboard doors dripping with tomato topping.

She grabbed her face, "Oh my god! Nick, why?" She began to cry.

Nick walked over to his mother, she looked up to see his face change from Nick to Lucifer; Jude scrambled to her feet and pushed past him and through the kitchen door.

"You can't run forever, Mother!"

Lucifer left the kitchen in pursuit. Jude had made it to the outside door, but it wouldn't open, although she didn't remember locking it.

"You can't escape me, after what your fucking son has done. I'm going to take my revenge. Time to die, Jude!"

She quickly leapt up the stairs, taking as many steps at

once as she could, and ran into her bedroom heading for the large bedroom window. She locked the bedroom door behind her and dived over the bed. She got to the window but the latch wouldn't move; neither would the other, the latches were stuck.

"If you're trying to open your windows they won't open. Hey, why don't you try smashing them?" mocked Lucifer.

He tried the handle on the door, but it was locked.

Jude looked around the room, searching for something heavy. She grabbed the stool by the window and launched it as hard as she could at the glass. The stool ricocheted off the window and bounced straight back at her, she ducked but it had failed to even crack it. Jude heard the handle being tried and double-checked that she had locked it.

"This would work easier if you just come out. I mean do you really think I can't get through this flimsy door?"

Lucifer turned the handle again; this time it opened freely. He looked around the room expecting to see Jude trying to open a window or ready to throw something, but she wasn't there.

Lucifer looked around and tried each closet door, quickly looking inside each one. He turned and looked at the bed.

"Really, Jude? Are you under the bed?" He lifted the bed with one gesture and Jude ran out through the open door.

Running down the stairs Jude slipped, pushing her arm out to stop her fall, but immediately she felt the pain shoot up her arm as her wrist made a snapping noise. She turned round to see Lucifer laughing at the top of the stairs.

"You don't even need me to hurt you; you're doing all the work yourself. It's a shame you didn't break your scrawny neck!"

Jude quickly got up from the bottom of the stairs, grasping her broken wrist, tenderly, and ran towards the back of the house. She grabbed the back door handle and tried it, it opened. She pulled and it was ripped out of her hand, slamming shut in front of her and keeping her on the wrong side of the door.

She started to cry once she realised there was no escape for her.

"Where is Nick, you bastard? What have you done to him?"

"Nothing yet, I have plans for your precious Nick. However, I no longer need you anymore." Lucifer moved in close; he grabbed her head and pulled her up.

Lucifer started to squeeze the top of her head and watched her scream as his fingers dug into her skull, he could hear her feet scraping the floor as they tried to make contact. He smiled at her then dropped her to the ground as she screamed in pain clutching her head with the hand that wasn't flopping in pain.

He knelt by Jude and moved his head in close.

"Your son for the past six months has been killing people in my name. Reaping souls in my name. Whilst I have lived here with you, listening to your controlling, smothering, sycophantic love of your son. How the hell does he do it? It has taken everything in my power not to strangle you! Every day your constant watching, never leaving me alone, only to go to work and then you still ring me. Oh my god, you never end! Get a fucking life…"

Lucifer stopped and tilted his head as he looked at her.

"Actually, that would be pretty pointless, considering that I'm about to end it. You see your son has been very, very bad. He needs to be punished for that. Seeing that I can't get to him, I will have to take it out on you!"

Jude started to crawl away from Lucifer. He crouched there, watching her crawl as she cried. He then stood back up, walked over to her and grabbed her by the hair and dragged her back to the kitchen, Jude howled in pain.

She tried to hold her hair to stop it from hurting as much, but with her broken wrist, her skull crushed in places – it was pointless. With blood and tears running down her face, she begged for mercy.

"Stop… I'm sorry… I…," Lucifer brought his fist cleanly down into her face, smashing her head into the floor and breaking her jaw in the process.

"Shut the fuck up, you whining BITCH! I gave you your son back! I gave you hope and how does your filthy son repay me?" Lucifer wiped his hand on a towel, clearing his hand of blood and mucous.

Just then a loud crack was heard in another room. Lucifer looked at Jude and plunged a carving knife through her chest and into her heart.

"Your son's home! Time to break his heart!"

Lucifer turned in time to see Nick run through the kitchen door. Lucifer smiled and with a loud crack, he was gone.

"Mum! Mum!" Nick grabbed Jude, trying to assess her status, "It's ok, I can sort this… It's going to be ok…"

Jude began to choke touching his cheek with the last of her energy.

"I'm sorry Nick… I love you…"

She stopped breathing.

Nick felt her last breath leave her body and her body became limp.

Nick moved his hands quickly over her to try to save her, begging for her to breathe, but whatever Lucifer had done, couldn't be reversed.

Nick laid his mother's head on the floor gently; he removed the knife from her chest.

"No mum, I'm sorry." Nick stood up and stared down at her.

He knew how sad this was, how everything he was working towards was now taken away from him, yet he couldn't feel the sadness, not one tear. Nick had started to realise that he was dead inside, numb, evil.

He picked up the phone and calmly asked for an ambulance. He knew he would be the key suspect and staying around to make sure his mum was found would be a mistake. He gave the address and hung up, opened the front door and shattered the door frame making it look like a break-in.

Nick knelt by his mother's side one last time, leaned in and kissed her forehead. He stood up and clicked his fingers. Nick disappeared leaving his mother staring at the wall with lifeless eyes, in a pool of her own blood, waiting for the ambulance.

Fifteen minutes later the EMTs arrived. Seeing the smashed-in door, they rushed in and found Jude cold and grey, slumped on the kitchen floor, staring at the wall.

Nick arrived back at the retreat, his mother's blood fresh on his hands. He ran out onto the veranda to see if Anton were still where he had left him, crucified to the side of the outside wall. But he was gone. His blood stained the wall where his body had touched the building. Nick kicked the furniture in anger, sending the chairs scattering across the floor.

His eyes caught something shiny, he touched his neck. He hadn't realised he had lost his necklace, and there it lay, glinting in the sun. He couldn't understand how he had just forgotten about it; he couldn't even remember losing it.

Grabbing it and putting into his pocket he turned and saw a note pinned to the door, he ripped it off and opened it.

Nick,

This was never meant to end this way; this was a gift for you to embrace, an adventure, for which you were chosen, yet you destroyed everything. You have broken my heart, and I hope you are suffering too, but I'm wondering if the lack of a soul would leave you emotionless, unable to feel your loss like I feel mine.

But, I still have your soul, and maybe one day I may return it. But in the meantime, I wish you nothing but hollowness and numbness – you ungrateful piece of shit.

Lucifer

"AAARRRRRGGGGHHHH!!!!"

Nick bellowed, tearing the note up in anger. He threw the furniture against the wall, smashing the chairs and table up. The broken pieces of plastic and wood lay mangled against the wall, strewn across the patio.

Nick ran into the kitchen throwing the furniture; he wanted to end this and destroying *his* sanctuary was the only way he felt he could. He went from room to room smashing, breaking, throwing, ripping; hoping that somehow this would affect *him*. He needed to bleed.

As Nick was going around destroying anything he could, he hadn't noticed the start of the collapse of the world he was in beginning. If he had been on the beach he would have witnessed the horizon start to fold into total blackness. The void grew larger as the ocean disappeared. But Nick's anger had him tearing down a place that was about to be removed from existence. The noise was growing like approaching thunder. The beach began to shake as the void drew in.

The noise finally attracted Nick's attention. He stopped his activity, and he ran out to see the black horizon hit the beach. He froze and watched it for a few seconds, realising what was happening. Nick clicked his fingers and jumped to the first place that came into his mind.

♕

He felt the softness of the sofa under him as his sight came back into focus, and he could see that he had successfully arrived at his intended location and still with his powers.

He sat for a few seconds staring at his hands, wondering why he hadn't lost them.

The room was the same as he remembered it.

A noise from another room made him jump and he refocused on the opening door. Jen stood there, aghast. Without a thought, she leapt onto Nick's lap, legs around him and grabbing his face, she repeatedly kissed him. She paused, hugged him again and started another round of kisses covering every inch of his face. Nick pulled his head back and grabbed her shoulders, pushing her back slightly.

"Jen, please let me breathe!"

She saw his hands were still blood-stained.

"Is that your blood? Are you ok?"

"It's not my blood, I wish it were, but it's not."

"What do you mean?" Jan sat back on him, holding his hands.

"It's my mother's blood, and maybe somebody else too, I'm not sure."

Nick looked at them still thinking about his Mum and Lucifer's ownership of his soul.

Nick looked up to Jen's eyes, "He took my soul Jen! My soul! He killed my Mother. I saw him stick a knife in her, and then he left her to bleed. She hadn't done anything to anyone." He looked back down to his bloodied hands.

"Nick, who did this?"

"*HIM*! Lucifer, it's always fucking *HIM*!" Nick pushed Jen to one side as he stood up and walked to the kitchen, she followed him.

"He killed your mother? Why?"

As Nick washed his hands in the sink, he watched the blood run off and down the drain.

"I killed his lover."

"What? Does Lucifer have a lover? Why did you kill her?"

"Him, he was a him. I killed him, and I didn't feel any remorse; in fact, I enjoyed it." Nick dried his hands and turned to Jen.

Jen was still in shock from the sudden appearance of Nick, but was very happy and excited regardless.

"Oh. I always imagined that he would have a harem of women who would do his bidding, like Dracula." Then she remembered what else Nick had said, "Sorry, did you say he took your soul?"

"Yes, I apparently don't have a soul because he has it. I don't really know anything else, it does explain a lot but apart from killing people, I don't really know what a soul is, I just did as I was told."

"But surely you die without a soul?" The conversation was starting to confuse Jen's mind as she tried to understand what was normal to Nick now.

"I don't know; maybe I am dead?" Nick walked past Jen and back into the living room, Jen followed.

"What are you going to do now? Are you here for good?"

"For now, if you don't mind? I don't have anywhere else to go, or anywhere else I want to go."

Jen's eyes lit up, "Stay here for as long as you want. I've missed you, Nick. I have craved you every day since you left."

Nick pulled Jen in closer and hugged her, "Me too, Jen. I am here for a while until I work out what I need to do next. I have to get my soul back, and maybe kill Lucifer." Jen pulled him in tighter.

"I don't care what you do, as long as you're here with me."

21

REFOCUS

Nick awoke to a strange sound, a sound he hadn't heard for a long time, the sound of drops of rain cascading on the window. He lay in bed staring up at the ceiling, holding Jen, listening to the drops of water hit the glass.

Months of dazzling sunshine, a huge bedroom, amazing secluded beach, had been nice but the whole thing was fake. This was real. Gritty as it was, it was real. He tightened his arm around Jen for a brief second, feeling her warmth and softness against his skin; he released her and slowly climbed out of bed.

Nick opened the curtains enough to take a peek outside, watching the droplets of water trickle down the window. He looked out onto the street below and watched the cars pass by, the people scurry off to work, protecting themselves from the cold downpour with umbrellas and newspapers.

He smiled to himself, thinking he would be happy just to be outside, feeling the real sky drenching his clothes. This was real; he was back in the actual world, but alone now. Yes, he had Jen, but he had no real life. He knew that the relationship he had with her was fake and that one day she would wake up and see this facade for what it was, a lie.

Jen stirred in bed and Nick broke out of his trance. He turned and watched Jen lying in bed. Part of her body covered by the duvet and half displayed, he stood there and admired her perfect body, shapely, slightly toned. He walked over to her and kissed her forehead. Jen stretched and opened her eyes slowly. She glanced immediately onto the thin, naked physique of Nick that stood over her; she smiled and reached for his hand and tried to pull him back into the warm bed.

"Not yet, coffee first!" Nick said teasingly and walked out of the bedroom.

She slammed her hand on the bed in disgust.

"Fine!"

She got up and grabbed her dressing gown from the side, wrapping it around her and followed Nick out of the bedroom.

He was already in the kitchen filling the kettle when Jen staggered in rubbing her eyes and yawning. She leaned on the side admiring Nick stroll around with no clothes on.

He grabbed two cups from the cupboard and added the instant coffee; he turned and looked at Jen leaning forward over the counter.

"I presume we are going to go back to bed after you've made these? I don't think I can pay attention to anything else whilst your strutting around naked, so be quick?" Jen insisted.

"I can go get some clothes on?"

"No! I didn't say that I'm not happy with the view; in fact, I'm very happy!"

Jen smiled and gave him a wolf whistle. She was happy again, not as on edge as she had been now that Nick was back, and looking like he could be around a bit longer. That was what she had wanted for a long time.

Nick finished the coffee off and stopped, still staring at the drinks, he paused.

"What am I, Jen?" Nick asked.

"Well… you're, you're you. The GREAT NICK, KING OF HELL!" she mocked in a deep voice.

Nick gave a sarcastic smirk, "You know what I mean, what am I? I don't have a soul, I kill people, I hurt people, I make people do bad things. I'm not Nick anymore. So what am I?"

Jen walked around the worktop and up to Nick; she grabbed him from behind and hugged him as he leaned against the counter where the drinks sat.

"Let's find that out together, ok? I'm here for you."

Nick turned around, and hugged her back, sliding her dressing gown off her shoulders and on to the floor. He lifted her up and she wrapped her legs around him. He walked back into the living room, carrying her, and they fell onto the sofa.

"What about the drinks?" Jen asked.

"Fuck the drinks!"

It had been three hours since they had fallen asleep. Nick woke in a panic; he realised that he had left them unprotected from Lucifer. He jumped to his feet and retained the note he had created with the spells on. Nick waved his hand whilst saying the words, feeling a wave beat out from his hand and throughout the flat.

This made him wonder: Why did he still have his powers? Surely Lucifer would have stripped him of everything if the contract were over. But here he was, still breathing and still powerful.

He waved his hand and created an internet screen resting

on a search engine in front of him. Nick asked for his address and any accidents; nothing useful returned. Nick then asked for his address and murders. Five news reports returned regarding his mother; the police were looking for him to answer some questions, just to rule him out of the investigations.

Nick continued to search the obituaries, looking for any details regarding her funeral. Nothing was showing yet. It had only been a day, and he wondered who was looking after the funeral arrangements. Nick waved his hand, cleared the object from the air in front of him and sat back wondering if he should attend.

He thought about going in disguise? He also wondered if he could change his appearance like Lucifer could.

Jen stirred on the sofa and reached for Nick who was sitting up; she rubbed her eyes and focused on him.

"Nick, you ok?"

"Yeah, just realised I hadn't protected your flat. I've done it now, but that could have been bad. Last thing I want it to lose you too." Nick stroked her hair.

She smiled and hugged Nick. "What's your plan? Have you decided what you're going to do yet?"

"Not yet, I still have my powers. I'm pretty sure I am going to go to my mum's funeral too. Once that is over and done with. I'm going to find Lucifer and try to end all this."

"I get that you need to say goodbye to your mother, but why go after him? Surely you're best staying away?"

"No, I want my soul back; I want this finished with. I want to understand why I still have my powers? My mother is dead, and his teen life is fucked! Jesus, I still have shit loads of questions that bastard needs to answer!"

Jen tried to hug Nick, but he stood up and walked into the bedroom to get dressed.

"Are you leaving me again?" Jen asked close to tears.

"No, I think I just need some air, being trapped inside that place is killing me."

Nick clicked his fingers and his trench coat appeared.

"Get dressed, let's go walk in the rain." Nick smiled and held his hand out to help her from the sofa.

"Ok."

Jen rose and she slapped his arse as she walked passed, Jen giggled as she ran into the bedroom.

They left the apartment and walked out on to the wet streets. Nick raised his face to the rain, feeling the cold water trickle down his neck and into his shirt. He had not felt anything but warm sunshine for months, and this was a million miles away from his recent life. The dirty streets, the pollution from the heavy traffic felt like poison in his throat. Within eight months, he had gone from being a regular seventeen-year-old finding where he fits in the world, from having fun and sampling the flavours that adult life brings, to being trapped in luxury, soulless and now motherless.

The toxic rain was a blessing which he reveled in.

"Jen, you got any money?" Nick asked.

"Not really, why? You wanna go for a drink?"

"Not really, but I want to go to a shop and buy things, I miss that!" Nick grabbed Jen by the hand and he started to run pulling her along with him.

"Let's have some fun!"

"Slow down, I can't run," Jen shouted.

"Come on; let's go get some bottles and play games with the shop keeper."

"What, why? Can't you just magic up some money? Do it that way?"

"I will, but let's play first, stay behind me, but close."

Nick opened the off-licence door and walked in nodding to the assistant behind the counter.

The assistant stood and watched his two customers walk down the alcohol aisle; he kept an eye on them, using the monitors behind the counter when they dropped out of his sight. He looked down at the screens and saw, what he could only explain later to the police, as a large black demon with wings and a woman without a face. He switched off the monitor and switched it back on, thinking a reboot would clear the defect on the screen. The demon was now grabbing multiple bottles from the shelf, whilst licking several others with an extremely enlarged tongue and then placing them back on to the shelf for others to find.

"Evening, sir, I will be taking these bottles and pass me ten of your best cigars." Nick boomed.

The assistant looked up from the monitors and into the eyes of a 7-foot black-winged demon. The assistant reached back into the cabinet, knocking several things over and trying not to take his eyes off the creature. He grabbed as many cigars as he could; then, without a word, passed them over to the beast. Nick had never seen anyone cry in silence before, but tears fell from the assistant as he stood there, fearing for his life.

They both departed the shop with their contraband, leaving a wet patch to form in between the legs of the assistant's trousers.

Nick now back in human form ran up the street laughing, whilst Jen tried to keep up carrying and dropping several cigars along the way.

"Why did you do that?"

"For the laugh, and at least I now know I can change my appearance, which means I can attend my mum's funeral."

"I don't think you should attend as him though; it might bring you unwanted attention!" Jen laughed as they reached her flat.

👑

Three days of alcohol-induced sex later and Nick and Jen had decided it was time at least to go outside again and get something more appetising than takeout.

As they got ready Nick quickly checked the papers for the obituaries, as he did every day, looking for a date for his mother's funeral to appear. Today was the day Nick had been waiting for; he sat and stared at the small box of text expecting her death to hit him hard; still, nothing emotional broke inside him. The funeral home seemed to have used a standard template which lacked love. As Nick was the only family Jude had, there was no one else to have arranged the funeral, and it was left to a stranger to say goodbye.

"Well, that's it I guess. I have two days to work out who I will attend as. I'm guessing the police will be there hoping to trap me if I turn up." Nick wiped his hand and the screen disappeared.

"Do you think he will be there though?" Jen asked as she dragged on her jeans.

"I should think it would be something he would do, even if it is just to see if I go. He will want a reaction. Did I tell you he was waiting until I got there before killing her and disappearing? He made sure I knew he had killed her."

"No, that must have been horrible?"

Nick shrugged his shoulders.

"What will you do if he is there?" Jen asked.

"Nothing, it's not worth it. I might just go as a tree; no one will suspect me then."

Jen laughed and slipped her jacket on, "You ready?"

"Do you miss your son?"

"Don't mention him, just don't, not now. I let him go. I needed you more than he needed me. God, you can be a soulless arsehole!" Jen stormed out of the room.

"Jen, that's harsh! You know I'm fucking soulless. One day I will get it back and you will see a different me. You might not even like me!" Nick followed her out.

"Let's not mention my past; I can't think about it. All I think about is you and the pain I feel when you're not with me!" She hugged Nick and they left the flat holding hands.

Jude's funeral had been gifted with torrential rain and a small parade of raised umbrellas filled the courtyard of the tiny chapel. Nick had waited nearby whilst the procession, made up of friends and distant relatives, passed by and into the small building.

Nick had changed his appearance slightly so it wouldn't look obvious or recognisable. He had changed his hair colour, eye colour and weight. He had also found that aging himself changed him a good amount so that people wouldn't think he was the same age. He had used the new look outside, in shops, many times, over the last few days as his face was starting to be shown in local papers.

The service was really nice. The vicar talked about her life growing up, shared funny stories that friends had passed on, but said nothing about Nick or his father. This broke Nick's heart to know how much Jude would have insisted he talk about how much Nick had meant to her, or it would have broken his heart if he had a soul to feel it with.

He stayed at the back, watching, and noticed the odd time when people would uneasily look around at the large wooden doors waiting for someone else to walk in at any moment. He guessed that would be him that they were all waiting for. That's when he saw a very familiar face.

Nick repositioned himself to look through the gap between the well-wishers, a man who was sitting in the third row on the far side. Was that Anton? Surely not, he had crucified him and skinned him, or was it Lucifer?

As the funeral concluded, Nick waited and watched Anton thank the vicar and leave through the doors with everyone else back out into the rain. Nick held back. He was one of the last ones to thank the vicar.

Nick finally shook the vicar's hand.

"Thank you, it was lovely. Why didn't you mention her son?" he asked

"Thank you, sir. We thought it was for the best that he wasn't mentioned." The vicar answered.

"We? Who do you mean when you say we? If you don't mind me asking that is?"

"The police. Did you know her well?"

"Not really, always seemed lovely though. I used to see her about with her son; they seemed happy. What a shame." Nick shook his hand again and started to leave.

"You say you saw them together a lot? Have you seen him since?"

"I'm sorry Father, I haven't. I just don't think he's the one. Or maybe he's dead too?" Nick shrugged at the same time and left.

He caught up with the rest of the crowd and scanned for Anton. He saw him again, by himself, smiling. Watching the people talk with each other, crying, hugging, reminiscing about Jude. He heard the odd mention of his name, but nothing positive. He kept his distance but not so far as to stand out. Then up walked Anton.

"You know I could kill you here, right now in front of him!" He said pointing up at a crucifixion of Christ.

"You sick bastard, coming here, as Anton too!"

Lucifer smiled, "I thought it would be funny watching your reaction, trying to work out is it really him? But, my you really have outdone yourself. I could see it was you immediately, but they won't, especially the five police officers who were dotted about."

"Is this over yet?"

"No, this isn't over till I say it is, and I still have one last thing for you to do for me."

"What?"

"Patience, Nick, all in good time. Oh and by the way, when you leave your" Lucifer air quoted, "lover, the protection leaves too." Lucifer smiled and disappeared.

Nick looked around for him, then made sure he was out of sight from people and disappeared too, back to Jen before Lucifer got to her.

22

THE EX

Nick arrived in the living room of the flat; Jen wasn't there. He ran to the bedroom, but she wasn't there either. Kitchen, no.

"Jen?" Nick shouted "Jen?" No answer.

Nick ran to the entrance door to check, it was locked.

Had she gone out or had Lucifer got to her before he could get there, again?

As Nick walked back to the room he heard the key turn in the lock and he turned. The door opened and in walked Jen, with a couple of bags.

She closed the door and locked it again.

"What?" She asked as Nick stared at her.

"I thought he had got you!"

"He was there?"

Nick nodded, "But he had come as Anton! He knew me immediately; no one else did, but he knew."

"Anton? The one you killed?"

Nick nodded again, "He warned me about leaving you; that's why I panicked. Are you ok?"

"I'm fine – hungry – but fine."

Jen stood in the corridor with two bags, Nick grabbed them and walked into the kitchen.

"Just a minute, I think I better protect us first."

Nick waved his hands and recited the protection spell, a blurred, distorted wave faded through the flat.

"Ok, we should be fine whilst I am here."

"What happens when you aren't here though?"

"I don't know yet; maybe we need to be in a better place, somewhere he will never find us."

Jen took off her coat and stood in front of Nick with her hand rested resting around his neck.

"So, how was your mother's funeral?"

"It was done nicely, very tasteful. However, they never mentioned me." Nick looked at his feet.

"Understandable, considering you're the only suspect."

Nick pulled away, walked into the room and sat on the sofa.

"The disguise worked; no one recognised me."

"Apart from Lucifer!" Jen straddled Nick's legs and cuddled him.

"Apart from Lucifer, yes. Maybe, I need to go looking for him and hide you, so he can't find you."

"How? Where would I go?"

"I think I have to build something like he had, but I don't know how. I'll figure it out; I have to."

"Well there's no rush because you're here, and there is no reason for you to leave, is there?" Jen asked, "So, let's just figure this out later. Come on let's get some food." Jen got up and led him by the hand into the kitchen.

The blackness faded, and the view of a city from high up came into focus. A view from an office window high up in a city skyscraper.

He could sense Lucifer in the room, he was not physically there, but there was a remnant as if he had been there. He scanned the office, empty apart from an old desk in front of the window. Filing cabinets opened, paperwork lolling out of them and cascading onto the floor. It seemed as if someone had left in a hurry.

He felt that Lucifer had been here, but had left quickly. As he crossed the empty office to leave, he noticed a small patch of blood, stained into the carpet, by the desk. He bent down and examined it closely.

He touched the bloodstain, smelt his fingers, and closed his eyes, absorbing the memory.

He opened his eyes again and he could see a scene play out in front of him, but without sound. He could see Lucifer smash the man's head against the desk and drag him round to the front. Pushing a scroll in front of him and forcing him to sign it, which he did. Lucifer took the scroll, rolled it up and placed it inside his trench coat.

The scene faded to black, a few seconds passed and the light came back again. He was face to face with Lucifer.

"Don't you understand, you are not needed anymore? You fucked it up!"

"But I did everything you wanted me to do; what did I do wrong?"

"No you didn't, all you had to do was kill the child, that was it, but you left him and now look at him!"

"But he was just a child, I thought I only had to take the evil souls?"

"That's the problem with you; you think way too much!"

Lucifer yelled at him, whilst tapping his head with his forefinger like a woodpecker tapping for food.

Anton stepped into his vision, "You see, you need to do this. In order for you to step up, you need to do something so bad, without thinking. Your soul is tying you down; you need to be free from it in order to be the chosen one."

Lucifer grabbed Anton and dragged him out of earshot, "...No...can't know..."

He heard the odd word but couldn't hear everything being said.

"Look, I think we need to end this now, I don't think you're the one."

"No, I can do this, I have nothing else if you take this away from me. Please, I'm begging you!"

"No, I think it's over, I will leave you with some powers, just enough to improve your life, for you to get out of the gutter, but I am ending this now."

"Don't you fucking dare leave me!" He lunged forward to grab Lucifer.

Lucifer threw him across the room, "Don't be stupid! Never, ever do that again. I, will kill you next time."

"You took away everything I had; you owe me!"

"I owe you nothing!" And with that Lucifer clapped his hands and the room went black.

Nick woke up sweating, looked around the room expecting to see Lucifer, but realised it was another vision, and dropped back into bed, breathing heavily. Jen stirred at his side and she moved her arm around him. Feeling her warmth against him, he relaxed and dropped back to sleep.

Several hours later, Nick woke and kissed Jen on the side of her head to wake her.

"Jen," Nick nudged her softly.

Jen sleepily opened one eye, "Morning?" she mumbled.

"I need to go, I have to find someone."

"What?"

"I'm going to have to go. I've had a vision. I think there is another someone, like me, looking for Lucifer, hunting him down,"

Nick climbed out of bed and slipped his jeans on.

"What about me? What happens if Lucifer comes for me?" Jen sat up in bed, worried.

"I don't know. Stay out? I will only be gone this morning."

"And what if you're not? And why stay outside?"

"Look, if you're outside with other people, it will be harder for him to do anything to you," Nick explained.

"Really? Lucifer doesn't work in crowds? Don you think he actually would give a shit who was there and who saw?"

Nick knew Jen had a point, Lucifer didn't care where she was. If Lucifer wanted her, he would just visit her, whereever she was. But finding the guy in the vision was key to his next step. It felt like he had had the vision for a very clear reason, but he wasn't sure what that was.

"I don't think he will bother us. He still needs me for something else; otherwise, I'm pretty sure I would be dead by now. But, I do think this guy that I need to find is our answer to most things, including hiding you from him."

Nick got his boots on and turned to Jen, "Get dressed, go out. Somewhere busy, but get outside in crowds soon, please? I have to go now, I won't be long."

He reached into his pocket and pulled out his necklace; Nick rolled it in his hands.

"Put this on, it always brought me luck growing up."

He tossed Jen the necklace.

"Really? I don't remember you wearing it."

"I lost it then found it again. Wear it."

Jen examined the worn leather lace and rusty fastenings, placed it around her neck and tucked it inside her t-shirt.

Nick stood up, hugged Jen and clicked his fingers, leaving the room empty. Jen quickly got dressed to leave the flat.

Nick arrived outside a twenty-four-hour roadside diner, the kind you see in the movies set in America in the '60s. As he walked up to the door he realised that this didn't feel like the location, he had visited in his vision, but he knew he was at the right place. He walked in and could hear country music playing in the background, sounded like Johnny Cash but Nick wasn't sure.

As he looked around he noticed a young couple in the corner booth holding hands across the table, whispering to each other, every now and then letting out a muffled giggle. He walked over to the counter and asked for a coffee.

Nick sat there scanning the other booths and noticed another male looking out the window, sipping from a coffee cup, lost in his thoughts.

"That will be one dollar forty, sir," the waitress prompted Nick in an American accent.

Nick reached into his pocket and took out two dollars, "Keep the change!" Nick said. He grabbed his coffee and walked over to the man watching the world go by and sat opposite him.

"Took you long enough, Nick. I was wondering if you were still under his control?" the stranger said.

Nick took a sip of his coffee and recoiled slightly from the taste, "Sorry, you are?"

The stranger put his hand out to shake Nick's hand, "Travis, did Lucifer ever mention me?"

"No, you worked for him?" Nick asked.

"I was supposed to be his apprentice, with the prospects of becoming the King of Hell. But, it looks like you took the mantle instead, congrats." Travis took a sip of his coffee and looked back out of the window.

"You think I wanted this? My mother, dead? Being on the run from *him*?"

"Being on the run from him? Why are you escaping him? Oh, and by the way, my entire family was killed, so stop bitching! So, what did you do for you to be hiding?"

"I killed Anton..." Nick mumbled.

Travis spilt a bit of his drink down his chin in shock, "Anton's dead? Why? How?"

"I flailed him, crucified him, and left him to be found, dead. Needless to say, Lucifer wasn't happy, and then he killed my mother in revenge."

Travis looked up at Nick curiously, "To hear you talk you don't sound that bothered, to be honest. Did you even like your mother?"

"Of course I did, but Lucifer has removed my soul, and now I don't feel much at all. I know I should, but the heart is cold." Nick tapped on his chest to indicate the hollowness. "So, what is the story here? I guess you sold your soul to him in return for power, and money?"

"Oh yeah, but it wasn't as simple as that. I lost everything because I couldn't kill the way he wanted me to, I couldn't kill innocent people as he instructed. Could you?"

"I could now," Nick tapped on his chest again, "Don't feel

a thing. You seem to still have some powers, too. How do we still have powers?" Nick asked.

"I really don't know. Did you spend a lot of time with him? Did he teach you everything?" Travis sat forward in the seat in anticipation.

"I spent no time with him; it was all with Anton. I learnt the usual stuff, I guess, twisting reality to confuse or make people see something different, basic illusion stuff. But it wasn't until I met someone else, a vampire that I learned some advanced stuff. She shared teleportation and protective spells with me, that helped more than anything Anton taught me."

"Right, that's how you got here; I wasn't sure if you would be able to get to me, just in case they got to you first. I got more to be fair, maybe too much, but the protection sounds good, I could do with that."

Nick moved in close too now, "So, do you know how to create something like that amazing retreat he had? Oh man, I would love to be to know how to do that!"

Travis sat back in his seat, and tapped his chin with his empty cup, "Yeah I do; wanna trade?"

Nick picked up his coffee cup and took a sip. He noticed that the couple had gone and the juke box was still playing someone who sounded like Johnny Cash. He looked at Travis again and looking at the counter realised it was just the three of them. Nick, Travis and Johnny Cash.

"This isn't real is it?" Nick looked at his host who shook his head slowly.

Travis clicked his fingers to blackness, just the two of them left sat facing each other in the booth, with nothing else but them and Johnny still playing. "I wondered how long it would take for you to see through it."

"For fuck sake, turn this fucking music off!" Nick rubbed

his eyes and looked around waiting to see something, anything in the blackness.

The music stopped and left them in silence, in darkness, with only some form of a spotlight on the place they sat.

"Let me tell you a story and explain what I know that might help you, and then you can help me to track him down and end him. Trust me when I say he is planning something large and has been for a very long time." Travis stood up and started to walk, Nick followed.

"So, I showed you how I met Lucifer, how he forced me into signing the contract and how things went wrong. But there is more, certain things I think you need to see." Travis explained.

Nick stopped walking and Travis stopped too, and turned to face Nick.

"Look, it's nice to meet you and everything, but do I really need to walk-through memory lane with you and listen to you telling me how you cried yourself to sleep every night?"

"Sorry, I forgot you are the Lord of the lower dwellings and you know all!" Travis bowed in mock homage to Nick.

Nick groaned and said, "OK, let's get this over and done with." He walked up at the side of Travis, "Look, I have left someone alone and I don't want that bastard getting her."

"I thought you had a protection spell?"

"I do, but it doesn't work when I'm not there."

"Right, I won't be long, but you need to see these things and understand them. I think there will be a few things you will need to know to help you on your journey."

Nick and Travis continued into the darkness.

Jennifer quickly got dressed, grabbed her purse and shot for the door.

As she grabbed the door handle and unlocked it, she heard a knock from the other side.

Opening the door slowly she was greeted by a tall, well-dressed man holding a book in his hands.

"Excuse me, Madame, I'm sorry to disturb you, but I was hoping I could have just two minutes of your time to discuss our Lord and Saviour?" He smiled a cock-eyed smile.

"Sorry, not now I need to go, I'm in a rush."

"You see that's the problem with today's younger generations, always in a rush, never time to stop and have a small chat."

"Look, I really don't have time for this."

"Oh, I think you do, Jennifer!" The tall man smiled again and pushed her into the flat, locking the door behind him.

23

TRAVIS

Nick followed Travis into the dark, a single beam of light shone above them illuminating them and their path. Travis was in his late twenties, but the last couple of years had taken its toll on him, and he looked as though he were in his late thirties. He had lost his job, his wife and his child; now, his whole life had become void. He was stuck in this life, unable to regain any kind of normal life. Like Nick, he was wanted by the police for the murder of his wife and young son; they had been massacred in cold blood, massacred at the hands of Lucifer in Travis's image.

A glow started to radiate to the right of them, revealing two men sitting in a room talking, Nick recognised the room as Anton's room, and the two men, as Lucifer and Anton.

Travis turned to Nick and explained, "OK, this is the first conversation I stumbled across. I decided one day to try and keep a close eye on them. I knew they weren't happy with me, but I didn't know why."

Travis began to walk around the scene, "I had been on a couple of so-called, missions and I hadn't done that well. To be honest, I was a little green around the collar, and I didn't want to do anything too bad. Well, what I considered bad, anyway, I didn't want to hurt or kill anyone. But, as you know that's what they really want from you." Travis waved his hand and the scene started to come to life.

Nick's concentration was on the glowing recreation of the conversation between Anton and Lucifer. He could only see it through a slight gap through a partially closed door as that was what Travis had seen with his own eyes.

Anton sat in a chair by the archway window in his room; he looked up at Lucifer who was pacing in front of the fireplace.

"What is wrong with him? Why does he find it so hard to kill someone? I mean, he's not a little girl, is he? I have given him powers, he now has magic. He doesn't even have to make it gory. A simple strangulation would be fine." Lucifer continued to pace backwards and forwards.

"You have to understand this is not his world, and where you might be able to smite a human without even thinking about it, he will struggle. You have had thousands of years to hone your skills of torture and murder. It will take time for him to be anything like you. Take your time, break him slowly."

"Oh Anton, you're always too soft with him. If it were up to you, you would want to keep him as a pet. He's not though; he's a tool, a means to an end. And as a tool, he's just not fit for my purpose. I actually think he might be slow, you know in the head." Lucifer tapped his left temple with his forefinger.

"That's not true, Luci, you know that. I know what he is, but that is not going to help you whilst he is still soft on the inside. If he doesn't want to kill, how do we make him? What about his family?" Anton smiled at Lucifer, knowing that that could be the answer they needed.

Lucifer stopped pacing and looked an Anton, "You bad boy! Are you suggesting we kill his family?"

"No, just explain why he needs to start killing and make some shit up about his family, and how they could be hurt by the balance of karma or whatever shite you can think of."

"And, if he doesn't do as I ask, I will kill his family?"

"No, just hurt his family. But make it look like something else did it, not you. He needs to trust you."

"Fuck that! If he doesn't do it, I will kill them and make him watch so that shit is stained in his memory for the rest of his life."

Lucifer suddenly spun his head in the direction from where Travis was watching, and the image shrunk and disappeared.

Nick turned to Travis, "Did he see you? What did he do to you?"

"Nothing, he heard me but didn't see me." Travis laughed, "I got out of there pretty quick, acted dumb, and I'm pretty sure he bought it."

"What about your family?" Nick asked.

Travis's head dropped, "Yeah, he followed through with that. He made me know it too, and live through it over and over again. I think he thought it would break me, and it did, but I never let him know that though."

Travis wiped his face, removing a tear that had trickled down his cheek.

"Anyway, as you can see, at this point I knew they needed me to kill but I wasn't sure why? It just seemed pointless. He explained about the souls, but I didn't see why I had to do the killing when he could do it so efficiently himself. This all seemed strange to me."

Nick seemed surprised that no-one had explained to him

why he needed to reap souls, he had been not been told, or at least he thought he hadn't.

"Really? Anton explained to me why I needed to take souls, but I didn't understand why I only needed to kill a few people and not, well, everyone who was dying. He explained it was only the evil ones, the suicides, but again why only a few, when there was so much evil on earth and why suicides? What was the issue there? Guess these were just plants so I would start killing."

Nick looked into the darkness, thinking.

"OK, so you sold him your soul for success? Is that right?" Nick asked.

"Yes, but he didn't want my soul he just wanted me to do him favours. It seemed strange compared to all the books I had read, and trust me I read some seriously dark shit. So, when I managed to actually summon him, and, when he didn't want my soul, it threw me. The business did amazingly well with his help, but he became pushier with the favours, each becoming darker and darker. Let me show you."

Travis waved his hand and another ball of light revealed another scene to the left of them.

It took a few seconds for Nick to understand what he was looking at, as his eyes grew accustomed to the dark blues and shadows of the image that was being shown. He could make out two small beds, and a wardrobe. Then as things started to develop more clearly, he realised he was looking at a child's bedroom. The window was slightly ajar, and the curtains were slowly dancing in the night's breeze. Looking down he realised the two beds had two small boys in them; they looked no older than two, the same age as Travis's son. The picture turned quickly to depict Lucifer behind him.

"Why are we here? Please don't tell me…"

Lucifer looked pleadingly, "You see, you must

understand, these two small innocent boys have been placed on this earth, by him upstairs, to end me. I need them to die before they reach an age where they understand why they are here. And now is the best time whilst they are still, innocent."

Lucifer let the last word roll on his tongue, tasting it.

"They won't put up a fight. Look they're asleep too; it would be so easy just to tippy-toe up to them and slowly slice their tiny, weak throats -- easy and so simple. Remember though, you are doing this to save me and your company. If I die, so does your whole life."

"No, anything but this, I can't do this, Lucifer, please?" Travis begged.

"Travis, really not even for me? The one who has built your empire? Made you rich, successful? And all I ask is this tiny, incey-wincey task?"

Travis looked as though he were going to cry.

"Ok, ok, let's not then. In fact, let's just say, they become teenagers and they come to kill me, and they succeed. And then let's say, I have put something in place where ermm... If I die your beautiful wife and child are brutally murdered, torn to bits. And you can't stop it. So it would all be your fault. Do you really think you could live with yourself, knowing you could have saved them, just by doing this one little iddy-biddy thing?"

Lucifer ended with his bottom, lip out like a child. He played with each scenario, danced with his words like a child, like this act was only a tiny job that would be done in seconds and forgotten about just as quickly.

"I gather you still said no, then?"

Travis put his head down again and nodded.

Nick's attention returned to the scene again.

"Trav, was that a no?!"

Lucifer stood with his mouth open in shock.

"What, two children you don't even know, for your own flesh and blood? Well, that's what will be left anyway, a pile of flesh and blood. You really do surprise me, Travis, you really fucking do!"

Lucifer produced a scalpel from the air and walked over to the two children, he slowly slit their throats. One at a time as they slept; they didn't make a sound or move.

Lucifer turned, made the scalpel disappear and he wiped his hands showing that his completion of the task was nothing. As Lucifer passed Travis he wiped his bloody hands on Travis's coat, leaned in and whispered.

"Your poor family."

Lucifer stood waiting by the portal doorway.

Travis looked down at the two dead children. They lay quiet and still, whilst a crimson liquid slowly seeped onto the white pillows. He felt vomit come to his throat; then he realised what Lucifer had said and turned quickly, "Wait, what? But you killed them! They're not a threat anymore."

"No Travis, I slit their throats; I didn't kill them. Only you could have killed them, but you didn't. Let's go." Lucifer stood with his arms folded standing at the portal, disappointment written over his face.

"But they're dead, I saw the blood. They're dead!"

"No, they are bleeding Travis, they will be saved." Lucifer's tone changed as he went from calm and disappointed to angry.

"I don't understand you. I mean, you want the world but are not willing to commit to the fight -- weak."

Travis entered the portal and the room went dark.

"Did he kill the kids then?" Nick looked at Travis.

"Yes, they were dead. He didn't lie; my family paid for me not killing the babies. But later, he told me that the two kids were innocent, and he needed me to kill them. There was a special task that he needed me to do, and I wouldn't have to do anymore. By killing them, I would have lost my soul; it was all about innocence. He never told me what that task was for though."

Travis started to walk again.

Nick reached out and grabbed Travis.

"Hang on, why didn't he just do to you what he did to me? He told me he has my soul. Do you think that's true?"

"Nick, I don't know where your soul is. It's not in you, I can see that. I know he found out a way to achieve that via magic. I know he didn't have it when I was with him. But around four months ago, he paid a visit to an old voodoo witch in New Orleans. He spent two weeks with her learning as much as he could. When I found out about this news, I tracked her down and I managed to speak to her. She told me that he was a nice man who just wanted to know about the creation and control of zombies."

"Zombies? Why Zombies?" Nick asked.

"Soul extraction is used when you are trying to control zombies. The Bokor would extract the soul to heighten their power and use that to control the zombie more easily, or so the legend goes. He would have to keep the soul close to him, so he may have it with him somehow."

"A what? Bokor?" Nick asked.

"Voodoo sorcerer."

"Right…So, I'm a zombie then?"

"No, you're not dead; you need to be dead, well almost dead, to be a zombie. You wouldn't be much use to him if you were dead. He has just removed your soul. The line of right and wrong will seem hazy for you, if not non-existent. I guess you still know right from wrong because that's your brain controlling that. But your heart, your soul, the part that makes you feel right from wrong – the remorse, the fear – that's all gone."

"Yep, bang on, living zombie! So I guess he perfected the skill of soul removal then. The question is how do I get it back?" Nick asked.

"I don't know, I never thought he would have achieved it so easily though," Travis said.

"Why did you think he wouldn't be able to learn magic like voodoo? It's Lucifer, the fallen angel, the light-bearer! All magic must be easy for him."

"I know, I know. Let me ask you, I presume you were advised, well, told to kill?"

"Yes," Nick answered.

"Did you decline?"

"Yes, at first, I tried different ways to get out of killing people. They didn't like it though, Anton kept pushing me to take more souls. Then one morning I woke up empty; I mean really empty. I thought I was just really hungry at first, and no matter what I ate, it wouldn't fill me. So I just gave up and then the killing didn't bother me. I knew certain things were wrong, but I didn't worry about them; they just seemed normal."

"Ok, so what they wanted me to do would have been the same, I guess. Maybe taking an innocent life may have destroyed my soul or at least removed it. I guess that could have been it, or that is what they believed anyway."

"Right, so what now? You mentioned a special task; any idea what he meant by that or what it was? And do you know where he is now?" Nick was eager to learn his fate, but also he now knew that Lucifer must still have his soul.

"I really don't have anything else, that's it. Oh, yes, one last thing, you want to learn how to create your own space, and I will need that protection spell off you too."

Nick explained the details of the protection spell, and how he learned it from Melina. In return, Travis explained how to build a space for his retreat and create each aspect including the environment. Nick realised he could combine the protection spell and the retreat spell. He was hopeful he would be able to protect Jen whilst he left her alone.

"Travis, I better get back, I have left someone alone, while he is still lurking somewhere. Thank you for everything, and I hope one of us finds him soon, and we can end all of this." Nick shook Travis's hand.

"Yes, go, and remember if you need me you know where to find me now." Travis pulled him in for a hug, "Good luck, Nick"

Travis clicked his fingers and they were back in the diner.

Nick looked around, "This is your retreat then?"

"We all need somewhere we feel safe and happy, I pretty much grew up in one of these. My mother worked in one when I was younger -- the best days of my life."

Nick smiled, took one last look around, clicked his fingers and he was gone.

24

TORTURE

Nick returned to the flat's hallway. He looked around to make sure Jennifer had taken his advice and had gone out. The dark hallway was empty apart from a couple of coats hanging on the hooks. Nick checked the door handle making sure it was locked and it was. Nick followed the shaft of light coming in from the living room door, he pushed the door open and immediately saw Jen sitting on the chair by the window, bleeding and unconscious. Her arms hung behind her, tied, and her head was slumped forward, blood slowly dripping from her mouth.

"Jen! Jen! What the fuck has happened? Jen?" Nick grabbed her shoulders and lifted up her head.

"Nick, let her sleep, she's had it rough over the last few hours."

Nick spun around to see Lucifer standing behind the door. He lunged for him, Lucifer raised his hand and telekinetically pushed Nick backwards and held him there.

"Calm down, don't run before you can walk. So, where have you been whilst we've been getting to know each other? By the way, she was delicious."

"You fucker! I will kill you!"

"No, Nick, you won't, not if you want her to live."

Lucifer smiled and stroked Jen's bloodied hair.

"I mean, it would be a shame for her to die, such a pretty whore. Well, she was pretty anyway. How old is she Nick, she seems older than you? Never took you to be a toy-boy. Mind you, you are a boy and you seem to be most people's toy."

Nick unable to move his limbs, gritted his teeth in rage, trying to get free, but without success.

"Leave her alone! I swear I will fucking destroy you one day!"

Nick tried to work free, but his struggles were useless.

"What do you want from me now?"

"I think I have an answer to end all of this, and maybe for you to get your mother back."

Lucifer stopped stroking Jen's hair and walked back to Nick.

"Do you want that? To get your mother back? Get your life back?"

"You know I do, but why would you give me this after what I did to Anton? Do you know he cried? He screamed your name!" Nick spat the image at Lucifer.

Lucifer brought a clenched fist around and it landed, hard, on the side of Nick's face. Nick could tell Lucifer held back on the power in the punch because it didn't kill him.

"How dare you even say his name! Do you want me to rip her fucking heart out, you fucking mag..." Lucifer stopped himself and refocused.

Nick, spat blood from his mouth, "What do you want?"

Lucifer shook his head as to dispel any negative thoughts.

"Right, yes. I just want you to pass a message onto someone for me, during your next task. It really is that simple, a simple message. Do you think you can do that without fucking it up?"

Lucifer's frustration was clear as he tried to hold it in.

Nick started to wonder just how sane Lucifer was. His mood swings were all over the place, completely erratic.

"Task? Where do want me to go? Who do I need to pass the message to? What's the message?"

"First of all, your mother. I think I can get her back to you. All you need to do is just beg for her, not me. You don't beg me; you need to beg Hades." Lucifer rested his chin on his palms and smiled.

"What? Have you completely lost your mind? How do I even get there, and won't he just kill me?"

"No, not you, Nick, King of Hell! He has to see you, he has to listen to you, You're Nick..."

"King of Hell... Yeah, yeah I get that. How do I even get there?"

Lucifer grinned, "I KILL YOU!" He laughed, then cupped his hand over his mouth to quiet himself, "Sorry, well, I sort of kill you."

"No, forget it; you're not killing me."

Lucifer stood holding his chin in thought.

"Ok, then I kill her then," he said pointing at Jen.

Jen stirred, and Nick quickly reconsidered. "Ok, just let me go and let's discuss this like adults. I won't attack you; just don't hurt her anymore. She doesn't need to be involved with this."

"Oh, yes, yes of course." Lucifer clapped his hands in excitement, and Nick dropped to the floor.

"So you will do it? Go see Hades?"

"If I do this, you leave us alone, forever?"

"Yes, of course, you have my word."

Lucifer crossed his chest where his heart should be.

"And you fix her now!" Nick demanded.

Lucifer paused, "Really? I'm very happy with my art on her, she bled so easily. I can see why you like her."

"Now!"

"Ok, ok. Honestly, no-one appreciates talent anymore. Fine."

Lucifer clapped his hands.

Jen started to cough, Nick grabbed her.

"Are you ok? Jen?"

He held her head and lifted it up to look at him. No blood was visible and the cuts had healed. Jen looked up at Nick and started to cry; then her eyes suddenly met Lucifer's, who sat near the door waving with his fingers and smiling. Her body jerked away, trying to escape.

"Get rid of him! Nick, get rid of him now! Please Nick, please!"

"Calm down, it's ok. He's not going to hurt you anymore. Jen, look at me! At me, Jen!"

Nick grabbed her head, turning it, forcing her to make eye contact with him.

"He needs me to do something for him, and in return, he will leave us alone."

"You can't trust him; its fucking Lucifer, he lies."

Lucifer put up a hand, "Actually, that's Beelzebub, my cousin. Don't lend him anything, you will never see it again!"

"Ignore him; just look at me, I just need to take a trip and pass a message on, that's all. Trust me, you will be fine."

Nick looked deep into her eyes, and she slowly nodded. Nick stroked Jen's hair and he smiled at her. Nick looked around at Lucifer.

"Any reason why you're still here? Can't we do this somewhere else? I need to sort a few things out, and I will come to you. OK?"

Lucifer looked at Nick and his expression went from excited to cautious within seconds.

"You won't know how to find me; you better just meet me here, Nick. You have forty-eight hours or I will be back here ripping your pet to pieces, and don't think I won't!"

Nick agreed and stood up in front of Lucifer; he looked small compared to Lucifer.

"I will be here. Now leave us alone."

"Forty-eight hours Nick. Don't be stupid."

Lucifer popped his head around Nick.

"Bye, Jen, nice playing with you." He finger waved again and gave Nick a threatening look, then he clapped his hands and vanished.

Jen jumped up and grabbed Nick. They clung on to each other, knowing just how close they had come to things going so very badly for them.

"What did he do to you, Jen? What did he do?" Nick asked pulling her away from him by her shoulders.

She patted herself down checking where he had cut her, stabbed her, punched and kicked her. She felt her jaw and checked for missing teeth, they had returned. Lucifer had tortured her straight for four hours, slowly. He had definitely introduced himself to her.

"I think I'm ok; everything he did, it's gone, nothing." Jen broke down in tears.

"Oh, Nick. Why did you take so long, I thought it was never going to end. I tried to leave as soon as you left, but he was at the door. He pretended to be a vicar, then before I knew it he had pushed me back in, locked the door and forced himself on me!" Jen grabbed Nick again crying and he embraced her again.

"He didn't.. you know, he didn't actually force himself on you did he?"

"No! Why did you presume that? No, he didn't rape me or do anything like that. He tortured me, Nick! Isn't that enough?" Jen pushed his hold off of her.

"You said he forced himself on you; I just wanted to understand what he had done. I want to know you're ok."

"I'm not ok, Nick. He hurt me, over and over again. I am pretty sure there were moments I died, but just as it started to go dark, he would bring me back. That was the worst part, not like being shocked back, like if I was defibrillated, but like being recharged slowly. Being made to relive each cut and gouge backwards, slowly. Four times that happened, Nick, four times I was made to go through that."

Jen screamed at him.

"So don't ask if I'm OK, because since I met you, I'm not ok, Nick! And where were you? Where did you go? Why weren't you here? It had better have been fucking worth it!"

Jen had made a clear space between them, separating them to vent her rage.

Nick made a grab for her arm to pull her close again, but Jen shoved his hand off her.

"Jen, I needed to find him; he has told me things that can help us."

Nick tried to pull her close again, but again she pushed his hand off of her.

"Jen, you need to be close, so we can teleport out of here. We can be safe." Nick pleaded.

"Where are you taking me?"

"Away from here, I can build us whatever we want; we will be safe." Nick pulled her in, and this time Jen let him.

"Can we ever return here?"

"Yes, but we need to get out of here and be somewhere safe. I need to get you safe. Are you ready?"

Jen held on to Nick and closed her eyes; Nick clicked his fingers.

Jen felt the floor disappear from under her feet, her whole body felt as though it were being torn apart, as though she was being stretched like toffee. She could feel her stomach trying to escape through her throat and into her mouth; she opened her eyes to see a vastness of nothing, oceans of black drifted on for miles, as far as she could see. She held on to Nick tighter and then suddenly something touched her feet. It was solid like earth, but she couldn't see it, just blackness.

Nick released his hold, and Jen stumbled, battling with her brain and the fear of falling into the emptiness. Nick clicked his fingers and shone a light on them.

"This will probably feel strange at first, but once we have something solid, some ground you will feel better." Nick looked around pleased with himself.

"This day just keeps getting worse, I feel sick." Jen bent forward and released the contents of her stomach.

"Yeah, I threw up a lot at first; teleportation is not good. But you get used to it." He rubbed her back and she stood up straight wiping her mouth. Nick clicked his fingers and the area below Jen's feet cleared.

"Where the hell are we, Nick? I thought you had brought me away, somewhere safe?"

"This is what Travis showed me. He said it's called the Dark Space; it's somewhere between reality, and what we use to create an image of what we want you to see."

Jen was confused, trying to keep herself from throwing up again.

"Let me explain. If I want you to see something, I can manipulate the area around us, create objects, buildings, nature, people – exactly how I want to. Or I can recreate something from your memory, watch."

Nick clicked his fingers and created a doorway in front of them. "Open it."

Jen walked forward and turned the handle on the hovering door. It opened onto a very familiar room.

"Nick, I know this house."

She slowly walked in and looked around the large living room.

"This is my Grandma's house, how is this possible? How do you know what it looks like? It even smells the same. How?"

"I can see your memories, sense what you sensed. I know how much this meant to you. I wanted you to feel safe."

"Does it have the garden too?"

"Go see."

Jen walked through the living room, the kitchen and the patio doors out into a long garden that was part grass then part sand as it joined the beach. She saw the ocean spread out before her, heard the seagulls above her. She looked up into a beautiful, clear, blue sky. And turned to see the cottage in all its glory secluded in such a perfect sweeping setting. The darkness had all gone, replaced by Jen's Grandma's beach cottage.

Nick was leaning on the patio door frame, smiling.

"Is this ok for the time being? However, I must warn you, there is no town, no other people, just us and this."

"It's perfect, I love it." She ran up to grab Nick, then paused, "Don't think I have forgotten that you left me to get tortured today; I'm still angry with you."

"Of course not, but don't forget, I have only two days before I have to go again. I get the feeling I have to do that. Even though this place is protected, it doesn't mean there isn't anything he can do to me. I mean, I don't know what happens if he suddenly decides to cut off my powers. I don't know what would happen to this place."

Nick stroked Jen's shoulder, "Look, I know I seem dead inside, and I should have reacted differently with Lucifer, but I saw he had healed you, and he didn't kill you or me, so I was grateful for that."

Jen held his hand.

"I know you're empty inside and that your head works differently from mine. Do you think you will ever get your soul back?"

"Maybe, I don't know, I will hopefully get it back after this last job. I'm not looking forward to it though. Wonder how bad it will be when I can feel again – you, my mum, the things I have done, with no remorse."

Nick leaned in and gently kissed Jen on her lips; she received him and pulled his body in closer. She could feel the heat from the afternoon sun beating down on her back. With the familiar scent from her Grandma's kitchen wafting into her nostrils, she relaxed, for the first time in months.

Nick picked her up and carried her down to the beach.

"And you say there's no-one else here, or able to watch us?" Jen asked.

"No, just us, this world belongs to us."

"Put me down then. Fancy a dip in the ocean?"

Nick put Jen down gently on the warm sand, laughing she removed her clothes and shouted.

"The last one in makes tonight's meal."

With that, she slipped off her underwear and ran for the sea. Nick followed suit and removed his clothes, running down the beach towards the sea throwing his garments off as he tried to catch Jen, before she jumped into the clear, crystal blue water.

"The sea was never this clear or warm when I was younger," Jen said.

"I know, but it can always be like this, every day for you now."

Nick grabbed Jen; they stood in the wet warm sand as it melted between their toes under the water. The gentle waves lashed around their naked bodies, but they were lost in their own arousal.

25

THE TRIAL

Nick woke to the sound of seagulls overhead, as he had done the past two mornings. He could feel the warmth from the sun as it radiated through the windows and engulfed his semi-exposed torso. The past forty hours had been beautiful but uneasy, knowing he would soon be facing a journey to somewhere he was pretty convinced that didn't exist, or if it did, he wouldn't be coming back from.

He had seen horrors over the past eight months that he hadn't believed could happen; he had endured scenes of violence that no one should ever have to see. But he had lived through them and come out the other side untouched.

Maybe it was just the lack of a soul that stopped him from feeling anything, or maybe it was something worse. Maybe he had become totally detached from the evils that he had seen and done. Seventeen-year-old Nick would never have understood the horrific lifestyle he now lived, nor should anyone else, he thought, no matter how old they were.

Nick walked to the window that looked out onto the garden blending into the sea. The glow warmed his skin as he bathed in the fake sunshine that he had created. This world they now occupied was nothing but a pocket of reality that was only there because he willed it.

The thought then hit him like a hammer between the eyes. What would happen to Jen in this world if Nick were to die on his journey? Would this place still exist? Would Jen die? If his magic were keeping this alive; how would she stay protected if anything went wrong?

But as soon as these questions arrived in his head, the thought of food entered and he felt that the last breakfast was more important. His brain, however, still asked the questions that his heart was no longer thinking of.

Jen reached out to wrap herself around Nick, but as her hand met an empty bed, she panicked and patted the area she expected him to be. She sat and looked around, paused her breathing, listened and then she heard the clattering around in the kitchen below. Grabbing a gown, she ventured downstairs.

"You scared me, Nick. You weren't there; I thought you had already gone!" Jen stressed.

"I woke up and was hungry; I thought it would be nice to bring you breakfast in bed."

"Why are you cooking? I thought you would just magic the food like normal?"

"I was going to, but I needed to do something, you know, to keep my mind from racing away. I woke up to so many questions in my head that I needed to re-focus."

"Like what?" Jen asked sliding on to a stool close to the kitchen counter.

"What would happen to you and this place if anything happened to me?"

"Do you think anything will happen to you? What *will* happen to me?"

"See, I had those questions too. I don't think anything will happen to me, but if it does I don't know. If I die, I don't know if this place dies too and everything inside it, or if it doesn't, how do you get out? Or do you pop back into reality, and he's there waiting for you? I don't know! Eggs?"

"Jesus Christ, Nick! Why aren't you panicking? I am! How are you so calm?"

Nick tapped on his chest then gestured with his forefinger as he pretended to slit his throat.

"I will be fine; I can't see any reason why he needs to kill me."

Nick then remembered what Lucifer had said about killing him.

Jen was starting to grasp her chest and breath heavily, Nick put his arms around her and pulled her close.

"Don't worry I will be back; it's just a little journey. I make them all the time. I killed a serial killer in America once."

She pushed him away, "I don't need to know that; I need to know you will be fine, I WILL die without you. Don't you understand how bad I get when you're not with me? How I need to have you with me? I crave you so bad!" Jen pulled him in again.

He stroked her hair, "I know, I know… do you want mushrooms?"

Jen pushed Nick away again, "Fuck sake, Nick! You know I hate mushrooms."

"I know, just joking."

For the rest of the morning, they had sex on the beach. Realising the sand was a little too real, they moved up onto the grass. At around two o'clock, Nick decided that he had better be getting ready and say his goodbyes before Lucifer came looking.

He promised to stay alive. Along with that promise, he vowed he would return and create a better life, a real-life together.

She had decided to stay, and if she were to die, she would die in something that was part of him. They embraced each other for what felt like the last time.

Jen started to cry and Nick lifted her face up to see his eyes.

"I will return Jen, I promise. There is nothing in my life that is more important than you. I will fight for you, Jen. I will live for you!"

Nick lifted her up and held her tight, her tears now covering his and his face. Nick put her down kissed her one last time and smiled. He clicked his fingers and vanished leaving Jen slumped on the floor hysterical.

Nick arrived back at Jen's flat; the place looked as though a break-in had just happened, with furniture strewn on the floor, broken and bloodstained. He started to try and tidy a few things up to pass the time.

"Should I get you a maid's outfit?" A voice came from behind Nick. Spinning round in surprise, Nick nearly stumbled over the coffee table.

"Fuck sake Lucifer, why do you do that?"

Lucifer sniggered, "It's funny watching you shit yourself."

"Fuck you!" he screamed, pointing at Lucifer and making sure that he knew that was aimed at him.

"Are we going to get this done or are you just going to insult me all day?"

Lucifer stuck his bottom lip out like a child.

"Nicholas, why are you always wanting to rush things? I mean it's like you never want to spend time with me. Do I frighten you that much?"

"I am not afraid of you, or what you intend to do to me. You did that by removing my soul. Now let's get this done."

Lucifer placed his left hand on Nick's shoulder, then with his right hand and another left hand, he clapped. The noise was deafening like sticking his head under a rushing river. Nick's legs buckled under the force of the landing as he hit the ground hard; Lucifer didn't buckle.

Nick stood up, having to pull his hand up from the soft, tacky floor. Looking around, he saw a wall that seemed to be made out of flesh, blood and bone, stretching from left to right as far as he could see. The sky, a dark, electric blue, was populated with odd red and grey clouds. This is what he imagined hell to be like. What he had seen so far was not hell, but this, he believed, was.

"Is this Hell?" Nick asked, trying to take it all in.

"This? No, Nick, this is your trial!"

"Trial? What trial? I thought you just wanted me to pass a message on?"

"Oh yes, that's right, I still do want that. But for you to enter Hades, you need to pass a trial. You see you're not dead, or dead as in naturally dead, and only the dead can enter there. Unless, you have what is at the centre of that maze."

"So, what do I have to do?"

"You have to enter the maze and find the Tri-Wizard Cup!"

"What?"

Lucifer stood there staring at the pulsing wall. "It's a maze." He pointed, again straight-faced.

Nick turned to face Lucifer, "Is this a joke? Are you taking the piss? The fucking Tri-Wizard Cup? The maze is made out of fucking faces and you're taking the piss? What the fuck is wrong with you?"

Lucifer burst out laughing.

"Your face!" He laughed, pointing at Nick. "Your fucking face. Oh god, I could do this all day, can't you?"

"Oh yeah, this is great. I mean as long as you're having a laugh! Get me out of here, now!"

"No, you can't leave unil you complete the test or die trying at least," Lucifer said, this time with no laughter.

"I'm sorry. I was only joking, about the cup; you have to find the Talisman of Fire in the middle though, you will need it to pass to Charon to travel the River of Styx."

"Charon?"

"Yes Charon, the ferryman, River of Styx?"

Nick just looked at Lucifer blankly.

"Really? Do you actually know nothing about the underworld?"

"The thing is, the books and TV in the real world," Nick air quoted the real world, "doesn't contain that much real, actual knowledge about down here. You see, when you die, you die. You don't go back and tell everyone, hold PowerPoint presentations with your work colleagues or share picture slides with the family. No-one really knows what happens after death." Nick looked at his watch, "Are we actually going to do anything today?"

"Fucking petulant child! You've changed Nick; you really have."

"Someone taking your soul will do that. That reminds me when do I get it back?"

Lucifer winced, sucking through his teeth.

"Not sure that you will want it back mate; it's a bit damaged now."

He looked back to the fleshy wall, clapped his hands, and

the wall opened in front of them. As the opening grew, the screaming began.

Lucifer looked at Nick and flashed his eyes in excitement. "Ooo! Goosebumps! Are you ready?"

Nick nodded and Lucifer screamed, "GO!" In a booming voice that shook Nick's skull.

Nick ran to the opening. The stench of rotting meat hit his nostrils as soon as he turned his first corner, this made him throw up. With each turn the smell faded, and he started to feel more at ease. Not really thinking about what direction he was going; he just wanted to get this over and done with.

Nick had always hated mazes after getting lost in one when he was nine. His mother had taken him to a local farm which hosted the largest maze in the country. They had entered and followed the instructions, but, as Jude had turned a corner, Nick had turned in the other direction, not paying attention. When Jude had turned to say something, Nick was gone, and she couldn't find him. It had taken the guides an hour to find him, crying huddled in a corner.

With each turn he made he expected some creature or something standing there to fight, but it was just him, alone in the dark, in the rotted-flesh maze.

He took the next left, which was a dead-end, turned back and took the right instead. He felt as though he had already been here for hours. The next corner had to be the one, then the next.

He was getting frustrated now, he took the next right and saw a long straight. Nick ran to the end, but it was another dead end. He stopped and screamed in frustration; the wall in front of him screamed back in a mocking response. He turned and ran to the end again, listening to the now laughing wall fade. He took the other turn instead.

As he turned the corner, the walls opened up and in the

centre. There in front of him, a pedestal sat and an amulet hovered above it. The pedestal was, however, surrounded by a ring of blue fire.

"Oh for fuck sake! Fire? Was the maze not enough?" Nick screamed into his hands.

A booming voice rained over him.

"NO!"

Nick also heard, what he thought was a giggle.

He walked over to the pedestal, took off his coat, and without thinking put his hand through the fire for the amulet, this made the flames grow taller. Instantly pain shot up through his arm into his chest, he pulled his arm back, quickly.

Nick checked his arm for burns but it was clear. He tried to produce something to use to reach through the fire for the amulet, but something wasn't clicking, and it seemed his magic wasn't working.

Looking around for something to use, he noticed a few limbs in the wall, slightly protruding. Nick walked over and stuck his fingers into the wall around the arm and pulled; as he did, the screaming started again.

"Ere, what do you think you're doing, that's my arm," a voice screamed from the wall.

Nick saw the face that the arm belonged to, but it didn't look to be in a position to be joined.

"Listen, I just need to borrow it, two minutes, then I will bring it back, I promise."

Nick continued to wriggle it loose from the wall.

A different face shouted at Nick, "Oi! That's my arm, shit bag!"

Nick looked to the other face.

"Really don't care. What are you going to do, spit at me?"

"Don't think I won't. Look 'ach ya, thinking you're better than us, just because you're not a wall!"

"I am better than you, you're a fucking wall."

Nick pulled the arm again and it plopped out, the screaming and insults continued. He walked over to the fire and stuck the severed arm through the flames, the voices from the wall shouted abuse at him. Slowly the screaming stopped and all four walls started shouting obscenities at him instead.

Nick managed to knock the amulet to himself, it rolled out of the flames and onto the tacky floor. He reached down to pick it up, but not before several fingers poked out of the floor and hooked onto it, he stamped on them and pulled the amulet free.

Nick threw the arm back at the wall, "Thanks boys; here's your arm back."

"Arsehole!"

The faces shouted back, spitting in his direction. Quickly all the rest of the faces began spitting at Nick.

"Nice!"

As he left the area to go back down around the corner, he heard a loud crack, and he was suddenly back with Lucifer. As he landed, his leg gave way again, and sent him spinning across the floor.

"Nicky, Nicky, Nicky, well done! You have the amulet. The arm was inspiring, by the way. Bet the boys were pleased?"

"They were not happy at all; dirty bastards were spitting."

Nick flipped the amulet round in his hands looking at the design.

"Ok, so you did the trial. You have the amulet. We now need to get you to the river. Shall we go?" Lucifer rubbed his hands together, whilst his shoulders danced in excitement.

"Ok, let's just do this. I'm not looking forward to this, for some reason, it doesn't feel right."

Lucifer crouched down to be eye level with Nick, then he placed his hands on each shoulder, "Nick, this is the part that you, *might* not like."

"What do you mean? I haven't liked any of this so far!" Nick replied.

"No, I mean, you *really* won't like the next bit."

Lucifer tightened his grip on Nick's shoulders and shook them a little.

"Let's just do it. Whatever it is, it can't be any worse than your fucking ugly, bad-breathed face directly in mine, grinning like a twat!"

"Ok, Nick. You want to be nasty about this then, sorry to do this buddy! Actually, I'm going to really enjoy doing this."

Lucifer looked down at his feet, raised his face, smiled at Nick, and very quickly grabbed both sides of Nick's head and twisted, hearing the snapping of his spine, Nick's eyes rolled back in his head and he collapsed to the floor, dead.

The waters gently lapped against the pebbles on the side of the river as the green mist crept along the shore. Nick's body lay motionless, his face to one side, his eyes, glazed over like clouded glass, staring up into his head.

The mist started to billow in the distance as a force pushed its way through the waters slowly. It eventually came to a stop on the shore. A dark-cloaked figure stepped out of the boat and into the shallow water. The pebbles crunched and creaked as the feet pressed against each other under the ferryman's weight. Slowly, he walked up the shore to the corpse laying on its back. The cloaked figure looked down inspecting his find. A Nike Air Jordan poked out beneath the cloak, and softly kicked Nick's arm, his body rocked slightly in response.

Charon crouched down and touched Nick's forehead with an ancient finger. Nothing happened. Charon rubbed his hands together to give them warmth and touched Nick's forehead again. Again nothing happened. He rubbed his hands and breathed hot air through his fingers bringing them to life as much as he could and touched Nick's forehead again.

A slight crackling sound was heard and Nick sat bolt upright, gasping for breath. Coughing, he spat out some congealed blood on to the pebbles. Looking around at the cloaked figure, he jumped to his feet panicking, bracing himself to fight.

Charon stepped back and flashed the palm of his hands to calm Nick down.

"Woh! Chill out dude, It's ok, I'm here for you; you're on my beach so you must be here to pass over?"

Nick stood shocked. He stared at Charon, puzzled by his surfer-dude accent.

"Where am I? I mean… What just happened?"

"Oh shit, you're not one of them are you? Sent straight here with no explanation? I hate it when that happens. Ok, it's cool; let's see, what was the last thing you remember?"

"Err… I don't know... it seems blurry…"

"That's fine, sometimes things take a while to spark to life again. Can you remember anything before now?"

"I vaguely remember a maze, lots of people shouting, screaming... erm... a medal... Ok! I had just done a trial; then there was a medallion… and then I came out of the maze back to… Oh, SHIT! The bastard! He killed me!"

"And there it is, you remember now? See I told you it just needs a moment for it to trigger. Right, so as you probably realised, you're dead, and by the sounds of it, you weren't expecting to die. It's not normal to be here and not be prepared for your journey. Normally, you would have a week or two to wander around with the living to get used to being dead, then, when you have your funeral you pass down here. You have accepted the inevitable. Well, most people do anyway."

"No, I think this just happened, or it feels like that anyway."

"Seems like you have been involved with some powerful shit coming straight here. To be fair, when I tried to wake you, I actually thought you wouldn't start. Everyone wakes on the first touch, the odd one takes the second touch, but the third, never. You're the first one, man. I was going to kick you into the waters, and let the others have you." Charon stood up, removing his ragged hood, revealing a shoulder-length bleach blonde head of hair, chiselled features and empty eye sockets.

"Sorry, this is going to sound ignorant of me, but who are you?" Nick asked.

"Hi, I'm Charon, I will be your ferryman tonight, bud." Charon bowed, "But first, I require payment, no obolus, no Hade's bus, ya get me?"

Charon held out a thin hand to Nick.

"I'm presuming you have payment then? Normally it's in your mouth." Charon asked pointing at his opened mouth.

"A what?" Nick asked.

"An obulus, a coin, payment."

Nick ran his tongue around his mouth and didn't find anything in his mouth. He then searched his pockets, rummaging for the talisman he had won in the trial.

"Err... I have this." Nick handed over the talisman to Charon.

He flipped the gold talisman over a few times in his hand, it was roughly the size of an Olympic gold medal. It had an image of an embossed burning Phoenix on one side and a skull on the other. He looked up at Nick, "Dude, who the fuck are you? This is the Talisman of Fire. I have seen this only once before, and that dude was after the throne of Hades. You better not be back to try to finish off what he started?"

Nick presumed he was talking about Lucifer; he felt it were best if he kept it to himself.

"Really? What happened?"

"Well, Lucifer, presume you have heard of him?"

Nick nodded trying to keep his face emotionless.

"Ok, well he did the trial to claim the Talisman of Fire. He had gained knowledge that you can use this to cross Styx to access Hades. Well, he was right. It is one of the six medallions in the world that can be used to make this journey without receiving an obulus. There is also another rule with these medallions and that is: If you have one of these, I have to take you, no questions asked."

"Ok, so what happened with Lucifer when he came down here?"

"Well he gave me the medallion, I took him and then he tried to take Hades out,"

Charon ran his finger across his neck.

"But he failed, and now there is a spell on him that stops him being able to pass the doors of Hades. Besides, I can never carry him again, and this is the only way anyone can pass to Hades. He might be the King of Hell, but he can't cross here anymore. So, how did you get the medallion?"

"I did the trial, I got the medallion. I had heard I could beg for my mother's life. She was killed."

"Oh, sorry dude. But how did you hear about the trial? I mean the trial is one of the darkest magics; it's not something humans hear of. You didn't ask for Lucifer's help did you?"

"No, the dark web is a very dark place."

"Ok dude, I don't know what the dark web is, but, I will take you, but I am really not happy about it. However, you do meet the requirements. You are dead, and you had payment, even though it is the Talisman of Fire."

Charon paused and looked Nick over again.

"Ya better climb aboard, buddy."

Charon walked back down the shore to the boat and climbed on.

Nick walked along the beach hearing the pebbles squeak below his feet, looking down he realised what he thought were pebbles were actually bones rounded and eroded with time. Nick climbed onto the boat a little faster.

"What are the chances of coming back with what I want?"

"All depends on what mood the big man is in."

Charon walked to the far end of the boat and he lifted his arm up summoning an orb out in front to shine the way. The orb of light and the boat slowly moved out into the river.

Nick looked behind him to see the small island of green haze get smaller as the boat moved out further onto the River Styx.

The darkness surrounded them on all sides, Nick could only hear the ripples of water hitting the boat and the odd moan from deep within the darkness.

"Charon, is it?" Nick asked.

"Or Haros, the new dudes call me that, but I prefer Charon, so Charon it is."

"You are not what I expected. I mean, I expected a silent, hooded skeleton or something eerie, but you sound like a stoner. It feels like you should be driving a kids' school bus. I mean, I have seen drawings and paintings. Okay, you do have the cloak, but your clothes beneath are definitely not as art portrays you."

"Yeah, every thousand years the God likes to keep things up to date, so it's easier to relate to the ferryman, and not be scared as much I guess. Then things change so quickly that I am out of sync with what is the norm."

"So when did you get… upgraded?"

"Eighties. I know, bad timing right. Still, need to keep the robe on though. Anyway, we're nearly there."

In the distance, floating in the darkness was another island, growing as they got closer. Nick saw only a short beach like the previous one, and he presumed it was made of bones too. A set of giant engraved doors loomed in front of him; it was hard to see if something was behind the doors or even if they were attached to anything, as the edges of the doors were enveloped in a green fog.

The boat pushed the mist to either side as it eased towards the shore of Hades. As the boat got closer, the giant wooden doorway towered above them.

Nick watched the boat ride up on to the beach, grinding the bones underneath.

"Well dude, your journey is over, you have crossed to the world of Hades. Good luck with trying to persuade him to hand over your mom; he's never done it before but you never know, he could be in a good mood." Charon helped Nick off the boat and onto the beach.

"Thanks, well I hope this works out, and I don't see you again for a very long time." Nick held out his hand to shake. Charon shook Nick's hand and stepped back on the boat.

"A few words of advice with the big man; be strong. He likes to hear confidence. Challenge the replies, he likes to argue. And, if he's in a particularly bad mood ask him about his dog; he loves his dog. Anyways, later dude."

Charon bowed and moved back to the far side of the boat. He lifted his arm, the orb rose, and the boat, with Charon, glided off into the mist.

Nick watched Charon fade into the distance; from behind him he started to hear a rumble. He turned to see the towering wooden doors begin to open slowly with a ground-shaking thunder.

The doors split open and the light from behind blinded Nick for a few moments. When his vision became clearer, he saw in front of him a vast hall. Marble and golds adorned the floors and walls, with huge pillars holding up the ceiling that was covered with the most beautifully painted murals that would shame the Sistine Chapel.

Once the shock of what was in front of him had subsided, he realised the masses of the dead in channels at either side of the entrance, flowing off into the distance. Sitting on an enormous throne at the far end of the hall, was Hades, and to the left of him sat Cerberus, his three-headed dog.

Nick began his long walk across the bridge, over the sea of moaning, writhing bodies below, towards the throne. As he approached, Nick realised Hades' size was exceptionally intimidating. The giant stopped stroking one of the heads of his dog and looked at Nick; he leant forward in his throne to speak.

"State your business, because you're not here to be judged?" bellowed Hades.

Nick looked up at Hades, whilst watching Cerberus out of the corner of his eye.

"I have come to plead for my mother's life back."

Hades looked down at Nick and boomed.

"And why would I do that? Who do you think you are? To come here and have the audacity to even ask this request?"

"My name is Nick Fitz…"

Hades cut Nick off before he could finish, "I know who you are. I am asking, who do you think you are, you filthy maggot!"

Nick cringed with the loudness of Hades' voice.

"Right, Ok, then you know who my mother is?"

"Of course, but I don't think you understand me. I am not going to help you as you are his toy."

Hades sat back in his throne and stroked his beard.

"Nick, it seems that you have made a mistake coming here. You cannot just arrive here and ask for your mother back. This is not how it works and *he* knows that."

Hades returned to petting his three-headed beast, looking at Nick with disdain.

Nick stepped closer and pointed his forefinger at Hades.

"I am not leaving here without her. You will return her to me or I will…"

Hades creased with laughter.

"What? What power do you think you have here? Do you think you can hurt me? Look at you! You're tiny, and even with the tiny bit of power you own, it's nothing compared to mine."

He laughed again, "Besides, and here is the kicker Nick, King of Hell. You're not leaving here soon; in fact, you're never leaving here."

Hades sat back stroking his long beard and looked down his nose at Nick waiting for his reply.

"Why do you beings think it is perfectly acceptable to fuck with my life? Lucifer first, now you – I am sick of this."

Hades raised an eyebrow at Nick's response.

"You brought me into your life, Nick. I didn't come looking for you. Besides, you have come for your mother, yet it is her choices that have led you here."

"No, Lucifer led me here."

"No Nick, your mother could have let nature take its cause, but her greed brought you this pain. It is nobody's fault but her's."

Nick knew he was right about his mother; not having a soul had made him see things in a different light. But, he was fighting for his mother because he knew he had to.

"That might be the truth, but she had no other option. She wanted me to live, to have a life."

Hades leaned forward in his giant throne, "And yet look at your life now, full of death. Even if I were to return your mother, it is too late."

"What? What does that mean?"

"She has been judged and has elevated."

Hades sat back and continued to stroke his beard.

"So all of this was a waste of time? I am dead, and it was all for nothing?"

Nick started to pace in front of the throne in anger.

"I'm afraid so, but for you, it gets worse. You're not going join her; you have done too many evil things to elevate."

"Wait, I know there is no hell; they told me it was just a state of mind."

"And you bought the lie, Nick. They lied about everything. You are not the King of Hell; you are nothing but a puppet."

"But, they gave me magic, I can control…"

"Nick, those are nothing but parlour tricks, they wouldn't give you true magic, the power to control worlds, to destroy universes. Your magic will not affect gods."

Hades looked at Nick for the first time with humanity, as he watched Nick start to realise what had happened over the past few months of his life.

Nick dropped to his knees, knowing that his life had ended on his eighteenth birthday, and even with no soul, he felt that kick hard. It was just easier to accept the inevitable.

"OK, Hades, let's get this finished with. One last thing, nice dog, or is it dogs?"

Hades smiled.

"Charon told you to ask about my dog, didn't he?"

Nick nodded.

"Yeah, that won't help, sorry. His advice is rarely helpful."

Nick braced himself for Hades to send him to hell, then he remembered he needed to give Hades Lucifer's message. For a split second, he wasn't going to mention it, but he decided that it might help to distract him.

"Wait, I have a message!"

Nick shouted whilst holding his hand up in a request for Hades to pause.

"What?"

"It's from Lucifer."

"Really, Lucifer? This should be good." Hades leaned forward to hear the message.

"I don't understand it, but he said you would."

"Ok, what is it?"

"The eagle has landed!"

"What? Time wasting; it's judgment day, Nick."

Hades raised a hand, said a few words that Nick didn't understand and then there was a thunderous crack and everything went dark.

27

THE JUDGING

Nick's eyes blinked open; his vision was slightly blurred, and his hearing was overwhelmed by a loud high pitched tone, created by the deafening noise just before the darkness came. The explosion seemed above him, or at least so close to him – it felt within touching distance.

As the whistling faded and his vision started to clear, he pushed himself up off the marble floor and looked around to see Lucifer standing at his side. He seemed taller than normal, but not as tall as Hades. However, his face seemed more twisted with insanity than usual.

Lucifer realised that Nick was awake.

"Hey there, Nick. Thanks for the blinding stupidity that oozes in your body."

Nick steadied himself as he regained his equilibrium.

"Oh fuck! How are you even here?"

Hades stirred; it seemed what had knocked Nick out had rendered Hades unconscious as well, along with his dog, who was sprawled on the floor.

"Urrgggh! What happened?" Hades boomed.

Lucifer waved at Hades, "Hey Honey, I'm home!"

"How did you get in here? You're forbidden to be here. I set magic to stop this from happening again."

Hades was stunned. He knew that Lucifer hadn't arrived with Nick; he was certain Nick was alone.

"Ah, not quite. You stopped me from being able to travel here and come through those doors."

Lucifer pointed at the Gates of Hades.

"You never stopped me from being *in* here. That's where your plan failed. You see Nick has allowed me to be anywhere he is and at any point to join him."

"What? I don't remember agreeing to anything like that with you," Nick said still dazed.

"Contract, Nick! You need to read the contracts you sign. I presume that you didn't read it then? It is very clearly explained in there."

"Well… yes… I think… I don't remember…"

Nick could remember reading the contract on many occasions, but as he forced himself to remember what he had read, he just remembered a blank scroll. The harder he pushed to remember, the more it seemed to be just some form of text in a different language than he couldn't understand.

"Let's face facts, you don't remember anything about the contract."

Lucifer flashed a knowing smile at Nick.

"I stopped you from remembering. The contract was a pretty hard spell to create; it took a long time to get right. Years of being patient, planning, losing loved ones."

Lucifer gave Nick an "I will kill you later" look and continued, "But now I'm finally here again. And you, Hades, will now die!"

Hades seemed to change his demeanour.

"Lucifer, what has happened to you? Last time you were here you were desperate but driven; this time you seem unstable. What has happened? Why are you even here? You won't defeat me."

"Don't patronise me, Hades. I am not a child, I am just seeing things in a different light, the way they should be – your death at my hands. I am here to fulfil that prophecy!"

Lucifer took a step closer.

"Prophecy! Lucifer, you are not a deity! You cannot claim an illusion of a crazed mind to be a prophecy. Prophecies are sent from God, and let's face it: He would not be talking to you. You're his rejected disappointment."

Hades was now perched at the end of his throne; Cerberus was coming back around and lifting his three giant heads off the ground.

Lucifer's voice got deeper and seemed more evil than the twisted one Nick knew.

"Don't call me crazy, Hades. I am not fucking *CRAZY*! I am controlled, I am focused, Moreover, I am here to take your throne, the throne that should be mine. You can either abdicate or die?"

Nick backed away sensing the two giant gods were about to do battle. He looked for somewhere to run to but decided to wait for the best time to hide. He decided to wait until they were fully distracted. For the time being, Nick just kept a low profile.

"You will never be the one who judges, Lucifer. You cannot be trusted and you will never beat my might." Hades booming voice rolled like thunder around the vast hall.

Cerberus was up and all three heads were now focused on Lucifer, snarling in unison. Hades placed a calming hand on one of its heads, trying to relax the beast.

Lucifer had bad memories from the last time he tried to take Hades throne, Cerberus was strong, but the power of Hades and his dog had been too much for him.

"Has nobody put that mutt down yet? It has three heads, it should have been killed at birth."

Lucifer mimed a knife running along his throat, "I think I might have to be the one to do it."

"Are you sure you want to try your luck with my dog again, trickster?"

Hades whistled a piercing note which sent the beast running for Lucifer.

Lucifer stood his ground, and as Nick watched, Cerberus bounded to Lucifer with all three heads barking and snapping. The sides of their mouths raised, bearing their sharp, stained teeth, saliva dripping. The beast lunged for Lucifer, enormous claws out as it flew towards him, knocking him back off his balance and on to the ground.

The hound was onto him immediately, tearing at him. Hades' laughter thundered around the hall. Nick started to slowly move back away from the fight. Lucifer twisted and turned trying to keep hold of the heads from making contact with him, and at the same time working an arm free. Seconds later, he had freed a hand and then, within a blink of an eye, there was an eruption of red and howls of pain as Cerberus was sliced into three.

Lucifer screamed with laughter.

"I killed the beast! HAHA... I killed your fucking, stupid dog."

Hades ran for Cerberus.

"What have you done? You..." he tried to hold his pet together, the three heads now limp and still, "You.. you... he's DEAD!"

Hades turned and faced Lucifer, who was now looking very pleased with himself, laughing.

This was it, Nick thought, Lucifer was now focused on Hades, Cerberus was dead and Hades had only one enemy in this hall. Nick made a run for a pillar that was nearby.

Lucifer saw him take flight. and without looking at him Nick found himself frozen in mid-stride as he had been before, unable to move, or talk.

"I haven't finished with you yet, boy." Lucifer sneered without taking an eye off Hades.

Hades screamed in anger, dropping his spliced animal onto the blooded floor and ran for his bident which was propped up against his throne. Grabbing it, he threw it with all his might; his aim was true and it pierced Lucifer in his gut.

Lucifer stumbled back and dropped to one knee, groaning he grabbed the shaft of the bident and pulled it out, tearing flesh from his torso. He stood and charged at Hades ramming the weapon into Hade's abdomen, twisting it, pushing and pulling.

Hades let out a loud cry as he tried to push Lucifer away by his face with one hand, as he attempted to stop the bident from being twisted with his other. Lucifer stood his ground, but it caused searing pain to flush through his massive form. Hades, bigger than Lucifer, managed to grab Lucifer's head and squeeze it. Lucifer let go of the bident and tried to push Hades hand away, he was now feeling the pressure from either side against his temples.

Hade's strength was greater, and he managed to pull Lucifer away from him. Hades let out a thundering cry and refocused his strength to shove Lucifer backwards, Lucifer lost his footing and fell into the river of the dead.

Lucifer fought to keep hold of the sides of the bridge, but the current was too strong and with all the un-judged beings tearing and grabbing at him to pull him down, he was soon carried away. His cries and screams rang through the hollow halls as he fought to keep his head above the water. Nick watched from a frozen position, waiting for his hold to cease.

Lucifer's head dropped under a couple of times before it finally disappeared under the rushing flow for the last time. His cries stopped, and Nick fell to the floor. Nick scrambled to the pillar and hid behind it, eyeing the large wooden, carved doors at the far end of the hall. He did not know whether he was going to get out of this massive mistake that he had made alive.

Hades removed the weapon from his stomach, slowly, as not to cause any more damage to himself and threw it to the floor. Crawling, he returned to his slaughtered dog, stroking each head in turn, he howled to the roof in pain for the loss of his pet.

"I'm sorry, I couldn't stop him, I... I didn't think he could..."

Hades howled again and turned in the direction of Nick as he hid behind the pillar.

"You! This is your fault, you little fucking flea!"

Hades held his hand out, Nick found himself being dragged towards the God. With nothing to hold onto, he couldn't stop the pull and was unable to defend himself. He clawed at the floor looking for a gap or lip, but the marble floor didn't have a break that he could get his fingers into. Nick decided to spin himself over to see the giant.

"You brought him here, hiding inside you. You knew what he was going to do, didn't you? You knew..."

"I didn't know; he wasn't inside me. I didn't even know

what the contract said. Please don't kill me, you have already ended him…"

"He can't just turn up like that. We stopped him! So, you must have done something to get him in here. What did you do?"

When Nick didn't answer immediately, Hades screamed again: "*WHAT DID YOU DO?*"

"I didn't do anything. He told me I could get my mother back; I could end all of this hell I have been living in for the past eight months. All I had to do was come here, ask for her and pass you a message – that was it. I didn't know anything about his plan; honestly, please believe me?"

"I don't believe you; my dog is dead, and *you* will pay."

Hades continued to pull him closer. Nick tried using his magic to stop him, but as Hades had mentioned earlier, it was just parlour tricks compared to his magic and it didn't touch his power. Nick couldn't stop him or help himself; even teleportation didn't work.

When Nick was within touching distance a gurgling noise came from the river. Hades stopped his pulling and turned to the noise. A whirlpool was growing in the waters, and as the screams began, the centre of the whirlpool opened and Lucifer flew out of the waters along with several bodies trying to pull him back in. He landed feet first onto the skulls of the bodies; there was a loud crack and a pop as the pressure forced the skull to shatter open on the marble floor.

Lucifer looked up, dripping with water and various other fluids, and turned his gaze to Hades, grinning.

"How are you still alive? No one has ever survived the rivers, how did you…"

Lucifer's eyes glowed red.

"I am Lucifer, the rightful ruler of this place. Heaven and Hell. I am no human. I am a fucking God!" Lucifer screamed.

Hades charged at Nick.

"I am going to slaughter your vessel like you killed my dog; let's see what kind of God you are then."

Lucifer made a run for Hades, grabbing him by his arm, and swinging him back away from Nick. He crashed into his throne, smashing his back on the throne's arm in the process.

"I don't need him to kill you! But he is not going to die by your hand. If anyone is going to kill him, it will be me. But that will not be happening yet."

Lucifer seemed larger now than before. He still wasn't as large as Hades, but there wasn't much difference between them. He climbed up towards Hades who was crouched and trying to get back up. Lucifer raised his hands in front of himself, a glowing force shot from his fingers wrapped itself around Hade's neck, lifting him high in the air.

Hades reached for the ethereal light, trying to pull the force away, but his fingers passed through the rope-like force. He struggled, kicking his legs out as they dangled below him, while he hovered above his throne.

"Stop Lucifer... stop... he will never accept you..."

"This is not your fight, Hades. Let me through or I will end your life, now." Lucifer tightened the force around his neck.

"I ... can't... stop..." Hades reached out with one hand trying to hit him with a blast of magic, each shot missing as he struggled to catch his breath.

"So be it. I am so sorry, brother, but I am taking back what belongs to me."

Lucifer shook the glowing light which held Hades high. Hades struggled more violently, grabbing and passing through the rope repeatedly. Lucifer pulled hard and eventually a breaking noise could be heard as Lucifer snapped Hade's neck, leaving him limp and motionless, hanging in the air.

"You killed him. Why did you have to kill him?" questioned Nick.

"He had to die; otherwise, I couldn't return home. I need to take what is rightfully mine now; he has ruled it too long."

"Home? Where's home?"

Lucifer pointed to a set of glowing white double doors way off in the corner of the vast hallway.

"It's time to go, Nick."

"But, I was supposed to go down. He told me."

"Not today. Today I choose, and you're going up. You're going to get your mother back."

Lucifer stood up, releasing the force around Hades' neck. And he dropped and crashed to the floor, shaking the hall as his limp body landed. Lucifer turned to Nick and walked towards him, shrinking in size to what Nick was used to, each limb cracking and popping as he resumed his old form.

"It's time to go, Nick. We better leave before the invasion from the river starts."

He grabbed Nick and pulled him along with him as he headed towards the double doors of the elevator.

Behind them, Nick heard groaning as bodies started to climb from the waters, heading towards Hades.

They reached the doors, and as they turned the floor was swarming with groaning, crawling bodies, covering Hades and his dog, feeding off them. Blood and flesh being ripped from the bone by hands and teeth. The noise was a loud rumble bubbling through the hall.

"What happens now?" Nick asked. "What happens to this place? To them?"

Lucifer placed his palm on the pillar at the side of the double doors, which opened up to a large elevator. It was playing the usual easy-listening medley of tunes from the eighties.

They stepped inside and watched the waves of bodies continue to crawl towards the dead god and his dog. As the doors closed, Nick noticed one of the bodies look up quickly as the noise distracted him; it screeched. And several beings started to head towards the doors in a frenzy.

28

ELEVATION

The doors closed and Nick was silent. Lucifer reached for the single button at the top of the panel and thumped it with his clenched fist. The button let out a glowing white light, shimmering from the edges, smiling to himself, Lucifer let out a snigger.

"This is not something to laugh at, I have just watched you kill Hades and his dog. Why did you have to do that?" Nick edged backwards into the corner, keeping an eye on Lucifer and an eye on the doors.

"Do you think we would have got in here without me slaying him? You would have gone to Hell, and I need you to be with me when I go visit Pop."

"You have got to be kidding me; you're off to take on God? Really? This just keeps getting more and more fucked up every time I'm with you." Nick slapped his face and dragged his hand off of his chin in disbelief.

Lucifer turned to face Nick who was propped up in the corner of the lift.

"I'm not joking Nick. My time has come. This is the furthest I have got since being thrown out, and I don't intend to waste it. Thousands of years I have planned for this moment, whilst I'm with you, I can get up there."

Nick slumped into the corner, slowly dropping to a sitting position.

"How long does this take? I'm so hoping he kills you."

"Nicholas! You've changed, saying such hateful things." Lucifer mocked, "For your sake, I hope he doesn't kill me, you don't want your soul being destroyed with me do you?"

"You have it with you?"

"Well, obviously, you can never trust someone else with important things."

Nick jumped up with a new source of energy, "It's here now? In this elevator? With us?"

Lucifer nodded, "Don't get excited; you can't grab it or even see it."

"So, where is it then?"

Lucifer tapped his chest, "In a safe place, don't you worry."

"What? It's inside you? With your soul?"

"Don't worry, I don't have one; besides it's asleep, enclosed in magic. That way I don't have to put up with its whining."

"When do I get it back?"

"When I have finished what I have come here to do today. You can have it back then."

Lucifer turned back to the panel; the lift was still travelling, and he started to get fidgety.

Nick could sense the frustration coming from Lucifer, as he watched him tap his fingers against the panel and stare up at the ceiling.

"Come on, Come on," Lucifer repeated impatiently.

"Why do you have my soul? What use is it to you?" Nick asked.

Lucifer turned to Nick to explain.

"The Trial of Fire, if you had entered that with a soul, we wouldn't be here. You would have burned alive, and I would have been very annoyed, like the first time, second, third…"

"What? How many people have you destroyed in getting what you want?"

"Five, six, not really sure."

"Five? Six? How can you not remember?"

Lucifer started to tap the panel again and look around the elevator's roof.

"It has taken me a very, very long time to get to this point; you just forget how you got here and what toys you broke in the process."

"But, I still don't understand, Hades told me you had lied to me, about everything. Did you ever rule Hell? I mean, Hades said I wasn't the King of Hell as you had said, so what's going on? Really?"

Lucifer's head dropped, "Nick, can you not smell a lie when one is slapped across your face? Just how gullible are you? No, you're not the King of Hell. Yes, I did rule Hell; I still do. But, there are no clean souls in Hell for a reason. I needed a clean soul, a good soul, a pure one."

"But I don't have it anymore, you took it!"

Lucifer looked at Nick in astonishment.

"I needed your soul; I needed to get into here and the pure soul was the key."

Nick thought about what he had said, then remembered that he had killed before he changed, he had killed Ethan, "But my soul wasn't pure, I had killed Ethan."

The demon laughed, "Oh Nick, there was no way I was going to let you kill him. I did that; in fact, I was at all of your killings, apart from Anton's." Lucifer hung his head again, "Poor Anton, I really am going to make you suffer for that after all this."

"You took my soul, I don't seem to have a conscience. I know what is right and wrong, but the lines are very blurred; in fact, they don't exist. I feel nothing after and forget easily. Anton was just a way of getting at you."

"Well done, you definitely succeeded. Are you sorry for killing him?"

Nick thought, "Not really, I didn't really feel that much when you killed my mother either."

"Shit, bet you're glad I have your soul now then?"

Nick just shrugged, "When do I get it back?"

"Not yet, I still need it"

Lucifer turned back to the lift's control panel and banged his head against it. "Come on!"

Nick moved back into the corner and slumped to the floor staring up at the row of light above the door. Where the floor number usually is, all that was displayed above them was a row of light slowly growing in length, filling the panel from left to right.

Lucifer started to pace back and forward in front of Nick, each time kicking his feet when he passed. Each turn glancing up at the light. Nick pulled his feet closer into him, trying to avoid Lucifer kicking him.

"How did you get to my mother before I got there? I presume we passed as soon as I left?" Nick asked.

"Nick, do you think I would give you a power that would enable you to have power over time? Do you realise how dangerous that would be, the power of time in the hands of a fool?" Lucifer let out a snort.

"You can control time? How?"

"No Nick. No, not ever, someone so young will never have this power, nice try though."

Nick stayed slumped in the corner, waiting, while Lucifer kept pacing. The light was nearly at the end of its journey, and Nick could only presume, some form of Heaven.

"How do you know where I am all the time? When we first met, I seemed to recognise you, why?"

Lucifer seemed pleased with himself.

"Your necklace. When you were eight you bought a necklace from a man on a beach. That was me, I have tracked and watched you ever since. Only recently though it doesn't seem to work."

Nick went to make a natural grab for it then forgot he had left it with Jen.

"What do you mean watch?" Panic set in.

"Calm down Nick. We have all been teenagers, just you have some weird tastes." Lucifer shuddered.

"Well, I'm glad I got rid of that then."

"Yeah, I know, you gave it to Jen. How do you think I got to her so quickly?"

"Shit!" Nick let out a defiant moan.

"I've told you plenty of times how stupid you are; don't be hard on yourself."

A few minutes of silence passed between Nick and Lucifer before the lift stopped at its destination. Lucifer braced himself in a charging position, Nick stayed slumped in the corner.

"Get up boy, get the fuck up. You will need to fight, fucking angels are cunts!" He spat on the ground in front of him.

Nick pushed himself up onto his feet, not bracing himself like Lucifer but like a reluctant teenager.

"Really? Not willing to fight for your soul?"

"Are they actually going to attack me?"

"Maybe they will leave you alone, but not me."

The doors to the elevator opened slowly, revealing a long white corridor vanishing off into the distance.

They stepped out slowly, Lucifer swinging his upper body left and right making sure nothing was there to jump out, but nothing did. They started the walk to the end of the white corridor. There were no doors to either side, just white walls. Lucifer a few steps in front of Nick, was on high alert, waiting for something to happen.

A creaking noise behind them caught both their attention, and they spun around on the spot to see a door on the right open. A middle-aged man stepped out into the corridor, oblivious to the visitors. He turned and closed the door behind him, then stopped suddenly when he caught sight of the two people in front of him.

Shocked on recognising who one of the men was, he sprinted back to his now invisible door, and reached for the handle. Lucifer barged past Nick, knocking him to the floor and charged for the scared man flapping at the handle, willing it to appear. The handle popped into existence and he opened the door. He almost got his body inside before Lucifer slammed into the door, forcing it to shut on him. He grabbed the man's arm and threw him against the corridor wall, knocking him to the floor. Lucifer showed his teeth.

"Hi, guess you recognised me?"

The man nodded scrambling backwards, keeping his face pointing at Lucifer.

"And you know what I'm going to do to you, too?"

Again the man nodded with a very scared look on his face, knowing that his day had turned very dark indeed.

Lucifer turned to Nick who was getting himself back up off the floor after being pushed over.

"Come over here Nick. Don't be shy, say hello to this... thing."

Lucifer waved Nick over.

Nick reluctantly strolled over to them both, showing all the disregard of a very sullen and moody teenager.

"Hi," Nick sighed.

The man just nodded in acceptance.

Lucifer got onto his knees and placed his head at the side of the man's head.

"Are you going to tell us where the door is to get out of here and into the Garden?"

The man mumbled a reply.

"What?" asked Lucifer.

The man mumbled again.

"Speak up, I can't hear you." Lucifer turned to Nick, "Can you hear what he's saying?"

Nicked shook his head.

"I can't show you, I don't know…" the man spoke softly but louder.

"Oh, but I think you can. Your whole being is being pulled towards it, a yearning that you can't fight."

Lucifer stroked the man's cheek.

"Let's try again. Where is the door?"

He left his hand resting on the man's neck.

The man gulped and said clearly, "I don't know."

The angel closed his eyes knowing what was about to come.

"Sorry to hear that."

Lucifer twisted the man's neck to one side filling the corridor with a distinctive cracking noise.

"Why did you do that? Now you won't find the door you're looking for."

Lucifer dropped his head and shook it.

"Nick, the key to anything is to listen, listen to the details.

I said he will know where the door is, Blood drives us all, Nick. Watch and learn."

Lucifer stood up and pulled a small dagger out from his inside pocket and slit the man's throat. The red liquid started to gush from his throat and down the dead angel's front. Sections spurted forward on the white walls.

The liquid started to congeal and slowly make its way up the corridor. Lucifer watched it lead the way, snaking, searching. They followed it closely, watched it cross the corridor to the other side and stop in front of a section of wall in front of them. A doorway appeared and the blood oozed underneath. Lucifer grabbed the handle and turned it.

"Every living thing yearns to be with my Father. The desire is that strong your blood will always drag you to him. Fucking weird, eh?"

The next corridor was in darkness, it reminded Nick of his safe place before he created the cottage. They both stepped forward and the door shut behind them. No noise could be heard and nothing could be seen. Nick reached out to his right to feel for a wall, but he couldn't feel anything either, so he decided to stand very still.

"Lucifer?"

He didn't reply immediately.

"Just wait. Don't move"

Nick froze, a pain shot through his head as though he had been punched in the temple. He dropped to his knees and screamed out in pain. Nick grabbed his head. Nick's eyes felt as though they would burst, and he screamed out again.

"Shut up! Keep your fucking screams to yourself," Lucifer whispered loudly at Nick.

"The pain will clear quickly; it's just you have to be altered to see clearly."

Nick was still grabbing his head in his hands, squeezing, trying to stop his head from erupting.

"I can't… I can't… it hurts too much… make it stop!" Nick pleaded.

"Shut up!" Lucifer ordered him again.

The pain started to ease, slowly at first, then the pressure started to abate. Nick caught his breath and released his grip. He could hear what sounded like a running stream and birds singing. He could feel a cool breeze as if he were outside, then he slowly opened his eyes.

His vision was blurred at first but within a few seconds, and a few blinks, he could see a magnificent woodland, with pathways through to a perfect landscape of views that grew to a wilderness of ravines, rivers and forests.

"Holy shit! This is amazing! Is this… this… I really don't want to say it, it sounds stupid, but is this Heaven?" asked Nick.

Lucifer shook his head in revulsion.

"Yes it's Heaven," he mocked, "or whatever you stupid creatures call it. To us it's known as The Garden, I don't know which is more ridiculous."

They both began walking towards the edge of the ravine, towards the pathway down. As they descended, Nick could see small buildings stretching along the valley floor at the side of the river. He followed the smooth, cobbled roads up towards a large building at the end of the valley.

Surrounding the grounds were what looked to be a white railed fence with enormous gates, closed to keep people out – or in, he wasn't sure.

"I'm presuming that the large building at the end is where you grew up?" Nick asked as they stopped to look at the distant building.

"Kind of, there is a lot more to it than that. I developed,

grew and trained by his side, I loved him, but he soon showed his true feelings. The moment I saw him slipping, I spoke to him, begged him to let me share the work he had put himself under. He turned on me and said I was trying to take his power; I wasn't. However, I am now."

"Is that why you was banished? Offering to help him?"

"He accused me of worshipping myself instead of him. I was crushed, but I'm here now and that is where we are going."

"Seriously, have you thought this through? How are going to fight him?"

"You don't know what he looks like Nick. He isn't what you all believe. Have you read his book? All men created in his image? Well, that's not a lie."

Lucifer set off walking again, and Nick followed. As they reached the bottom Lucifer stopped and looked around, a few beings went about their general business not paying attention to the two visitors. They walked through the small village and up towards the large gates. The closer they got, the clearer the fence and gates became; they gleamed and sparkled in the sun. As they made their way closer, Nick could see just how beautiful the pearl-encrusted gates were.

The reality of where he was suddenly hit him: He was dead and in Heaven.

He had just followed like a puppet, and now he was about to face God. Just how far was Lucifer going to go, and how easy would it be for him to get out of this situation? Could he get back to Jen? Was Jen still alive and in the cottage?

Nick and Lucifer arrived at the gates. Nick stood slightly behind Lucifer, and he realised that they were not alone. Nick turned to see about twenty armed beings behind them ready to attack.

"Lucifer... we have company," Nick whispered.

29

THE GARDEN

Lucifer dropped his head and muttered something under his breath. Lifting his head, he turned to face the surrounding guards. He bowed elegantly.

"Gentlemen, Gentlemen, Good morning to you all. What a glorious day that greets us in such a breathtaking land."

One of the guards stepped forward, whilst the rest kept their spears pointing at the two visitors.

"Lucifer, you must leave, now."

"I am not leaving until I have seen him." Lucifer pointed at the house behind him. He continued, "This is not your fight, you don't have to do this."

"Lucifer, we guard the Garden, and you shouldn't be here; therefore, this *is* our fight. You must leave, now."

Lucifer sighed and stepped forward, the guards in turn repositioned to make it clear they were there to see it through.

"You know that there is no way I am going to step away and leave without doing what I came to do. You know that your next move is critical to your survival. And you know that I am way too powerful for you to stop me."

Lucifer stepped within touching distance of the guard who in turn had stepped forward.

"We cannot allow you to continue with your journey. Our Lord cannot be allowed to know you are here. If you do not leave now, we *will* have to use force."

The guards braced themselves.

"OK, your choice, bloodshed in the Valley it is then."

Lucifer turned to Nick, "You better step back, I don't want you to be involved in this."

Nick stepped back as one of the guards jumped forward before the order had been given, eager to prove himself. The guard master tried to stop his junior soldier but it was too late.

He lunged forward with his spear raised towards Lucifer. Lucifer reached out and grabbed the end of the spear with both hands. That split second the young, naive soldier regretted his early attack. Lucifer pushed the spear back instantly forcing the guard to let go. Lucifer repositioned and rammed the spear through the guard master's neck.

The master dropped his weapon instantly reaching for his throat, choking on the hole spurting blood from the wound. He dropped to his knees and that was the moment that the rest launched their spears at the King of Hell.

Lucifer dropped his spear and just before the guard's weapons hit him, he dropped to his knees, raised his hands and muttered a few words to himself. The spears disintegrated, showering him with dust. As Lucifer stood, the guards stopped their movement forward. He pushed forward with his hands towards the guards, Nick couldn't see what he was pushing at first then it all became clear as one by one the guards dropped. Lucifer had forced a grid of energy at the guards, like a hot butter knife the grid sliced through the guards, dicing them. Nick watched as the guards slowly fell into cubes of flesh, skin and bones – blood covering the pathway below their feet.

Nick heard screams coming from the houses that covered the valley, but his attention was broken by a loud banging noise coming from behind them, from the building behind the pearly gates. Nick turned quickly to see the large wooden doors open.

"Lucifer, someone's coming." Nick nudged Lucifer out of his trance as he watched the blood run away to the grass at the side of the paving.

Both the visitors turned back to the opening doors, waiting to see who would come through them. The visitors slowly walked up to the gates waiting for the first view of who would appear. Even though the screaming was still going on behind them, their focus was on the doors.

Several guards ran out and lined either side of the doors, followed by a young, teenage boy dressed differently from the guards who were all dressed in the same white uniforms. He was dressed in just jeans and a t-shirt; he turned to speak to the guards who were behind him and pointed towards the gates.

Nick looked at Lucifer who was now beaming in excitement.

"Who's that? Who's the kid?" Nick asked.

"It's him!"

"Who?"

"Really? Him, your God. My creator. My next victim!" Lucifer snarled.

"You have got to be joking, that is what he looks like? He's just a kid?"

"Looks can be very deceiving."

The guards ran towards the gate, leaving God standing in the doorway, his hands on his hips. The gates opened fully, and the guards shot past Lucifer and Nick towards the pile of gore. Nick watched Lucifer and realised he was not moving.

"What's wrong? Why aren't you trying to get into the courtyard? Are you broken?" Nick whispered.

"I can't move; he hasn't allowed it yet."

"What? You have to wait?" Nick tried to prod him but he was solid, staring at the boy who was wearing a very wide smile.

"Yes, he has to address me," Lucifer strained through his teeth.

God stood in the doorway looking disappointedly at Lucifer. The guards had somehow got the pools of flesh into several containers, carried them past the visitors and into the yard. God waited to see the guards walk past him; they stopped for him to look in the containers, and Nick watched God shake his head. He said something to the guards as they left and turned back to the gates again.

"WHAT THE FUCK HAVE YOU DONE THIS TIME?"

God asked Lucifer in a voice that hurt Nick's ears and sent him to his knees.

Lucifer stood with a painful extremely wide grin fixed on his face, "They wouldn't let me see you; I had to see you," he said through clenched teeth.

God turned to one of the guards; Nick could see him gesture for them to open the gates and let them in. He then turned around and disappeared through the doors. Lucifer slumped down as though he were a marionette and he had just had his strings cut.

"You ok?" asked Nick.

"You understand why I hate him now?"

"Why did you have that grin on your face?"

"He's a fucking sadist; he finds it funny to force us to

greet him that way. I thought he would have got bored of that by now, but…"

The two guards arrived at the gates as they started to open, Lucifer stood impatiently, tapping his feet like a child waiting to piss.

"Are we going in?" Nick asked.

Giddily Lucifer replied, "Yes, nothing changes though."

He leaned in closer to whisper to Nick. "I'm still taking his fucking place." And then he winked

"I reckon the kid will give you a good fight though."

The two guards reached the gate; the guard to the left stepped forward to Lucifer.

"The Lord wants to see you in the dining room; you know the way. Also, he said touch anyone else, or anything else, and he will make sure you leave here in a bin liner."

"Getting grumpy in his old age then," Lucifer sneered.

"How dare you talk about the Lord like that!"

Lucifer pretended to zip his mouth shut, lock it and throw away the key, whilst laughing to Nick.

The guard stepped-up to Lucifer. "You're going to pay for what you did earlier, I hope he sends you back to Hell!"

Lucifer lunged at him, the guard stumbled and fell backwards, tripping over his own foot.

"He's very angry, I wouldn't want to be you."

"Let's get this over and done with; I want to get out of here," Nick said grabbing Lucifer's arm to drag him towards the building, Lucifer waved goodbye to the guards.

Nick and Lucifer reached the large doors. Nick noticed they were nothing in terms of grandeur compared to the ones at the entrance of Hades. Lucifer's walk was getting cockier as they passed through the white doors, and he was looking around as though he owned the hallways. The low sun was shining through the windows, catching the dust in its wake.

Nick noticed a strong smell of polish and roses in the air; it reminded him of Sunday mornings when he was a kid, his mother cleaning whilst listening to her record collection.

Lucifer stopped ahead of Nick in front of a set of double doors to his left. He paused with his hands on the door handles; he looked nervous and seemed a little shaky. He took a deep breath, looked down then back up at Nick, smiling a half-smile.

"This is it, Nick. I'm finally here. I knew it would happen one day. Stay back and don't get in the way."

He pulled the handles down and pushed the doors open, and Nick followed behind.

The room was an enormous dining room; it looked as though it could hold around two hundred guests. A long table stretched the full length; small tabletop lights were positioned every few seats, and chairs surrounded the oak masterpiece of furniture.

A short, lonely, figure sat at the head of the table flicking through a book. He lifted his head up as his two visitors arrived at the top end of the table.

God looked at Nick and nodded in recognition.

"Nick."

Then he cast his eyes on Lucifer in disgust.

"Lucifer, why are you here? Why have you butchered Hades, his dog and my guards? Do you realise how long this is going to take to resolve? I mean you left the Hall of Hades in chaos. That I will need to sort personally, and that is a place I really don't want to go."

Lucifer sat in the chair at the left-hand side of God, shuffled it to face him and leaned in.

"They all got in my way, all stopped or tried to stop me. If you would have only listened to me, answered my calls, this could have all been avoided. But you cast me out and ignored me; you forgot about me. You must have known this was bound to happen and that I was coming."

God's voice was now a little louder, and Nick could feel the pain at the back of his ears and his eardrums pounded again.

"Don't you dare blame me; this was all your fault. You went against me, against my word; you deserved what you got."

"There you go again, your word, not all of your sons and daughters believe in you anymore. They have started to look for a new ruler."

Lucifer smiled and sat back in his chair, with a smug look on his face.

"And you, Lucifer Morningstar, believe you can take my place?"

God laughed loudly making Nick grab his ears as the pain speared his head.

"I might be old, but I am still more powerful than you, or any of the beings that I created. If I ever decide to walk away, you will not be my successor. And I think you will find nobody will back you either."

"Maybe I don't want to wait until you decide to walk away. What if I decide to take it now?"

Nick raised his head, realising this was a room he didn't want to be in just before two gods went head to head again.

The room began to tingle with electricity from the two ancient powers. Nick began to look around for a place in case he needed to run for cover. God's laughter filled the room and the heaviness thundered in Nick's head, striking pain through his whole body this time. He wasn't sure how much more he could take of hearing God's laughter or voice; he clearly wasn't made to hear him.

"You? Take my throne? You're more deluded than what people whisper about you."

Lucifer quickly jumped up to his feet.

"You! You did this to me, you! You made me the villain, the leper, just something to throw away. I loved you; all I wanted to do was impress you. I wanted you to see me."

"Lucifer, I saw you, I saw what you had become, how you turned against my creations. It makes me laugh to know you need one of them to return to me. How you have come to depend on them, and how you're carrying his soul inside you. You haven't changed. You're still working against me: therefore, no-one will ever follow you."

"I don't need anyone's permission or approval, I'm taking what I came for…"

Lucifer swung his fist around making a perfect connection on God's jaw. His head having taken most of the impact, God moved his head to one side from the hit.

"Is that it Lucifer, is that all you have? Did you learn how to do that from your friend here?" God pointed at Nick.

Lucifer smiled at God, "No, I don't think my friend here knows this magic. Enjoy."

God's smile started to fade as he started to feel the pain begin to throb through his jaw. He touched the corner of his mouth and came away with blood on his fingers. As he stood up, God felt his knees start to buckle; he grabbed the table to keep himself from falling.

"What did you do?" God fell into another chair and crashed to the floor.

Lucifer walked around the chair at the top of the table, and stood over God, as he tried to turn himself round to face Lucifer.

"What's the matter, old man? That was some old, dirty, dark magic for you. Looks like the old voodoo queen knew her stuff, after all. I reckon a few more of them will kill you off."

God started to mumble something under his breath. The static in the room became heightened, making the hairs on the back of Nick's neck rise. Nick couldn't work out any of the words from God. He watched him raise a hand to stop Lucifer, But Lucifer came down with another blow to his head. God dropped to the floor with force, blood splattered from his nose and mouth.

Lucifer stood above God's bloodied head.

"I'm not strong enough? I'm not good enough? Look who's weak, you're finished you old bastard; time to take what's mine."

As Lucifer drove another punch to God's head, the static in the room became unbearable as it flowed through Nick. It filled every inch of Nick's body, and the voice came loud and clear in his head, blurring his vision.

'Stop him, Nick. Raise your hand, picture the electricity running through your body, reach out and hurt him. Reach out, Nick, you must do it. He will end your world if you don't."

Nick raised his hand and pictured the electricity leaving his fingers towards Lucifer, forcing him against the wall. As Lucifer raised his hand again for another blow against God's head, Nick closed his eyes and pushed the electricity down his arm, As the blast left Nick's hand he was thrown back against the wall. The electricity bolt hit Lucifer full on and sent him crashing into the opposite wall.

"What the fuck Nick? What was that?"

Lucifer pulled himself back up onto his feet and looked over at Nick.

"How did you do that? That fucking hurt me. You're going to pay for that, Nick."

Lucifer turned back to God. "Now where were we?"

Nick dragged himself up using the table. He raised his hand again and sent another blast towards Lucifer, with the same outcome blasting him back against the wall. The bolt hit Lucifer on his shoulder twisting his body and spinning him through the air and smashing him into the wall again.

This time Lucifer didn't get up immediately; instead, Nick got up first and peered over the table to see Lucifer getting to this feet.

"Nick, you're going to die!"

Lucifer launched himself over the table and grabbed Nick by the neck, picking him up and throwing him over the table where he landed like a marionette doll at the side of God.

Lucifer jumped over the table and landed on his feet at the side of the two of them.

"Sorry Nick, but you're about to get the same as the old man here."

Lucifer raised his fist and flashed a grin at Nick, as his fist came down towards his head.

Nick raised his hands to protect himself from Lucifer's coming blows; however, he felt the energy pulse through his arms repeatedly. Again aiming at Lucifer, he released the blast upwards forcing Lucifer against the ceiling. As he dropped down to the floor, the blasts from Nick continued to come and sent him flying through the air and into the wall.

Nick could hear slight groans from God as his limp teenage body lay motionless, blood seeping from his face. Lucifer dragged himself up onto his feet, using the table to balance, but collapsed and slumped back down at the head of the table.

He slowly rolled onto his back and closed his eyes. Nick watched him lay with his hands across his chest as though he were trying to find the strength within.

Lucifer levitated his body up off the floor and into the air, turning into a standing position; slowly he stretched his arms out into a crucified position, dropping his head to down to face his chest.

"Eli, Eli, lema sabachthani?" Lucifer cried.

"Is that what he cried when you ignored him? Left forsaken, dying! Father, I will not die like your weak, pathetic human son. His precious blood dripping in the daylight, his murderers standing around, mocking, laughing as he died."

Lucifer paused for a moment to feel the atmosphere.

"Did you know, I was the one who whispered in Pilate's ear on the day of the trial? I changed his mind, told him he would look weak if he decided not to crucify him. He was so easy to manipulate, very much like you Nick. So weak."

A warm glow started to crawl up through Nick's legs, from the floor, pulsating, growing. He tried to hide the feeling of euphoria filling his body. The power coursing through his veins, his muscles. Nick was breathing faster, trying to catch his breath. His heart was racing; he couldn't slow down the energy, it seemed beyond his control.

Lucifer had not finished; he was having fun detailing the death of God's son, still in his crucifixion pose.

"I watched his last breath leaving his body, I made sure he was dead. Left as an example of fear for the ones who dare challenge the state. Then you interfered bringing him back; all that hard work I had done, wasted. Time after time you stopped my work. But, that was the time, the time I decided to come back and take your place. And now that time is here…"

The energy now had taken over, Nick felt invincible; his breath was shorter and quicker. He felt extremely light-headed, and his heart was racing. He levitated up to the same level as Lucifer; shocked, Lucifer stopped talking.

"Nick, what are you doing? This is my time…"

Trying to catch his breath, Nick wanted to speak; he wanted to scream, but he couldn't. He opened his mouth and tried to shout for help, feeling his heart trying to launch itself out of his chest. Nick felt as though he were about to die.

He couldn't think; the glowing began, from the centre of his chest at first then radiating down through his arms, his legs, until Nick's whole body shone, filling the room with light. Without Nick speaking, he heard God's voice. Throwing Nick's head back, violently as though the voice needed more room to move.

"Lucifer, I know what you did, I know everything you do, but, I just didn't see this, you hid behind Nick's soul, like a coward. You should have finished me off when you had the chance. Even now you have failed, like usual. I should never have created you. I am so disappointed in you."

"No!" Screamed Lucifer forcing himself towards Nick's floating body, trying to stop him from retaliating, but it was too late.

Nick's body arched as far as it could go backwards, and he screamed in pain as a blinding light blasted out of his torso, destroying all in its path.

Lucifer, muscles flapping in the blast, screamed as the flesh was torn from his body, still trying to stop Nick. His screaming ceased as his face melted and blood cascaded on the walls behind. His skeletal frame stopped holding Nick and was flung against the wall smashing into pieces from the impact.

The light stopped, and Nick slumped to the floor, not breathing, then the blackness came.

♛

"Nick? Nick? Are you ok?"

A familiar voice was trying to wake Nick.

A voice he had heard so many times before.

He didn't want to wake though; his body was hurting so badly, it felt as if every inch of him had been stretched and beaten. He slowly opened his eyes to see a woman's face, so close to his.

His eyes took a few seconds to re-focus, It was the face of his mother.

"Mum?" Nick lifted his head up from the floor, slowly, feeling the pounding beat of his heart in his head. Quietly Nick spoke.

"I thought you were… gone, but how?"

"I am, dear. I'm sorry, I didn't mean to scare you."

"I don't scare that easily anymore."

Nick sat up and looked around to see guards cleaning the mess that had been Lucifer. His flesh, blood, and bone, pulped together. Nick looked round to see God sitting in a chair close by, dabbing a cloth on his own face.

"Is he dead?" Nick asked watching the guards leave.

God laughed, "What do you think?"

Nick grimaced.

"How did I do that?"

"You didn't Nick, I did. I just worked through your being. I am, however, sorry to tell you that your soul didn't survive either."

"Great, so am I dead then?"

"Oh no, Nick. You're going back, soulless, but alive."

Jude sat on the floor at Nick's side, smiling and touching his arm, there was a tear in her eye.

"Nick, they showed me everything you had to go through: How I died. I never meant for you to have to go through that. I was selfish, wanting you to live."

"No, Mum, I know you only wanted what was right. Like now,"

Nick turned to God, "Please, let her live? Give us our lives back? This was taken from us. We were tricked into death; you must see this?"

"I do and I understand, but the choice has already been made. The path has already been woven, Nick."

"No, we haven't even asked or discussed this. We want our lives back, I know you have the power to fix things."

"I do, but you both want different things. Look, I will leave you two alone to talk. Jude, I will be just outside." God disappeared from the chair he was sitting in.

Nick got up off the floor and helped his mother up. Nick grabbed and hugged her, squeezing her. Tears ran down Jude's cheeks onto Nick's chest.

"Mum, I am so sorry. I thought I could get to you before he did, I tried."

Jude grabbed Nick's face, holding his cheeks in her hands.

"I know, I know you tried, but what's happened has happened. And I have decided I don't want to return. I am happy here, and I know I couldn't watch you walking around without a soul, knowing that it was all my fault."

"I have survived without a soul for months; sometimes I wonder if it's better to be like this -- numb. Come on, let's get out of here. Let's go home and have a cuppa. Watch something on TV, like we used to do?"

Nick grabbed his mother's hands and held them.

"No, Nick. You have a life now that I couldn't live with. He needs you to continue what you are doing. You are needed to stop others who destroy lives, who terrorise souls. He has no-one to do that, to help with the evil in your world."

"No, I have fought for what seems to be forever to get our lives back. I came here to take you home." Nick refused to understand why his mother wanted to stay.

"Nick, you need to go. Go and help the suffering. Starting with that poor girl, Jennifer. You need to release her."

"What? Release her? What do you mean?" Nick sat back down.

"She is with you because she needs you, but you need to sever that tie. She needs to have her life back; you must understand that?"

"She wants to be with me."

"She is your prisoner. Let her go."

Nick rubbed his face with his hands.

"How?"

The door creaked open, and God walked through.

"Give her this." God said handing Nick a small glass vial. "There are only two drops in there, and that is the exact dose you need. She won't forget you, but she won't have that pull to you either. You are stopping her getting her son and life back. Love is a strong emotion, Nick. But, obsession is stronger."

Nick took the small vessel, held it up to the light.

"What is it?"

"That, Nick, is repulsion. She will see everything, very clearly and understand everything that has happened. After a period of time, the repulsion will fade, but she will not desire you anymore."

Nick grabbed his head and pulled it towards his knees in disbelief.

"So, let me get this straight. I lose my Mother and Jen? And I am left with no-one and nothing?"

God patted Nick's shoulder.

"You know it's right."

"Is that it? Well, that is just fucking awesome, I lose everything? Do you have anything positive to tell me?" Nick asked God.

"Power and magic, you get all the power you had before,

but now you have no restrictions. I will keep an eye on you, so don't misuse them."

Nick stood up, standing taller than God; he held his hand out to shake God's hand.

"Well, thanks for everything. You know I don't mean that, right? You and Lucifer have fucking ruined my existence."

"Nick! You better apologise to God; it is not his fault." Jude shouted.

"It's fine, Jude, I understand your son's anger. Listen, I have spoken to Steve Harper, and he will help you, guide you and stay in touch here. I believe you both got along with each other when you helped him?"

"I get Steve? A ghost?"

Nick shook his head in disbelief.

"Right, get me back to Jen."

Nick walked over to his mother and hugged his mother again.

"You sure?"

"Yes, I am staying here. Apart from you, I had nothing to live for. And seeing that you won't be around anymore, I am happier here."

"Right, how do I get back?"

God and Jude walked out of the room, Nick followed.

God opened a door on the left; the room was filled with a blinding white light. Nick covered his eyes with his arm as he turned to say goodbye. Nick hugged his mother one last time, kissed her head and turned and walked through the door.

The light engulfed Nick as he heard the door close behind him. He felt his body lift into the air and the oxygen got harder to breathe. He didn't panic, the calmness settled him.

He felt something pulling him forward, levitating him towards darkness.

As Nick sank into the black, his body began to warm. It

seemed cosy at first, heating his body like the sun on a warm morning, but it quickly became uncomfortable. As the intensity grew, the darkness gave way to a vivid bright light.

Nick covered his face to protect his eyes from the brightness. The intensity grew with every second. Nick felt the world around him close in, and the pressure grew to the point where he passed out.

♔

What felt like only moments later was actually hours.

He felt the soothing warmth again of the morning sun on his face, and he discovered he was back on the floor. Nick placed his hand down into the sand to feel his surroundings. He slowly opened his eyes to see a beach and the vivid blue, clear blue ocean in front of him. Pushing himself up, he realised that he was back at the cottage in his own world, where he had left Jennifer.

His body ached; it felt as though it had been minutes ago when he left his mother and hours since leaving Jennifer.

He was happy to see his surroundings, knowing that there was nothing now to ruin his existence. He decided not to rush giving Jen the repulsion that he could feel sitting in his pocket.

Walking up to the house he couldn't see any movement from inside. All the lights were off, and all he could hear was the lapping of the ocean behind him.

Nick walked in through the kitchen door, but Jen was nowhere to be seen.

He continued through the living room to the staircase that wrapped around one side of the room.

Something caught Nick's eye as he walked up the stairs, a

splash of red on the wooden steps. As he continued up, he realised the red was blood and it was getting worse.

Nick bounded up the rest of the stairs, realising how stupid he had been.

He should have known he couldn't stop Lucifer from destroying the final bit of normality he had.

Following the trail into the bathroom, Nick swung the door open expecting to see Jen lying on the floor. She wasn't there; he ran out to the bedroom, but the door was already ajar.

Jen lay on the bed face down, the blood on the bedsheets at her side had dried.

Nick jumped onto the bed and flipped her over. Jen swung round with a knife to his throat, nicking his neck slightly.

"Nick! It's you!" Jen screamed and threw the knife to the floor. She pulled him down onto her. Nick held her tight and kissed her neck.

"What happened? Are we safe? Where's your mum?"

"I saw her Jen, I held her. But she didn't want to return. Basically she said that since I didn't have a soul anymore, I would be a monster."

"What? What happened to your soul? Didn't you get it back? Did he double-cross you?"

"No. He's dead and took my soul with him, there was no other way. God had to destroy him."

Jen let out a slight laugh in disbelief.

"God? Did you meet God? Fuck off!"

"You were tortured by Lucifer, and you don't think God exists?"

"Oh my God, really? What... what did he... she look like?" she asked.

Nick laughed, "He is a teenage boy, explains a lot really!"

"What? Seriously?"

"Oh yes, but Hades was fucking huge."

Nick looked back at the knife and the blood. "What happened? Why is there blood and a knife?"

"When you left I didn't know what to do or where to go. I just grabbed a knife from the kitchen and ran upstairs. I tripped and caught my hand, then washed it off in the bathroom, then waited here on the bed. I fell asleep until you came back."

Jen checked her arm. She saw the blood was dry and the cut wasn't as bad as she had thought.

"So Lucifer is dead? Really? So we can be together, with no fear of him?"

Something clicked in her head.

"Sorry, did you say a teenage kid?"

"Yep. His voice was hard to listen to though, it was so painful."

Nick rubbed his ears remembering the pain he had gone through during the fight. Nick went on and told Jen about the battle between God and Lucifer, and how he was dragged into it, about the trial, Hades and everything else.

"Come on, I need a drink."

Nick grabbed Jen's hand and they descended to the kitchen and poured a drink.

"Let's stay here for a couple of days before we decide what to do next. I need to spend some time not thinking about what has just happened."

Nick held Jen, savouring the moment but dreading what he had to do. He just didn't want to be left all alone, not just yet anyway.

SEPERATION

For the next couple of days, Nick and Jennifer spent their time enjoying each other's company. He was happy that he had decided to postpone giving her the potion; he wished that it could just stay like this forever. Even the fake weather was becoming a comfort; he felt as if he could continue and embrace this lie of a life he was playing a part in.

There were times when he thought he almost felt a love growing for Jen, but knowing she was under his spell, and the fact that he didn't have a soul to feel love, he decided to just ignore it and enjoy the sex while it lasted.

Nick decided on the last night together he would do something a little special. They sat outside in the garden eating and drinking, laughing and talking about their time together. And as the evening drew on and it got close to eleven o'clock, Nick slowly altered the weather, making it colder. He prompted Jen to look into the sky and they watched the first snowflake drift down, slowly followed by more.

"Nick, it's snowing!"

Jen held out a hand and watched the delicate creation land and melt in her hand.

"The last time I saw snow was with Eddie..." Jen dropped her head.

"Eddie? Who's Eddie?" Nick lifted her chin up to look into her eyes.

"Sorry, I shouldn't have said his name."

"Who is he?"

"My son, Eddie, he's my son." A tear came to her eye and she wiped it away.

"You miss him, don't you? I'm sorry, that should be a given."

"Obviously I do, but he is better where he is and who he is with, I would only destroy his life. I've been a shit mother."

Nick pulled her close and Jen cried. The snow continued to fall silently and cover the garden.

"Do you want me to stop it snowing?"

"No, it's nice. I'm sorry, I just miss him."

Nick tightened his hold, squeezing her harder.

"I can make all this go away and give you a chance to rescue your life again, the option to try again with your son."

Jen pushed him away.

"No, I would still want you. And both of you together, I know he would be the one to suffer."

"No, I could make your hunger for me go. You wouldn't *need* me anymore; you could live your life the way you want to."

"Nick, no, leave it. I am wrong for him," Jen begged.

"Ok." Nick pulled her in again, "Ok."

At least Nick knew that she couldn't be told what his plan was. She would stop him with no thought, and Nick still felt as though they could be together. Hopefully, the potion, or whatever it was, would work and the dependency on Nick would disappear. She deserved a chance to get her life and her son back.

Nick had gone through so much with losing his mother to Lucifer that he didn't want to be the monster to take away Eddie's mother.

Nick decided to give Jen the drops in her morning coffee; she wouldn't know.

👑

The morning soon came, and Nick lay in bed holding her close to him.

Laying there, thinking about losing her, even though he knew it was the right thing to do, he didn't want to. Not having a soul should make things like this easier, but he was now having to learn about how to go by what he knew was right and wrong, rather than waiting for the inner voice to say yes or no.

Jen stirred, she pulled Nick close to her and kissed his chest.

She wrapped a leg around him and squeezed him.

Nick stayed still and stroked her hair.

"Do you want coffee?" Nick asked.

"Mmm," she released Nick as he slipped out and disappeared downstairs, grabbing the vial of repulsion from its hiding place.

Ten minutes later Nick returned to the bedroom with two drinks.

Jen sat up in bed and took the cup from Nick and sipped.

Nick, tried not to stare at her as the first sip that went down.

"What?" Jen asked as Nick stared.

"Nothing, I just want to remember this moment; our life won't be like this after today. I will be on a mission for God."

Jen smiled, then within a few seconds, her smile dropped.

"I can't go with you."

Nick's dropped his head.

"I know."

She put the drink down and slumped back in the bed and started to cry.

Nick put his drink down and climbed onto the bed to comfort her, but she pushed him away.

"No, Nick. I'm sorry, but this is wrong. How did I let things get to this point? I need to go home."

Jen threw herself out of bed and pulled her clothes on.

Nick followed suit. "Where do you need to go?"

"Get me back to my flat. Are you sure he won't return?"

"Lucifer? He's gone forever," Nick said.

"Ok, flat it is then."

Jen grabbed him and she closed her eyes as the walls around them melted away.

Within seconds they were back in her flat; it looked exactly how they had left it.

Jen was now flapping around, rushing into the bedroom and throwing things into a suitcase.

"Jen, don't you think we should talk about this?"

"Sorry… maybe…but look, something clicked in my head this morning, telling me I can do this. To start again, just me and Eddie. I don't know where it came from, but it was like a bolt of lightning. It was like I was under a spell or something, and now I am not. I'm sorry, Nick. Also, you being here actually makes me feel a little uneasy and to be honest a little... sick," Jen winced telling him.

Nick had been warned, but he didn't expect things to turn sour so quickly.

"Right, ok. Well, I better leave then."

"Yeah, you should." Jen returned to her packing.

"Was it that bad?"

"Was what that bad?"

"Us?"

Jen stopped packing.

"Nick, it's as though I have been dead for the past few months, even though I haven't. And even though I feel this way now, it doesn't mean I have felt this way before; understand? I obsessed over you, craved you, but now, I am over you."

Jen stroked his cheek.

"Sorry but it's over. You're young enough to get over me quickly. And to be blunt, with no soul, it should be very easy." Jen smiled and returned to her speed packing.

Nick stood watching her, he reached out to touch her again but decided to just leave.

"Goodbye, Jen, I hope everything goes to plan. And, if you ever need me, you know how to reach me."

"Thanks, but I won't." Jen smiled as Nick walked out the front door.

He left the building, shocked by just how fast the potion had worked. But what threw him the most was how brutal the parting was. He was soulless, but he felt the repulsion from Jen, in every word. Nick was glad to not have a soul right now.

He walked away, down the street and out of sight, glancing back every couple of minutes to see if she were watching him leave.

But Jen wasn't to be seen. It felt strange to go from being obsessed over to being pushed away. Lucifer had done him a favour finally, to not feel love and not to be killed by it either.

Nick stopped by a small coffee shop, walked in and sat down at a table.

He ordered a coffee and a full English.

After 10 minutes the waitress returned with his drink and breakfast.

"Is there anything else I can get you?" The waitress asked.

"No, no. I think that's it. Thanks."

A thin, young man, mid-twenties, walked past and sat opposite Nick.

He took his jacket off and starred at him. Nick paused as he was about to put some bacon into his mouth.

"Hey, Nick. Any chance you could get me one of them too? I haven't eaten for a while and I really would like to."

Aghast, Nick paused for it to sink in. "Steve? You're not a ghost!"

"Well, I am not really sure what I am yet. I know I am on a mission from, you know who," said Steve as he pointed towards the ceiling of the cafe.

Nick waved the waitress down and ordered the same for Steve.

"You here to keep me in check then?"

"Something like that. Think it's just to help you more than watching you. But I'm back solid again. So…"

Steve leaned over and grabbed a sausage from Nick's plate, immediately shoving the whole thing into his mouth.

"Oh, shit! That's amazing!" orgasmed Steve, licking his fingers.

"How's the wife and kid now? All ok?"

"Not sure, last time I checked they were."

Steve took the plate and cup from the waitress as she returned to the table. "Thanks love."

Steve watched her leave.

"So, me and you eh? Jesus, what a fucking pair!"

Steve looked up from shovelling tomatoes into his mouth.

They raised their cups and chinked them together.

"Cheers."

And then they continued to eat their breakfasts.

ACKNOWLEDGMENTS

Writing isn't easy, maybe for the likes of Stephen King, but not for me. I may have a story, ideas or at least a flash of a twisted image but it takes talent to make those words shine and I don't own any polish (actually I do but you get what I mean).

These people, however, have the talent and have helped to make my scribblings English and readable. Richard Ryan, my editor, who has been extremely patient and guiding, asked the right questions to make me ask myself the correct questions to improve many scenes. He didn't take over, I had a fear of this, just prodded me into seeing things differently. I now understand more of the craft of writing, I will never be a master, but happy being a student.

My original First Edition cover was created by a very talented artist, Elina Laaksonen from Mistvale Covers. I asked for a moon on a stick, she delivered a galaxy. My mind is a strange place, and to explain what I want from the shadows and screams, she understood and created the artwork you see. This can still be found on the original cover that still is about.

The new Second Edition cover was created round a photo from an artist called Andrey Kiselev. As I was looking around trying to find something to inspire a new cover, as Amazon owned the rights to the first edition and they had deleted my account for some crazy reason, I saw this picture and I knew it was my Lucifer. So, I worked the cover into what you see now and again I love it.

Martin Stephens, for reading my painful scratchings, also known as my first draft, he saw it before it was rewritten and cleaned up, he saw the turd before it was rolled in glitter.

Dylan Morgan, for answering the constant questions without losing his shit.

Cindy Schneider for her time dumbing down how she approached self-publishing and marketing.

Isaac Thorne, along with Dylan for being my other ARC reader, thanks for the blurb.

Nikita Malone for formatting my manuscript and making it look amazing.

I am sure there are plenty more people to mention during this novel being thrown together, especially in the early days.

Thank you to all the above for your guidance, help and kind words, it all made things easier to get through.

CHILL

A SHORT STORY BY

LEIGH HADDINGTON

"Do you realise how long it has taken me to find you? The time I have spent looking for you? Fifteen years, FIFTEEN FUCKING YEARS! And now it's come to this: just me, and you."

I look down and watch the blood run from the blade into the stainless steel sink. Hot steam rises to cloud my vision and I struggle to see my reflection. I wipe the vapour off the mirror, leaving a faint blood streak behind. The black makeup smudged around my bloodshot eyes dances with the beads of sweat on my cheeks and my eyes pierce my enemy's reflection behind me.

I look down and watch water run over the blade, light from the mirror bouncing off the steel as I roll it in my hand.

Memories flood my mind, reminding me of all the years I've hunted him since he murdered my parents in front of me; in cold blood, in the rain, with no regret. My mother's scream lingers as it always has done and then the second shot rings in my mind again, echoing, tearing through the flesh of memory.

I pick up his wallet to make sure it is him. The licence reads Joe Chill, but I do not recognise his name; Yet his face is the one that has been nailed to the walls of my tortured memories.

I face him, he's silent and slumped forward, tied to the metal chair.

"Do you know who I am? Why I have been looking for you?"

I walk over to him, my heart pounding, excitement churning in my gut.

A chill runs up my legs as I step onto the plastic that covers the rough wooden floorboards, each splinter screaming to break through.

I stop in front of the slumped, shirtless, bleeding obsession. My dominance over him, I am finally in control; yet motionless he sits.

I loom over my prey, my black wings drag behind me and I catch my reflection of a stranger in the mirror to my right, a limp bloodstained man. On a second glance, he's gone and I am back, strong, dark, dominant.

"You took my parents' lives. I watched you take their light. I watched their souls swim up through the rain, and you ran, like a coward. But tonight I have you. You cannot run."

I step closer, placing my face against his ear, the cold of his cheek against mine like a morgue slab.

"You are a virus. You infect people. You spread your disease and rot their lives." Whispering into his ear I inhale his stale fragrance of dirty body odour.

"Tonight I stop you, for I am the CURE!"

I step back and flick my cloak off my shoulders,

embracing the moment. A cold flush runs up my back, the hair on the back of my neck raises with excitement.

He is still, quiescent, and even the blood from his head wound has ceased dripping onto the floor. I'm not sure when it stopped, it ran so freely before. I slowly remove the knife from his skull, taking my time to enjoy it, feeling it scrape against the bone, the noise it makes. It comes out much easier than when it went in.

The blood begins to run again, only for a minute. I can get so lost watching the blood flow and my victims squirm; not always, sometimes they just sit there, like he is now.

I throw my cloak back off my arms and I grab his head, yanking it up to stare into his evil virus-ridden eyes.

"You can never escape me. Your virus won't kill me. Nothing kills me. But I KNOW pain, sometimes I share it, I share it with scum like you!"

Still no response from him. I kick his leg, nothing. I run my hand over his ice-cold face, the chill awakens my touch and I slap him. Nothing.

His shell is hollow now, his light has gone, and my work here is done.

I stand there watching him, despondent, mocking me.

My legs grow heavy and the weight buckles my knees, sending me to the floor. The cold reality of the plastic and the pools of drying crimson freeze me. I stare at my reflection again and the weak creature is back. The darkness of my soul, empty of love and void of regret.

I don't know how long I stared at the maggot in the mirror, it could have been seconds, maybe minutes. Closing my eyes I catch a whiff of the body above me and I heave, vomit mixing in with the blood on the plastic and it's at that point I acknowledge my surroundings.

Somehow I manage to get onto my knees and I look up; the evil is sitting looking down at me, cold, empty eyes staring through me. The smell hits me again and I lose more fluid.

Quickly, I cut the pull ties and shake the body out of the chair onto the plastic sheeting below; he collapses like a marionette and its limbs sprawl out. Pulling in the corners of the sheet I catch my bare foot on a wooden splinter and the pain surges through me. Wincing, I slip on my boots and grab my jacket and some cable ties. Fastening the sheeting into a bundle with the ties, I remember his wallet and snatch it. I check for cash, check once more at his driving licence - Mark Gomez - and pocket the wallet. I can't let that drop in with the body.

Dragging the object out of the doorway, down the hall and into the garage, I realise just how much heavier it is than the ones before. I struggle to lift it, with each attempt it changes shape and I drop it again. Looking around I notice my winch on the bench. I strap it to an overhead beam and clip the shape onto the hook, then raise it. As it gets level with the trunk, I give it a shove into the rear of the car, along with the spade and rope.

An arm spills out, why is there an arm? I force the appendage back into the bundle and push the shape deeper into the trunk, releasing the hook and slamming the trunk shut. I breathe again, fumble for my keys in my pocket and release the garage door. One last check, making sure I haven't left anything behind. No, I'm good. I rush into my car and drive off into the cold night air.

***

It's been two weeks since my last blackout. I get them once in a while, I seem to lose time more often these days. Sometimes it's one day, sometimes five, seven, whole weeks just gone. I don't even know if it's getting worse or if I have always had these problems.

But tonight I am back out again, mingling with the people, the city folk. Food, music, it doesn't matter, I'm trying to get my life back to normal. Fingers crossed that was the last blackout.

New York can be so vibrant in the evenings, yet during the day I feel the constant rush of anxiety getting through the throngs of traffic and suits. But the evenings are so inviting and I enjoy the happiness and frivolity that alcohol brings to the crowds.

I slip into a local café for a coffee to wake me up, ordering my usual dark, black. I like it here: I don't need to learn a whole menu with weird names just to get a simple black coffee. Those places make me feel stupid, not knowing what I'm going to get. But this place also has a wonderful area to sit and watch the world go by.

I position myself on one of the raised stools near a window, looking out across an open road facing one of the busiest nightclubs in town, watching people coming and going. It's like being invisible, no-one sees you sitting here, watching, even though it's like you're a mannequin in a shop window, posed for the seller's pleasure to entice the shopper.

It's been an hour now, and apart from the odd angry drunk being dragged outside by the bouncer, nothing has really happened.

A small group spills out of the door onto the pavement and road; shouting, laughing, hugging. I see him and my heart starts racing. I spill my cold coffee across the surface of the counter in front of me. I mop it up quickly with multiple napkins. Leaving the fallen cup and my half-assed attempt at cleaning, I shoot out the café door.

Where did he go?

I saw him a minute ago, where is he?

I sidestep a few times back and forth, trying to see him through the crowds.

I see him again and this time I know it's him!

My parents… he killed them… fifteen years I have looked for him…

Fifteen long years.

He's not getting away from me this time.

Not this fucking time.

ALSO BY LEIGH HADDINGTON

Emotion Corrosion

… poetry from a distressed mind …

A collection of dark poetry that kept Leigh sane over a year of depression, anxiety and loss. Touching on subjects ranging from suicide, serial killers, pandemic and death.

100 pages of sickness, sadness and somethings more sinister.

Available from all online bookstores.

Paperback ISBN: 9781838261122

eBook ISBN: 9781838261139